CHARLES ELTON was a director of the literary agency Curtis Brown before becoming an independent TV producer in 1991. In 2000 he joined ITV as executive producer in drama and left in 2010 when his bestselling first novel *Mr Toppit*, a Richard & Judy Book Club pick, was published. He lives in London and Somerset. *The Songs* is his second novel.

ALSO BY CHARLES ELTON

Mr Toppit

THE
SONGS

CHARLES ELTON

BLOOMSBURY PUBLISHING
LONDON · OXFORD · NEW YORK · NEW DELHI · SYDNEY

BLOOMSBURY PUBLISHING
Bloomsbury Publishing Plc
50 Bedford Square, London, WC1B 3DP, UK

BLOOMSBURY, BLOOMSBURY PUBLISHING and the Diana logo are trademarks
of Bloomsbury Publishing Plc

First published in Great Britain 2017
This edition published 2018

Copyright © Darkwood Ltd, 2017

A catalogue record for this book is available from the British Library.

ISBN: HB: 978-1-4088-8239-9; TPB: 978-1-4088-8238-2; EBOOK: 978-1-4088-8236-8;
PB: 978-1-4088-8234-4

2 4 6 8 10 9 7 5 3 1

Typeset by Integra Software Services Pvt. Ltd.
Printed and bound in Great Britain by CPI Group (UK) Ltd, Croydon CR0 4YY

To find out more about our authors and books visit www.bloomsbury.com
and sign up for our newsletters

For Julia Elton and Rebecca Elton Fitzsimons

Rose

My brother Huddie said that we must be in the very small percentile of people who had a mother who fell out of the same window twice. Even dogs don't do that: they learn from experience.

Huddie and I liked statistics and research. We were both good at maths; we liked to set each other problems: what percentage of the world population has eaten oysters or what the odds are on a dog in China being neutered. Huddie spent a lot of the day on the computer and told me all the things he had found when I got back from school. There were fewer of them now because he had become so slow on the keyboard.

Our mother died when she fell out of the window the second time so he had done some research on falling. He had found out that it is better if your body is floppy, but the problem is that you instinctively tense up in a danger-ous situation like falling out of a window and that's why bones get broken and people get killed. Being drunk – like our mother was – can sometimes help you: the cognitive processes are slower and the tensing-up instinct does not kick in so quickly and that can save your life. It certainly did for our mother the first time she fell: no bones were broken. Her spleen was ruptured, but luckily that wasn't an organ in constant use, unlike her liver.

Of course, being drunk is not an infallible method of falling from a window safely. Our mother was also drunk the second time, but she fell differently and her head hit the pavement first. She was in a coma for three days before they switched off the machine. Iz told us he had taken us to the hospital to see her but because I was only three and Huddie two we did not remember it. That was almost the only thing he ever told us about our mother, and we knew better than to ask him more.

Iz was our father, Isaac Herzl, which was the name you saw in newspaper profiles and on concert posters and CD covers but because he was eighty now there were almost none of those things any more. Everyone called him Iz even if they did not know him. I think that's what it's like with well-known people: patches of knowledge seep in like damp and make you feel you have some special connection with them even though the same patches of knowledge – his flight from Germany as a child before the war, fighting in Israel with the Jewish underground in 1947, his songs at his concerts, the causes he had championed – were actually shared by everybody else as well. When strangers talked about him – about the power of his personality or the intimacy of his singing or the passion of his commitment – their connection to him seemed forged from links as strong as steel; ours sometimes felt flimsier than that.

We had an unusual childhood, certainly more interesting than children whose fathers were doctors or lawyers or bus drivers. Even the names he had given us were unusual: I was called Rose Sharon Herzl, named after a character in his favourite book *The Grapes of Wrath*, and Huddie was Huddie Ledbetter Herzl, after a black American blues singer from the 1930s.

When we were young Iz took us to concerts or meetings or demonstrations, although he did not seem to have the time or inclination to tell us what the meetings or demonstrations were about. Iz always said that children should work things out for themselves. We were exposed to all sorts of people who came from all sorts of countries and spoke all sorts of languages. We heard a lot of songs in those languages.

But as children, it did not make much difference to us whether he was a pioneer of the folk movement or had sung protest songs at demonstrations in Trafalgar Square and been arrested or had been on fact-finding missions to countries accused of ethnic cleansing. Even now, when I was sixteen and Huddie fifteen and we understood all the things he had done, it still did not make much difference to us.

When I was small and was asked what job Iz did, I said that he was an 'Active Singer'. That was not the kind of job that other children at school were familiar with and they probably thought that it meant that he sang while taking exercise. I really meant 'Activist Singer', but I was not exactly sure what that involved. I knew that his songs were about a lot of different things but they seemed filled with ambiguities. Why was it fine for some people to die but not others? Were all people of one colour good and people of another colour bad? Why weren't all people who worked called working class? Maybe the ambiguities were why I wanted logic and precision so badly later. Maybe that was my version of teenage rebellion, better than smoking or stealing your parents' vodka.

Iz was a mystery really, but maybe all parents are a mystery to their children. Iz always believed that the important thing was what a man did, not who he was or where he came from. He had always said to us, 'It is the future not the past you must concentrate on.' You might say that's a sophisticated concept for a child to grasp, but I was a sophisticated child.

He certainly never talked about his past. He didn't even bother to fill in any of the gaps in his early life: his Wikipedia entry was headed 'This page has issues' and there were a lot of things with question marks and [citation needed] next to them. His birthplace was listed as 'Leipzig?', his father's profession was 'Lawyer?' and the date he was put on a *Kindertransport* boat to get him out of Germany was '1938?' Obviously, Iz was the one person who knew what the facts were and could have corrected them if he had wanted to, but now he was eighty it was too late: his memory had begun to fail.

There were other gaps: he had another child, our half-brother, Joseph, who he never talked about. We had never met him: he was years older than us. Of course we were intrigued by the idea of having a brother. We had researched him: he was quite a famous songwriter but not the kind of songwriter Iz was – he wrote the lyrics for musicals. He was Iz's child by someone who had died a long time ago and Iz did not talk about whoever that was either, just as he did not talk about our mother.

Her name was Molly Pierce and she was a singer and songwriter, too. People generally believed that she had killed herself when she fell from the window that second time but we tried to stay open-minded about it. If a suicide note had been found at the time, or if one turned up later lost behind a sofa, we would have had to accept it but until then we could believe what we liked and we believed that the fall was accidental. We were not just trying to make ourselves feel better: we had thought it through logically. I know it doesn't look good having a mother who keeps falling out of windows, but that was actually the point: if you had fallen out of a window once and survived, you wouldn't choose that method if you were trying to kill yourself.

Obviously with the drink and the drugs she was always self-destructive, but that didn't mean she wanted to die. Huddie and I looked at other forms of self-destructive behaviour: if you are anorexic all you are trying to do is lose weight and be as thin as possible. You're not trying to kill yourself. If you're an alcoholic you just want to get drunk, not die of some horrible liver disease. The trick is to stop at the right moment. You need to be disciplined about self-destruction otherwise you can die like our mother did.

Despite the fact that our mother had died thirteen years before, people on the Internet were still fascinated by her life and death. We did not like the fact that there were so many strong opinions from people who did not know her, many of them lifted from the book about her life which was called, *Icarus's Valentine: The Legacy of Molly Pierce*. I had found it in a second-hand bookshop and kept it hidden in my bedroom. It was not a book that would have been very welcome in our house. Some people say is it is full of inaccuracies, particularly about Iz and the part he played in her death. That was another part of his past that he did not bother to correct.

Huddie and I, the closest people in the world to her – genetically at least – could talk about her in a calmer and more rational way. In fact, I would go so far as to say that we managed to neutralise her. You wouldn't have found us bursting into tears at the mention of her name. It was better that way.

When I last looked, there were 55,265 references to our mother on Google. That's still quite a lot even though obviously it's not up there with Stalin or Madonna. Anyway, she was not famous in that way – she was more of a cult thing. If you walked down Oxford Street and asked people if they had heard of her, I don't suppose that many people would have. But lots of people know her most famous song 'Icarus's Valentine' because it's been covered by so many other singers.

I can't even remember the last time I listened to one of her records. I think Huddie did it more often than me, then pretended he was listening to something else. The albums were certainly on his iPod, I know that. I suppose I would have liked her to have recorded some songs that were specifically about us, like the one about Mama's going to buy you a diamond ring, but she certainly never did that. If I'm honest I'd say that what she sang was not really my kind of music which makes me feel disloyal, so that's sad too, but I'm not going to suspend my critical faculties just because she was our mother. If you're not objective you can't hold any real opinions, or at least any opinions that are worth anything.

Actually, I didn't even know if I really regarded her as my mother. You might think there would have been a hole in my life where she ought to have been, but there wasn't really. Occasionally she came up in conversation with people and I could see them doing that funny little thing with their mouth, a little downturn of the lips, that's meant to express solidarity and show that they understand my pain. That was irritating.

Still, even after all this time, her name cropped up so we couldn't just forget about her. There had been a review of a recent album by Mockingbird, the group our mother had once been part of, which lamented the absence of 'the late, sublime Molly Pierce' from the line-up. The original line-up was the one that everyone loved, particularly Niall McCarthy, who had started the group, and our mother. She played the piano and sang in a clear, pure voice that, so the biography said, was so full of emotion and pain that people were held spellbound.

All of the group were interviewed for the biography of her. Some of them talked about her drinking and her many erratic performances but they all seemed to be in awe of her talent. They obviously disliked Iz because he had persuaded her to leave the group and only work with him. Niall McCarthy had other reasons: he and our mother had lived and sung together for years. Their duets were always the heart of Mockingbird concerts, particularly when they sang 'Icarus's Valentine'. He was so distraught when she left him for Iz, apparently, that he went to live in a Sufi commune in Eastbourne. I suppose creative people are more sensitive than other people.

Ironically, it was at a Mockingbird concert that Iz and she first met – a benefit concert for El Salvador after the Civil War ended. The climax of the evening was when, as a surprise guest, Iz had joined Mockingbird onstage – a coup for one of the acknowledged legends of Folk to shine his light on a group of younger musicians, only compromised by the speed with which he got together with our mother and made her pregnant with me – that very night according to some sources. He was sixty-two. She was thirty.

For the final number of the evening, Iz and our mother sang the national anthem of El Salvador in Spanish. One of the verses began:

> *Libertad es su dogma, es su guía*
> *Que mil veces logró defender*

Those words translated into English were on our mother's gravestone in Highgate Cemetery: 'Freedom is her dogma and her guide; a thousand times she has defended it.'

I've only ever found one photograph of us with her. We are perched on the control desk in a recording studio looking at our mother through the glass. The sharpness is on her: her head tilted into the microphone, her hand cupping her ear as she sings with her eyes closed. Our faces are fuzzy and out of focus. Huddie always said that it was a sort of metaphor. I wish there had been other pictures. I do not think that photograph defines the unbreakable bond between mother and child.

At the time Iz and our mother broke up, when she left the house taking us with her, she was recording her only solo album, *Magnetic North*: it was called that because she said in one of her last interviews that her music was a perfect construct in her head but when she tried to get it on to a record, it did not turn out the way she had hoped. It was like heading for the North Pole, she said, but finding herself at Magnetic North instead, which is not the exact top of the world, but the point at which the earth's magnetic field points vertically downwards.

The recording of *Magnetic North* is still the subject of debate. Iz was producing it, but only about six tracks were completed before she left and it was abandoned. The songs are very different from her work with Mockingbird. Iz got her to do a completely different version – just with piano and oboe – of 'Icarus's Valentine', which was always the highlight of the Mockingbird concerts.

On the live recordings it was much more like a rock song. She was on her own for the early verses, then gradually the rest of the group came in on their instruments and it built through a long guitar solo until the end when the whole group sang. I knew the words by heart:

> *When the moon is in its quarter*
> *And the sun is at its height*
> *When you've followed nothing that you ought to*
> *And chosen wrong from right*
> *When you've broken everything –*
> *Everything that's fine*
> *I know that Icarus will send his valentine*
>
> *His feathers wet with melting wax*
> *You watch him falling from the sky*
> *On life you hope there is no tax.*
> *On death you cannot say goodbye*
> *And when you've stolen everything –*
> *Everything that's mine*
> *I know that Icarus will send his valentine*

People have always loved the song and I do now. I regret that Huddie and I were so pedantic then – we always had to analyse everything: we wanted everything to be logical and accurate. We debated whether melting wax could be 'wet' because it is oil-based not water-based. We discussed the fact that, as far as it can be dated, Icarus lived in the Mycenaean Age, around 1500 BC, while the origins of Valentine greetings were in the Middle Ages so we thought the song had a fundamental flaw in it. I'm not sure why we believed that songs should be logical. Nothing else seemed to be.

After she left, in the year that led up to her death, it is well documented that her drinking became out of control. She went back to Mockingbird for a while, but there were cancelled dates and reports of shambling, embarrassing concerts. And there were obviously drugs – the autopsy after her death found heroin in her system.

She lived in a rented flat in Maida Vale with Huddie and me after she left, but I have no idea who was looking after us when she was falling to pieces – ours were not the kind of parents who employed nannies. Maybe Iz sent over one of the political refugees he rescued from some corrupt regime. I can't even count the number of evenings Huddie and I had sat listening to somebody who had escaped from political oppression singing one of their incomprehensible songs of freedom. There were a lot of them over the years: they did things like mow the lawn and do repairs round the house.

A few weeks before she died, Iz did something that caused outrage: he took us away from our mother – an act that was referred to as 'kidnapping' in the biography. People who took our mother's side believe that was the reason for the downward spiral that led to her death. Those who supported Iz took a different line: he had done everything he could to help our mother, and now it was time to protect his children from her self-destructive behaviour.

We found it hard to piece together a coherent account of the days leading up to our mother's death. There were a variety of conflicting opinions on various fan sites, often tirades against Iz for his real or perceived failings as a husband and half-formed interpretations of what had happened. Someone had even posted a timeline of the days before her death: places she may or may not have gone to, bars and restaurants she may or may not have been in and people who may or may not have been in them with her.

What was not in question was that some kind of party was in progress at the flat when she died. The balcony from which she fell was in the bedroom off the living room. The varying testimonies of the people there did not vary on one point: she was in the living room with everyone else, and then she wasn't. Nobody saw her again. We always wondered what she was thinking about in the bedroom on her own. Maybe she was thinking about us, and Iz taking us away from her. Huddie said – half-jokingly – that she must have been talking about Iz when she wrote, 'When you've stolen from me everything, every-thing that's mine' but, of course, she was no more able to look into the future than anyone else.

It was a hot evening – July – and the windows of the bedroom must have been open. The flat was on the second floor and there were two big French windows in the bedroom, both opening on to a ledge with a low cast-iron parapet. Our mother must have been out there before, at least once anyway, because that was where she fell from the first time, the time she didn't die.

She was a chain-smoker. Perhaps she had a cigarette out there and threw it down to the street. Perhaps she was worried it had fallen into a dustbin full of dry paper and might catch fire. Perhaps she looked over the edge to check and slipped, but Huddie and I did not really think that she was the kind of person who might be concerned about litter or fire.

By the time the police arrived there were fewer people in the flat than when they had been called. We thought that a body hitting the pavement would clear a party pretty quickly, particularly if there were drugs around. Statements were taken in the usual way but there did not seem to have been an exhaustive investigation. There was no implication that foul play was involved, not even the conspiracy theorists have suggested that.

There was an inquest and the coroner pronounced an open verdict. It was impossible to say what her intentions might have been because of the amount of drink and drugs inside her – what the papers called 'a lethal cocktail' – but whatever was in her system was not the lethal thing. It was the fall that was lethal. Huddie said that the drink and drugs were just the icing on the cake.

Magnetic North was released only after she died, and some live recordings had to be added to bulk out the songs our mother had recorded in the studio. The track that people loved most was a version of Iz's song 'Let Them See Your Scars' sung unaccompanied, recorded at the concert for El Salvador where Iz and she had first met.

> *If they take you from the light*
> *And force you into darkest night*
> *If they cut your bodies with their knives*
> *And you are frightened for your lives*
> *Do not bow your head in shame*
> *Let no man hide your name*
> *Come proudly through those iron bars*
> *And let them see your scars*

Although her version is often played – it had been used a couple of years before in a documentary about Nelson Mandela – it's really Iz's signature song. It was always his encore and people still talk about him singing it at the concert for his seventieth birthday. I don't remember much about the concert – I was only seven then – but I do remember Huddie and I walking down a dark corridor. Someone was holding my hand and I was holding Huddie's, not just out of reassurance but because he was a little unsteady on his feet. His illness was starting but we did not know it yet.

It felt as if we were moles in a tunnel. I could hear music in the distance and there was a bright light ahead of us. We got closer and closer to it and then suddenly we were bathed in it. Noise enveloped us and I realised we were being taken onstage. People were shouting and cheering. Huddie began crying and I did not let go of his hand. We were taken to stand by Iz at the front of the stage, and he began playing the first chords of one of his silly children's songs. The cheering grew louder as he began to sing:

> *Don't you cry*
> *Don't you cry*
> *Don't you cry any more*
> *It's only the gooseberry moon overhead*
>
> *Don't you cry*
> *Don't you cry*
> *Don't you cry any more*
> *The sun will come back, it's just gone to bed*

Huddie began to bawl. What was odd was that this made everyone cheer more, as if a child weeping was somehow endearing. He had never been as tough as me – even then, when he had the ability to be tough. That particular ability, like all of the others, would go within a few years.

I suppose that people thought that Iz was singing the song to us because it was an old family favourite, that he sat on the edge of our beds at night singing us to sleep with his children's songs like 'Gooseberry Moon' and 'Take Your Tractor for a Dance'. In fact, the song was completely unfamiliar to us – I expect he had written it for children somewhere else, maybe for the children of the Disappeared in Chile, one of his many causes.

Anyway, I never remember Iz putting us to bed. Carla always did that.

Carla was our stepmother. The facts of how she and Iz got together were well known, but like most things about Iz's life, finding any meat on the bones of the facts was difficult.

Carla's father was called Theodore Wasserman. He taught anthropology at Harvard and was a famous song collector. Iz and he had known each other since the 1950s when they went on a field trip to the southern states of America in search of old folk songs. Years later, Iz went to Boston to give a lecture on the assimilation of Yiddish songs into Hebrew culture and had dinner with his old friend where he met his daughter Carla who he married after our mother died. He was sixty-six, Carla was thirty.

It sounds a bit like a gothic fairy tale: an evil woman who steals a father and supplants the mother who died in mysterious circumstances; a little girl in rags sweeping the floor, lying down at night on straw matting in the cellar, holding a tattered photograph of her dead mother and crying herself to sleep. I'm not sure how Huddie would fit into this story: I'm not sure they have wheelchairs in fairy tales.

But it wasn't like that. Carla had her faults but as stepmothers go she did not do too badly. You would not have caught Carla falling out of the same window twice. I sometimes think that a person's best quality can also be their worst and Carla's detachment towards us was both of those. She just got on with her life and let us get on with ours. What Carla was not detached about was music: she was a multi-instrumentalist and could play the guitar, the banjo, the dulcimer, the autoharp, the penny whistle, the recorder and probably other things too, many more than Iz could. He had just picked things up as he went along.

Mostly she sang traditional folk songs. She didn't interpret songs, like people say our mother did.

Carla came into our lives a few months after our mother died. She was certainly around for the court case in which our grandmother, Evelyn, tried to get custody of us by proving that Iz was an unfit father. I suppose you could look at that as an act of love on her part, but I thought it was unfair. After all, her own daughter was someone who might be thought of as an unfit mother.

Against everybody's advice, Iz refused to hire a lawyer and represented himself in court. Evelyn brought up everything she considered bad about Iz: his various marriages, his 'itinerant' and 'unsuitable' lifestyle, his political affiliations, his time in jail, the fact that he was already living with Carla, and so on. She even brought up how Iz had treated his first child, his elder son, Joseph.

There was a lot of debate about his 'kidnapping' of us – her lawyers interpreted this as the act of a deranged and unstable father – but what impressed the judge was Iz's quiet dignity. The thing that finally turned the tables in his favour was when, to everyone's astonishment, he picked up his guitar and sang a song. Although it had been written about the children of Soweto, it seemed strangely pertinent to the children of Muswell Hill. After the judge had deliberated, Iz was granted full custody.

Carla had told us all this. When we were small it was like a magical fairy tale in which good triumphed over evil. It was certainly a wonderful story, and one that I've seen people go misty-eyed over. I feel slightly less misty-eyed about it: reading about Iz on the Internet and putting dates together, I discovered that two days after the custody hearing ended he flew to Chile for six weeks, presumably leaving us in the care of Carla who we hardly knew. I don't know whether it makes it better that those concerts in Chile were among the most famous he ever gave and drew the attention of the world to what was happening there. Apparently 3,000 people singing 'Let Them See Your Scars' was an extraordinary sight. People who look into the past still talk about it.

So: in their own ways, both our parents had left us. I could forgive Iz – after all, there was some kind of purpose to what he was doing in Chile and all the other places that he went to even though it meant he was never at home. It was different with our mother. At Highgate cemetery, apparently, people still put fresh flowers on her grave sometimes. If that is true, there's one thing I can tell you for certain: it would not be me. I cannot forgive her. I cannot forgive her for leading a life so utterly devoid of logic.

Maurice

At the beginning of July 1947, when he was seventeen, Maurice Gifford was sent by his parents to his uncle's farm in Kent, the consequence of events that had taken place in his home town of Godalming, somewhere that now seemed as far away to him as the moon. Although he had waited for as long as he could remember for his life to change, for some force to shake him out of the skin into which he had been born, this was not the change or the force he would have wished for. But when he first met the boy called Isaac Herzl there he had no idea that he had stumbled on what he had always been searching for.

Maurice rather liked the idea that he had been banished by his parents because of his beliefs. There was a fine tradition of that happening throughout history. He had read many books on the subject. Everything was so clearly delineated there: the oppressor and the oppressed in *Darkness at Noon*, the proletariat and the ruling class in *Das Kapital*, not that he had really made much headway with that one even though he religiously carried it in his satchel to school and produced it as ostentatiously as he could when he took his books out. The level of ignorance among his peers was staggering: some boys thought *Das Kapital* was a German book about the alphabet. To search for truth and only find indifference: that was his lot in life, he thought mournfully, a biblical curse sent to punish him by a non-existent God, a curse that seemed to have accompanied him like an old dog from his school to his uncle's bleak farm.

One of the many things he could not forgive his parents for was the name they had given him. No Fifth Columnist worth his salt would be called 'Maurice'. It wasn't a shame that could be hidden, like athlete's foot or the angry red spots on his back. It was in his school books and above his peg in the sports pavilion. It was name-taped to his clothes, written in chalk on blackboards and on an oval ceramic plaque in cursive script with a floral surround on his bedroom door: a present from his parents several Christmases ago and – symbolically – a companion piece to the one that said 'Toilet' on the door of the downstairs lavatory. The name pursued him like a sinister doppelgänger. 'I Am Not That Maurice,' he wanted to shout. 'I Am Not Any Maurice!'

It had been his grandfather's name: a pathetic attempt by his parents to engender some kind of quasi-aristocratic tradition in a family that had none. If asked, his mother would modestly disclose that they came from 'a landowning family in Kent', a generous description of a clan of illiterate tenant farmers who had managed to buy a few hundred acres and a decrepit farmhouse a couple of generations ago. One day, on the assumption that his uncle was unlikely to marry and have children, it would all go to Maurice as 'next in line', a phrase of his father's that made him think of a slow procession towards the firing squad.

His father was a doctor. Although he would have preferred him to be at the forefront of experimental medicine, like the surgeon who pioneered skin grafts on burnt RAF pilots during the war, being a GP was a perfectly honourable profession in Maurice's eyes. What he could not bear was that his father had grown dizzy with upward mobility: he had recently been in touch with the College of Arms in order to ascertain whether any of his antecedents had been granted arms, were 'armigerous', as he called it, and if not, whether a crest might now be bestowed on such a distinguished family.

Once, his father had forced him to look at a glossy book containing other families' coats of arms. In order to acquire one, it seemed less a matter of how grand you were than simply whether you were prepared to hand over a ridiculous sum of money to the College of Arms. With the war just over, with poverty and starvation and displaced people all over Europe, you might think there were better things to do with your money. There were certainly better things to do with your time than wondering if your Serpent should be Torqued Erect or whether the Ermine should be reversed between Three Swords Points Upwards.

The other unforgivable thing his parents had done was to send him to King George's College, a threadbare minor public school outside Godalming with delusions of being, as it said in the prospectus, 'The Eton of Surrey'. All public schools were totalitarian institutions, of course – even a pathetic one like KG which had all the backbone of a bowl of blancmange – but he would rather his parents had actually sent him to somewhere like Eton where he might have at least found worthy adversaries and something solid to fight against.

But his parents, preferring to spend their money on expensive Daimlers and a wine cellar – although, of course, there was no cellar and the bottles were kept in the boot room – had sent him to KG for one reason: he had got a choral scholarship. It saved them money. When he was twelve, his voice unbroken, he had what his mother proudly called, in the days when she was proud of him, 'A voice like an angel'. At his interview at the school he had sung 'Blow the Wind Southerly', which his mother had got him to learn from a Kathleen Ferrier record and, by her account at least, the headmaster's eyes filled with tears.

It seemed a long time ago, but when he had started at KG at thirteen he supposed he must have been the Maurice that everyone thought he still was now, a combination of name and talents as integrated as the matching tie and handkerchief sets his father ordered from a gentleman's outfitter in London, a plausible construct of a bright boy who could make people cry with his voice, whose exam results swelled his parents' breasts. Now, at seventeen, he had become somebody quite different but nobody seemed to realise it.

He still sang in the choir every morning and practised most evenings. His voice breaking was not the disaster it was for some boys whose perfect sopranos vanished to be replaced by a gruff stranger in their throats. For Maurice, after a few months of vocal uncertainty, his voice had settled into a clear, warm tenor, but by then something other than his voice had changed: some tectonic shift of the kind you get before an earthquake, a redistribution of strength that frightened and excited him at the same time.

Sometimes, on Saturdays, telling his parents he was going to visit the British Museum or the Tate Gallery, he would take the train to London and wander around Soho.

All the excitement missing in Godalming lurked in those narrow streets. Everything thrilled him there. He found second-hand bookshops – on Brewer Street he bought a battered copy of Engels's *The Peasant War in Germany* for a shilling, but it was such heavy-going that he went back to reading *King Solomon's Mines* on the train home. There were dingy record stalls with racks of old discs that he pored over. If he had any money saved, he would buy scratched 78s of Paul Robeson or the Almanac Singers. They sang about important things. Imagine! Songs about war or building a dam or supporting a trade's union – not just mindless music in praise of God.

One evening at the beginning of that summer term, Mr Costello, who was in charge of music at King George, drew him to one side as he and his fellow choristers were leaving choir practice. It was the moment he had been hoping for: Mr Costello had a proposition for him. The end of year concert – Elgar's *The Apostles* – was being planned and he had known that, with one of the best voices in the choir, he might be offered a solo. Now it was happening.

'How do you feel about John?' Mr Costello asked.

He said, 'I'm sorry, sir?' and arranged a look of confusion on his face. He knew exactly what Mr Costello was talking about.

'St John the Apostle. Keep up, man! In the Elgar! Lovely tenor stuff. It's a big commitment, a lot of rehearsal time.'

Maurice tried to stay very still. Now the time had come, he was not sure he would be able to go through with it.

'I don't know, sir.'

'You don't know *what?*' Mr Costello said impatiently.

'I don't know whether I can do it, sir.'

'For God's sake, you'll just have to make the time.'

'It's not that.' Maurice paused for a moment. 'It would contradict my beliefs,' he finally said.

'Your *beliefs*?'

'Yes. I'm an atheist,' he said clearly. 'I don't feel I can sing religious music. There is no god, sir. In my opinion.' There: he had done it.

Mr Costello was gratifyingly stunned. 'I'm not interested in your opinion,' he said contemptuously.

'But why not, sir?'

'Because you haven't earnt a licence to speak.'

'Is that licence granted simply on the basis of age?'

'Yes! And at your age you know nothing.'

'Actually, sir, I'm quite well read. I've moved beyond *Swallows and Amazons*.'

Mr Costello narrowed his eyes and raised a single finger in a gesture of caution. 'I warn you, Gifford: you are sailing dangerously close to the edge.'

Maurice liked that. Yes, he was in a small boat being buffeted by the waves and teetering on the edge of one of those apocalyptic waterfalls you saw in German romantic paintings.

'I don't think you would want me to compromise my beliefs,' Maurice said quietly.

'I don't give a fig about your beliefs. Who put you up to this?'

'Spinoza, sir.' It was a risky card to play. The last thing Maurice wanted was to get into too involved a discussion. He had looked up 'Atheism' the week before in the many-volumed set of an old *Encyclopædia Britannica* that his father had bought in the local saleroom. It had come in a special mahogany cabinet with sliding glass doors and there had been a spat the day it was delivered when Maurice said scornfully, 'Knowledge is not furniture.'

Now he could not quite remember the specific views of Spinoza as opposed to Wittgenstein or Hume.

'Don't get clever with me, young man.'

'Isn't that the point of being at school? To be clever.'

Mr Costello ignored him. 'So: you'd like our end-of-term concert to make no reference to Our Lord, is that it?'

'There are other kinds of music, sir.'

'Is that so?' Mr Costello said sarcastically. 'And what shall we have at our hypothetical pagan concert? Jazz? Schoenberg? Victor Silvester? Perhaps a music-hall show with jugglers and performing dogs?'

'What about a tribute to Paul Robeson, sir?'

'*Paul Robeson*? That Negro communist? I presume you're joking.'

'He has a wonderful repertoire.'

'Oh does he?'

'"Joe Hill", "Ol' Man River", "Song of the Volga Boatmen"…'

'Yes, I know his songs,' he snapped. 'I also know that whenever he opens his blubbery black mouth there's some kind of trouble.'

That was what Maurice liked about Paul Robeson. He had read how he had got involved with a miners' strike in Wales.

'You could say the same thing about Jesus, sir. Apart from the blubbery black mouth.'

Mr Costello had had enough. 'I don't know what you're up to,' he hissed, leaning into Maurice's face, 'But let me tell you this: you're quite an ordinary boy. Not at the bottom of your year, but by no means the top. I doubt if you're going to feature in the Oxbridge intake, let me put it like that.' He gave a nasty little laugh. 'Sport? Not picked for many teams, are you? Friends? You've got a few,

I suppose, but not the golden boys, not the elite. You're one of the grey ones, aren't you? One of the colourless ones. A tiny glimmer of youthful promise beginning to dissipate already. Oh yes – you've got an unexpected gift for music. It won't make you stand out from the crowd, but if you're lucky it might just give you a bit of definition. I'd say it's a lifeline for you. I wouldn't throw it away too quickly, if I were you.'

'I'm not going to throw it away. I love music,' Maurice said quietly.

'Well then, you better begin learning the part and forget about this nonsense. You're not the only one who can sing John, you know.'

Maurice was wavering and he hated the feeling. He forced himself to speak before it got worse. 'I won't,' he said. 'I can't.'

Afterwards, after Mr Costello had stalked out of the room, he felt a small sense of peace, a feeling that something had started – no, not as passive as that: it was he alone who started it – that would leave him in control for the first time in his life. The next thing would be a summons from the headmaster, perhaps a refreshingly abrasive discussion about personal integrity. His schoolmates might collar him in the corridor and ask breathlessly if what they had heard was true, that he had taken on the might of King George.

Then, he supposed, there would be a drab confrontation with his parents – they didn't like the texture of their lives being ruffled – that would involve some sordid discussion about whether refusing to sing in the choir might remove the pathetic scholarship he had. He didn't really care if he had to leave the school, but not yet: he wanted the full effect of his stand to be felt.

The strange thing was that, in the succeeding days, nothing happened at all. Nobody mentioned it. He was not called to see the headmaster. His parents had obviously not been told. When he did not turn up for choir practice later in the week, he expected a note from Mr Costello, normally rigid about attendance, but there was nothing. Maurice saw him coming out of lunch the next day and slowed down his walk, preparing to look surprised when Mr Costello collared him, but there was just a small breeze as the master swept past him like a giant ocean liner oblivious to the pathetic dinghy in his path.

All in all, he had the uneasy feeling that Mr Costello had managed to get the better of him. In a way, he rather admired him. It was a classic technique, a textbook way to neutralise rebellion: destroy the printing presses, blow up the railway line, barricade the radio station – he had simply starved Maurice of oxygen. General Franco couldn't have done it better.

In fact, the only implicit acknowledgement was a list pinned up on the noticeboard outside the music rooms with the names of the soloists for the concert. Arthur Mayall, one of the few boys Maurice might have called a friend, was to sing St John. Of course, they had no ideological bond, but Arthur's old man was a GP in the same practice as his father and their families occasionally had Sunday lunch together.

A couple of years before, when Maurice wondered, on the basis of no real evidence, whether he might be a homosexual, they had masturbated together. Arthur had clearly enjoyed it more than Maurice did – there was an awkward moment when Arthur leaned down and looked as if he was about to put his penis in his mouth. Maurice had to move backwards quickly and pretend not to have noticed. He wanted to experience everything to the fullest, of course, but on balance he felt that just using their hands would be enough to get the gist of this particular one.

Now he was in an impossible position. His absence from choir practice must look like sour grapes and if he told the truth about why Arthur was singing St John instead of him, it would sound like an implausible invention to save face. When he ran into Arthur and the others as they were heading to the chapel, hastily pulling surplices over their dark green cassocks, most of them averted their eyes. Even Arthur had difficulty managing a hollow greeting. Already they thought of him as a sore loser.

He had made a fatal mistake with Mr Costello. He had not thought it through. He should have accepted St John and then, once it had been announced, maybe even after the programmes had been printed, he could have taken his stand and refused. That would have really shaken things up.

Now he seemed to have ended up with nothing. He had not realised he would miss the choir so much. If only you could just ignore the words, filter them out and bathe in the music itself. But even then there would be the taint of God or Country or something unacceptable. He was not going to go back now. Anyway, he had come up with a new idea, something that might cause the kind of stir he knew he was capable of.

Rose

It was not just Huddie who seemed to be losing his strength. Iz had become old in the last few years. He could still get around but he did not really move much outside his study. In her practical way, Carla had begun to make adjustments for him. His legs were slightly shaky so a metal bar had been attached to the wall by his bed so he could pull himself to his feet. Once on his feet, though, he could walk reasonably well even though he had to be careful on the stairs and use a stick. I hoped that Carla was not going to install a stairlift. It would have been undignified for him to be whizzed up and down as if he was on a funfair ride.

In other circumstances, Iz might have moved to the ground floor where he would not have to climb any stairs but there was not enough room for both him and Huddie there and Huddie's wheelchair trumped Iz's various infirmities. He seemed to have shrunk into old age. He had become broody and silent: I wanted to think of him as he had been when we were children, big and bearded and buzzing with energy, although his energy always seemed reserved for other people rather than us. We never saw much of him then. He was often away from home, and when he was at home he always seemed to be about to go away again. Now he was old and never went away, we did not really see much more of him. I would go up to his room sometimes when I got back from school, but he was not someone you would have a cosy chat with. He had somehow become more intimidating over the years. Carla always said rather proudly that he was too concerned with others to share the secrets of his soul. I wondered if that could be construed as selfishness on his part.

His domain was on the first floor where he had a large study with a bed in it. He spent the day there with Lally, who called herself, only half-jokingly, the Curator of the Isaac Herzl Archive. For a man who had always said that you should never look back, there were certainly a lot of newspaper articles and photographs from his past that Lally was collating and putting into fat scrapbooks.

Carla's quarters were on the top floor where she had a study and bedroom of her own. I was not sure when Iz and Carla had stopped sharing a bedroom but I had an uneasy feeling it was when Joan arrived to help Carla. Joan lived in Muswell Hill as well and they were involved in a lot of local activities: supporting an AIDS hospice, trying to get more speed bumps on side roads and starting petitions about the lack of residents' parking. Protest seemed to have got downsized.

Joan did not live with us, but she was there most days and sometimes stayed the night when they worked late. They did that a lot. By then, the house had divided into factions: me and Huddie on the ground floor, Iz and Lally on the first, Carla and Joan on the second.

They were writing a book together about the depiction of women in nineteenth-century folk songs. Folk music was a specialised area, but enough folk obsessives had come to the house for us to know that someone would be interested in the book. Iz himself had published several, the first ones on the origins of Israeli folk songs but later he had concentrated more on Britain and America and the history of the protest song.

Huddie and I never liked folk songs much. We preferred the protest songs – at least they were about something. The folk ones seemed so silly: people sang them in strange nasal voices with odd regional accents. In idle moments, of which there were many in Huddie's life, we amused each other by inventing ridiculous folk songs that piled disaster on top of disaster: lairds being poisoned by their lovers and ships being dashed on rocks and doomed maidens left in the lurch at the altar and all of these crazy things being crammed into the Merry Month of May. It made Huddie laugh, and there were fewer and fewer opportunities to do that these days. We needed to find funny things on the edges of his illness, already spreading outwards through his life like an ink stain on a piece of blotting paper. We laughed about his funeral a lot. I suppose it was a kind of aversion therapy. Maybe Huddie's sense of humour was morbid but I'm not going to apologise for it: he had the right to do whatever he wanted with the concept of death.

Iz sang both traditional folk songs and protest songs. I think one of the reasons they were so popular was that they were rather unspecific. 'Let Them See Your Scars' had been appropriated for a lot of causes, just as relevant to South America as South Africa or South Korea. His songs multitasked.

Lally probably knew his songs better than Iz did. She knew everything about Iz. We could not remember a time when she had not seemed part of the family. In a way, of course, she actually was part of the family: she had been Iz's first wife. They had known each other for fifty-one years, as Lally was always telling us, but had only been properly together for a couple of years, even though they did not get divorced until years later when Iz met our mother. There was no awkwardness between Lally and Carla: after all, for Carla, thirty years younger than her, there was nothing much to fear, and for Lally, it was our mother whom Iz had left her for, not Carla.

Lally was almost as old as Iz, but in better shape, except for her deafness. She lived in Tufnell Park and she walked the four miles to Muswell Hill and back whatever the weather. Her job had expanded into being the Curator of Isaac Herzl himself as well as his archive. Like I did with Huddie, she was the one in the house who cared for Iz and kept him company and cooked for him.

Huddie and I were fond of Lally even though she had ridiculous opinions. For someone who professed to be such a radical, she was very right wing. I did not even mind that Lally always called me Rosie and kept losing her glasses, which I had to find for her. Anyway, she spent time talking to Huddie, which was certainly more than Carla and Joan did. They were always too busy with their projects.

Lally came most days. On one particular day at the beginning of the time when things began to change for us, she arrived at the house early and came in to say hello to us as she normally did.

'And how's Huddie this morning?' Lally said looking at me. Like a lot of people, she had difficulty asking direct questions to someone disabled.

I turned to Huddie: 'How's Huddie this morning?'

'Huddie has a terminal illness this morning,' Huddie said in my direction.

I turned to Lally: 'Huddie has a terminal illness this morning. How's Lally this morning?'

'Super! Glad it's going well.' Her deafness was getting worse.

She went upstairs to see Iz but came down after a few minutes. Iz was still asleep. 'Look what I found in the archives? Isn't that fun?'

She handed me a photograph, and I moved over to Huddie so he could see it as well. It was a picture of Lally when she was young, her hair done up in braids, holding a strange-looking instrument that looked like an elongated guitar.

Huddie snorted. 'Did you actually play that?'

'Yes, I did,' Lally said defensively. 'It's a rebec. It's a medieval fiddle. I've always thought you should play traditional songs on the original instruments.'

There were a lot of strange rules in the folk world.

'When was it taken?' I asked.

'I suppose just after I'd left home and come to London. I must have been about eighteen.'

'Was that when you met Iz?' Huddie asked cautiously.

Lally was predictably reticent about the past, but she had become more forthcoming recently. Maybe it was because Iz seemed to be failing and – just as for Huddie – there was not much future to talk about.

'Oh, I just had my little nose pressed to the window in those days. I was shy. It was all I could do to get up onstage and sing, let alone speak to the famous Iz Herzl. He was like a lion then – everyone wanted to be in his orbit. Gazelles like me didn't dare approach him. It must have been in the mid-fifties, that's when the folk music boom really took off. He had come back to England from Israel with all those songs he had translated.

'Those awful Hebrew songs?' Huddie said, making a face.

'They weren't just Hebrew songs, Huddie,' Lally said sternly. 'They were also the songs that Jewish immigrants from places like Lithuania and Poland had brought with them. He did very important work with those songs at the beginning but he moved on. Israel's a small country, dear – he needed a bigger canvas than that. When he came back to England, he began writing those wonderful protest songs of his, one after another. He was a bit of a legend by then, playing at the Ballads and Blues Club in Soho with the big boys like MacColl and Lomax, then doing all those radio things and concerts.'

'So when did you get friendly with him?' I asked.

'Have you listened to his albums of Appalachian songs? Breathtaking! That's how I really got to know him. I was concentrating on my tuppeny-halfpenny life working as a little nobody in the library at Cecil Sharp House and he came in to do some research because he was going on a trip through Virginia to find old songs. I helped him because I knew where all the books were – I was mad for those songs! – and to my astonishment, he asked me to be his assistant on the trip.'

'He must have fancied you,' Huddie said, laughing.

'Certainly not. He just needed my help.'

'So what did you do on the trip?'

'Oh, lots of things. Operating those big tape recorders they had then, indexing the tapes, keeping a record of the songs we found. Extraordinary stuff! There were eighty-year-olds who were still singing songs they had heard their grandparents sing. So many lovely ones!'

She began to sing in a croaky little voice:

> *Send for the fiddle and send for the bow*
> *And send for the blue-eyed daisy.*
> *Send for the girl that broke my heart*
> *And almost drove me crazy*

'I think I fell in love with Iz when he sang that. We were friends, then we became romantic friends. I knew I could never have all of him. I was just grateful for what he gave me.' She looked mistily into the distance and sighed like a Victorian heroine uttering her last words: 'I must have done something right to have had such a remarkable man love me.'

I could see Huddie trying not to laugh.

'And he was so kind to marry me.'

'Kind?' I said.

'Well, I got pregnant by accident, and I suppose I didn't want to hurt my parents. Do you mind me telling you this?'

'No, not at all,' I said. It was fascinating to hear a seventy-five-year-old woman talking about her sex life.

'But I lost the baby.' She wiped her eyes. 'Silly to cry after all these years. As I always say: it's the future not the past you must concentrate on.'

Everybody had so many secrets in our house: we had not known any of this. 'That's awful, Lally.'

'I had problems in the ladies' department afterwards. I couldn't get pregnant again. I think he would have liked a child. Afterwards, really, Iz and I went back to being just friends. Occasionally we were loving friends, but not often.'

'Radicals with Benefits,' Huddie said softly to me. I tried not to smile.

'What?'

'Nothing.'

'Anyway, it all ended well. You both came along. But when our baby died, it was painful for Iz. Poor man, he has so many areas of pain.'

'I think everyone has those, Lally,' I said pointedly, trying not to look at Huddie.

Lally was not one for irony. 'Iz has more than most,' she said briskly. 'You know what he's been through.

Germany – so traumatic he can't even talk about it. I've known the man for fifty-one years: never a word about his parents being murdered. That terrifying journey to Israel on the ship – and then the bombs and the fighting. Friends being killed. Death everywhere! So brave to hold it all in and concentrate on others. I found a newspaper piece the other day which called him "part working-class hero, part cipher". Isn't that a lovely description?'

'No,' Huddie said. 'It's just gobbledegook.'

'You just be grateful that someone's saying nice things about him, Huddie Herzl! It doesn't happen very often these days. After all he's done! If you stand up and be counted, people try to pull you down. Maybe he's stood up and been counted once too often.' Then she gave a mournful little laugh. 'Well, he's certainly let everyone see his scars from fighting in Israel, hasn't he? He did what all of us tried to do: he fought and was wounded and went on fighting. Even the *Jewish Chronicle* is horrid to him now: they accused him of not being Jewish enough! I'm certainly not putting that piece in the archive!'

Huddie and I had seen it – a profile of Iz on his seventy-fifth birthday. There was a bit of praise for Iz in it – fighting for the Haganah after the British left Israel, his research into the folk tradition of the diaspora – but there were also snide intimations that he had become less supportive of Zionism when it became unfashionable, that he blew with the fickle winds of protest, as if he had left the Zion cocktail party early because the El Salvador one served better canapés.

Even his popularisation of Hebrew songs was questioned. The implication was that by making the songs more universal, he had made them less Jewish. They cited his version of 'Hatikva', the Israeli national anthem:

As long as your heart yearns
As long as your soul burns
Finally you will turn
To the place that you must love

We had found a literal translation of it. The problem was that Iz had made it unspecific: in the original, the soul that was burning was a Jewish soul; the place that you were meant to love was Zion.

'So now he's not Zionist enough for the Jews and too Zionist for everyone else! Remember all the heckling at that concert when he sang the Hebrew songs? *He's* not responsible for the situation in Israel! And when he sang "Scars"? Oh, that was awful.'

Once people used to light matches and hold them up when he sang it. That time they didn't. A few years before, Iz had allowed the song to be used in a television commercial for an antiseptic cream. A small boy in shorts and school cap limped through cobbled streets in the rain. His knee was bleeding and when he got close to a picturesque cottage with smoke coming out of the chimney, the door opened and his mother stood there with her arms open. Over this, a male voice choir with brass-band accompaniment sang rewritten words:

If you find yourself in pain
And the sky is full of rain
If your find your body aching
And you think your heart is breaking
Do not bow your head in shame
Just call your mother's name
Come running to her from afar
And let her heal your scars

At the concert, when Iz was singing the original version, someone shouted out, 'Where's your mother?' and people began to laugh.

'He's never performed again since then, has he?' Lally said. 'It breaks my heart. He only sold the song to get the money to convert the ground floor for Huddie, which must have been *very* expensive.'

Huddie looked hurt and fell silent. In a while I could see him falling asleep. He was doing that a lot by then.

Lally was on a roll. 'It's so unfair: this is a man who has borne slights and criticism all his life, not just for his beliefs but for his personal life too. That's so intrusive, isn't it?'

'You mean our mother?' I said tentatively.

'Well, it's not for me to say.'

'Say it anyway, Lally.'

'I only met the woman a few times. She certainly didn't want me around. Of course I didn't mind getting divorced so Iz could marry her. In fact, I wanted to make it easy for them. I even admitted adultery, which was completely untrue – I would never have been unfaithful to Iz. I asked for nothing. He had already given me so much.'

'What was she like? Naturally, Iz never talks about her,' I said, a little sarcastically.

'Too painful, I expect. What she put him through! I didn't see Iz for a long time when he was with her, which broke my heart, of course, but I've heard things from other people.'

'What?' I asked.

'Well, she led... a very chaotic lifestyle.'

'Didn't Iz?'

'No, he was bohemian. That's quite different, Rosie,' Lally said sternly. 'The thing was, she came from a different world. Iz didn't fit into it. His was a world of pure song, not fizzed-up rock music.'

'It's called folk-rock, Lally. What's wrong with that?'

'Folk isn't rock.'

'Maybe she didn't play the crumhorn, but that doesn't mean her music didn't mean something.'

'She wouldn't have known the crumhorn from the sackbut.'

'But you wouldn't know the rhythm guitar from the bass, Lally.'

'Thank God.'

'You're not being logical.'

'Oh Rosie – you're putting me in the position of bad-mouthing your mother. I don't want to do that. I mean, a lot of people did love her and that group she was in,' Lally said. 'They still do, I hear. So I suppose that's good. I won't mention the drugs and all those things,' Lally said primly. 'Of course she was talented. Her voice was lovely, except she ruined it blaring out all those rock songs. If you want to remember one thing about her, listen to that unaccompanied version of "Let Them See Your Scars" she did. That shows you the purity she could have achieved. Oh, Rosie, let's not talk about this any more. You must hang on to your memories of her.'

'I don't have any memories of her,' I said.

Lally looked at her watch. 'I should see if Iz is awake. We've got a lot to do.'

'Lally…' I had suddenly remembered something: 'When you said that Iz would have liked a child.'

'Yes?'

'Didn't he already have one? Joseph.'

'Oh – Joseph,' Lally said dismissively. 'The less said about him the better. Sometimes the apple falls a very long way from the tree.'

Joseph

Joseph dreamt in rhyme. It was his country. Words have jagged edges: they cut you, they catch on your clothes. Rhyme smooths things out. It puts oil on a scratchy engine, honey on a raspy throat. Add rhyme to life, Joseph thought, and you could alter everything: the mean-spirited would become keen-spirited, the acrimonious harmonious. Those were rhymes that particularly applied to his father, Isaac Herzl.

Over the years Joseph had spent more than his fair share of time thinking about rhymes in hotel rooms at night in New Haven or Boston or Plymouth and now, in Manchester. He always found it hard to sleep in them. It was not much better at home but at least there was more in the fridge there than a bag of peanuts and miniatures of Johnnie Walker. Hotels were frustrating for Joseph – the tiny bars of soap that slipped through your fingers in the shower where you could not work out how to change the temperature of the water; the many switches by the side of the bed that only seemed to turn on the light by the door or the bathroom, even though at least one of them had turned off the bedside light when you

had gone to sleep; the key card that worked only inter-
mittently, and certainly never after midnight when the
night porter who spoke no known language had to be
summoned.

What he liked to do in those rooms late at night was
invent additions to other people's songs. Although he
wrote songs of his own for a living, he found thinking
about the ones that he did not have to write strangely
soothing. For the last few weeks he had been toying with
some embellishments to 'Manhattan'. He kept going back
to it like a half-finished crossword puzzle

All songwriters have their perfect song. This song, that
Ella Fitzgerald had sung, was his. He loved the rhymes:
'Manhattan' with 'Staten'; 'Fancy' with 'Delancey'; 'Take
a' with 'Jamaica'. It was perfect. Tonight he was trying
to add a verse that might make the song more topical.
These days you couldn't write a song called 'Manhattan'
without making some reference to the Twin Towers. He
was trying to recast it as the thoughts of someone yearning for New York from abroad. So far, he had come up
with:

> *I dream of old Manhattan*
> *Before they flattened*
> *Those skyscrapers. How I ache*
> *For some New York cheesecake*
> *Before those kamikazes make*
> *An increased quake*

It was not perfect by any means. He had had some trouble
with rhyming 'Cheesecake.' 'Increased quake' was on the
edge of being a false rhyme, but it just about worked.
Before he came up with 'Kamikazes make', he had toyed

with 'Chimpanzees make'. It was a better rhyme, but he worried that equating terrorists with chimpanzees might not play these days. Even in fantasy you're not allowed to cause offence. It also reminded him of some lines in a song called 'Tell Me on a Sunday' which he had a particular aversion to.

The song is about a girl being left by her lover and she's singing about the places in which she would like to hear the bad news. She wants the deed to be done at a zoo where there are chimpanzees, and to be told on a Sunday 'please'. There was no truth to that. It was just rhyme for rhyme's sake. Who – even in the bizarre alternative reality of the musical – would do that? And assuming she did have a preferred setting, Joseph could not understand why it would be in front of a lot of screeching chimpanzees. And why Sunday? Wouldn't the girl rather be left in the middle of the week when at least she had work to distract her? Joseph knew how empty Sundays could be.

To make those lines truthful, it would be better to do something like:

> *Put a box of Kleenex on my knees*
> *Tell me on a Thursday, please*

The sad thing was that, after all these years, he was happier trying to improve other people's lyrics than writing his own. If only he could made a living doing that – he could not see anything enviable in writing musicals, not in Manchester anyway, not when the last show they had written had had crippling reviews and quickly closed there two years ago, not when the first performance of their new show *A Taste of Honey* was tonight, not when the show was in crisis, not when there seemed to be no shred of human comfort coming his way.

It was Alan, Joseph's writing partner, who had come up with the idea of turning Shelagh Delaney's play, *A Taste of Honey*, into a musical. They needed to work: in the last few years their unbroken run of successes seemed to have dried up.

The original play had been written in the late 1950s and was considered rather shocking then: the heroine, Jo, was an art student in Bolton who gets herself knocked up by a black sailor, is seen through the pregnancy by her gay best friend, while her nightmare of a mother causes havoc. It was rather plotless, without the through-line that drives a musical and it was very dated.

Alan came up with the idea of changing the period. Bolton in the 1950s seemed so drab. They moved the time to 1963 and made it about England on the cusp of change: the Beatles, the Lady Chatterley trial, Harold Wilson coming to power. *A Taste of Honey* was what the decade would bring. It was always good to have some cheap symbolism in a musical, Joseph thought.

Then Kevin Lever became involved. He had never produced a show before but he had money, or so they were led to believe. They were swayed by the fact he had been in the music business, talked about a record label underwriting the show and took them to meet 'his investors', who said they loved the show. It was Kevin's idea to get Michelle to play the mother, which had seemed rather inspired at first.

She had not sung onstage for a while, but her voice was still in good shape. She was in a rock band before she went into the soap that made her famous. She was as keen to do the show as Kevin was to have her. He said her coming aboard was going to be the key that would unlock the short-fall. 'Shortfall' was not a word that filled Alan and Joseph with confidence. Still, this would not be the first show – and certainly not the first for Joseph and Alan – that had had money problems. Everybody in the theatre was used to that.

Although she was a big enough name to bring the inves-tors in, she also became the problem: Michelle was the star of the show, top-billed, but the part she played – the mother – was not the biggest part. Jo, the daughter, was the biggest part. Michelle began to make demands that Kevin agreed to: she wanted her part to be bigger, she wanted more songs. Alan and Joseph went crazy trying to give her more lines and crowbar her into scenes she was not meant to be in. The show began to list dangerously.

They had another problem when the part of the daugh-ter went to Toni. The daughter was meant to be scrawny and working class: Toni was a well-fed girl from the Home Counties, all puppy fat and peachy complexion, who had won some TV talent show. And after all the changes, the story made little sense: at the end of the show, Jo was going to take the train down to London in search of her dream, despite knowing nobody there, being nine months pregnant and having no money. They were in the middle of rehearsals and the show was already in crisis.

The only thing that everyone liked was the title song, which the daughter sang at the end of Act 1. Kevin had kept asking for a song that 'came from the heart', and Joseph knew that this one did: it was really about himself:

> *All the hurt you've ever seen*
> *The things you might have been*
> *Put them all in quarantine*

All the hurts you wanted healed
All the thoughts you wanted freed
Grown to flowers in the field
That's what I need

On the afternoon of the first preview, before heading for the theatre, Joseph had been sitting in the bar of the hotel with Alan and Shirley, having a drink to prepare themselves for the onslaught ahead. He hardly taken a sip of vodka when the assistant manager came over to them and asked rather aggressively if they had any idea when their room bills would be settled.

He could see Shirley's face becoming red, not an uncommon occurrence. He knew she was about to blow, also not an uncommon occurrence in the last few weeks. Alan put his hand on her arm and, with the telepathic stun-gun he had perfected after thirty-five years of marriage, managed to calm her down before she broadcast to the whole of the bar the financial mismanagement of the production, her opinion of Kevin, and how badly they had been treated. Once Alan had got rid of the man, Shirley started on a smaller tirade: she simply didn't understand why the stars were living in smart penthouse apartments round the corner from the theatre, while they just had standard doubles in this godforsaken hotel.

'All they have to do is run their lines, for God's sake! You two are doing the real work. You have to write the bloody thing. Remember when we were in Baltimore with *Monte Cristo*? They were so nice that they had a piano shipped up to the suite for you without even being asked. When we did the Dickens show at the Ahmanson, *those* producers were professional. And charming! Remember the leather-bound first editions they gave us inscribed by the cast?'

'I don't think they were first editions, Shirley,' Joseph said. 'First edition Dickens would cost more than putting on the show.'

'Well, it was a giant success! They could have afforded it. And when we did—'

'Please don't go through all our shows, Shirley,' Joseph said wearily.

Just when it seemed as if she might be winding down, he saw Kevin heading through the lobby. Shirley called him over. Joseph could see him freeze. He must have wondered whether he could make a run for it, but there was no escaping Shirley. By the time Kevin got to them he had arranged a smile on his face.

'Did you get my First Night presents?' Kevin said nervously. 'They're only small.'

'I dare say,' Shirley said sourly, 'if you left them at reception, it'll be a decade before they're delivered to our rooms.'

He ignored her. 'I thought the tech run went great. I think we're in pretty good shape, fingers crossed, touch wood, don't walk under ladders.'

In turn, Shirley ignored him. 'Kevin – why is it that, when Alan and Joseph are working all the hours God gave them to come up with yet another song for Michelle, we have to be hassled by the hotel asking about unpaid room bills?'

He looked shifty. 'You'll have to ask the accountant.'

'I don't want to ask the accountant,' she said. 'The accountant is never around. I'm asking you.'

'I'm concept not detail, Shirley,' Kevin said dismissively.

'Actually, Kevin, you're the producer: you're detail not concept. Alan and Joseph are concept.'

Kevin shifted gear. 'Look, you know how hard it's been.' There was a little catch in his voice. 'The last tranche of money's coming through this week. It's been quite a roller coaster. I'll sort out the hotel. And listen – thanks for everything you've done.'

'Are doing,' Shirley corrected him.

'Oh – and I've booked the pizza place opposite after the show. A little celebration.' As Kevin scuttled off, he turned back and gave them a double thumbs-up.

'Pizza!' Shirley said. 'This production is in worse shape than I thought.'

They should change the billing on the posters, Joseph thought: 'Book and Lyrics by Joseph Carter, Music by Alan Isaacs, Anger by Shirley Isaacs'. She was very experienced at it. She had made herself the hurdle that had to be overcome to get to Alan and Joseph. She was finish-the-vegetables-if you-want-pudding. When a meeting was arranged for them to discuss a project, Joseph could hear the person on the other end of the phone saying to Alan, 'Shirley wants to come? What a shame – I don't think they can do another place at the table on Thursday.'

But there she was on Thursday with her hair buffed up by a visit to the hairdresser, her bangley jewellery clanking, lipstick the same shade as her nails, asking questions about contracts and giving the waiters a hard time because she had asked for her tuna well done, not swimming off the plate.

In many ways, though, Joseph loved her. She was like a Rottweiler puppy. He had known her as long as he had Alan. They had all been at school together. Over the years she had been kind and generous to him, but he still reserved the right to have murderous thoughts about her when she threatened to take him shopping to smarten up his wardrobe or brushed the dandruff off the shoulder of his tux. But she was brave. Although it could be embarrassing, Joseph was always impressed by her willingness to be unpopular on their behalf. Why did they pay their agent 10 per cent? Shirley did most of the work. Still, it filled up her life and gave her something to do. Maybe it would have been different if her daughter had not died. Maybe it would have been different if one of the psychics Shirley had been to in the last fifteen years since Sally died had actually got in touch with her. Then she could have interfered with her life on the other side instead of interfering with theirs. Joseph did not want to think about Sally. He did not want to think about holding her bony, fleshless hand in the hospital as insubstantial as a chicken wing.

After all these years Joseph was frightened every time they did a new show. Even their successes, the ones that yielded the songs that were recorded by many singers and made him and Alan a great deal of money, had had difficult starts. This time he was not handling it well. There was too much displacement activity, too many late nights. Normally he was very disciplined, but something surprising had happened to him, something terrifying and exciting at the same time. Shirley had noticed that something was up. She had put her hand on his arm one evening as he was leaving and said meaningfully, 'Take care, Joseph. I'm worried about you.'

He had always taken care before; he had avoided things because he was frightened of the consequences. He didn't know why it was different now. Maybe it was because Gaz was different. He told people he was called Gavin, but in fact his name was Gavriel, an Old Testament variation on Gabriel. He had been brought up by parents who were part of an isolationist Christian Fundamentalist sect and adhered to every commandment in the Old Testament. The name Gavriel meant strong or powerful. He certainly worked out in the gym enough – Joseph paid for his membership.

There was a time when Joseph thought Gaz might become part of his life, but now he knew that it was not going to be. Maybe that was just as well. In his line of work he had seen enough of those kind of boys dragged around by an older actor or director, boys who wanted to act or dance or sing and quickly got a taste for tables at expensive restaurants and private islands in the Caribbean and then began to feel resentful that their talent was not being taking seriously enough.

At least Gaz didn't want to be in show business. He had no interest in it. Although Joseph had invited him, he didn't come to the last day of rehearsals in London when they filled the hall with friends and did a run-through of the show to see how it would play to an audience. Not well, it turned out. There was probably some biblical law about musicals: you were unclean if you saw one. There were laws about everything else. Not that the laws seemed to stop Gaz. He felt bad afterwards, but you didn't have to be a fundamentalist to feel bad afterwards. Christians didn't hold a monopoly on regret. Gaz, drunk – one of the many things forbidden by his religion – sometimes sent him texts late at night quoting commandments from the Bible. They're not my laws, Joseph thought.

Did Gaz believe any of them? He told lies all the time. He told Joseph he did security on the last Take That tour. He told him he had been offered a model-ling contract by *Vogue*. He said his father was an elder in their church, but in fact he was only a lay preacher. He had no idea where Gaz even lived. For a long time he didn't even have his number, but then Gaz broke his phone because he threw it against the wall in a temper and Joseph bought him a new one and got his number that way. Not that he ever answered it. He would just turn up at odd times. Sometimes Joseph came home and Gaz was standing outside on the street waiting, lost and afraid. Something awful had usually happened – his wallet had been stolen or he had been mugged. Who knew if any of it was true?

Gaz always laughed about his parents and their beliefs. At the end of Lent, when his parents were celebrating finishing their forty days of fasting and abstaining from secular pleasures, Gaz suggested that he and Joseph should have their own celebration. Joseph did not think that Lent had necessarily been a period of fasting and abstinence for Gaz. How Gaz wanted to celebrate was with an expensive meal and a lot of coke. Normally, he was the one who had it, but he said he couldn't get any because Joseph never gave him any money, which was not entirely true.

Joseph had done embarrassing things in his time. He called a PR guy who had worked on their last show. Joseph could tell he was taken aback by the request although he was nice enough to put on a breezy no-prob-mate voice as if he organised coke deliveries all the time, which he probably did but not usually for fifty-six-year-olds. He was not to know that this particular one was already a dab hand at squatting in the lavatory of smart restaurants chopping out lines on the seat. Gaz had introduced him to that.

Amazingly quickly, no more than twenty minutes – Joseph would have liked to find someone who would come to repair a leaking pipe with such efficiency – a leather-clad motorbike messenger arrived and the deal was done. Gaz, briefly, was happy.

His therapist once said to Joseph: 'The life you lead is the life you have chosen.' Joseph didn't ask him what the choice would be if you were born in a slum in Delhi or found yourself in Auschwitz. What he did not tell his therapist was that choice was the last thing he was looking for. He wanted not to have control, to be devoid of power like a child, to be encircled by someone else's strength: bound and powerless and with no regrets. It was only conditioning that made you feel regret. Or the Bible. Or the blue morning light and the mess and the credit cards with the white residue on their edges and the empty bottles and the broken glasses.

Joseph's father had once written a song that Joseph could relate to. It was called 'Let Them See Your Scars'. It could have just been about him, but it was also about everyone: in great songs the specific becomes general, the objective personal. People who have never been to America understand 'New York, New York'. We all know that The First Cut Is The Deepest. We always think You'll Never Walk Alone.

He wondered sometimes – not often – if his father had ever seen any of his shows. Joseph doubted it: not pure enough for him. Dinner and a West End show might not be his thing. Of course, Joseph did not know for certain. He had only seen him once in his life.

Luckily, most people did not know that Iz Herzl was his father. Sometimes it was mentioned in interviews in a believe-it-or-not kind of way – 'Surprisingly, lyricist Joseph Carter's father is the famed political activist and singer Iz Herzl but he scoffs at any notion that song-writing might be in the genes...' – but with a different surname he normally managed to fly under the radar. It was not that he was embarrassed by him – he was distinguished if you liked that kind of thing: a father you could admire, probably – it was just that Iz Herzl didn't feel like his father. He was like a rhyme that works but doesn't connect, like the one Joseph had come up with the other night: Hierarchy and Teriyaki. Even Cole Porter couldn't fit that into a song.

A long time ago, Iz Herzl had rejected him. In a letter that was sent a few years after their only meeting Joseph was told that he would be cut out of his father's life 'like a canker'. Joseph supposed that 'canker' must be an archaic word used in folk songs and he had looked it up: it was a destructive growth on a tree that required excision before it killed it. He apparently had 'betrayed' Iz Herzl, and maybe he had. Joseph didn't care much. And yet, there was something intriguing about their connection, some itch that Joseph needed to scratch from time to time. After all, the man was his only living relative apart from his other children who Joseph knew nothing about. His mother had died long ago. He hardly remembered her. She was gone by the time he was five. His grandparents, her parents who were named Carter, brought him up. At any rate, he lived at their house – a house in which the name of Iz Herzl was not to be mentioned.

Although they had only met once, Joseph had seen Iz Herzl another time, ten years before. Their new show on Broadway, *Monte Cristo*, regarded as a sure-fire hit, had opened disastrously and closed after a week. The first night party was held at the Oyster Bar in Grand Central Station. By midnight in New York you can get the morning papers and someone had gone to find them: there was a whisper in Joseph's ear, 'We've got a problem with the

Times...' That was one way of putting it. *'Those who doubt the sterling qualities of* Les Miserables *might find their minds changed by a trip to the Shubert Theatre where they will discover the noisy and witless facsimile that calls itself* Monte Cristo. *The audience's desire to escape may well turn out to be as desperate as that of the count himself, limply portrayed by...* As if a yellow fever flag had been hoisted, the party emptied out in about five minutes. Failure is catching on Broadway. Shirley was weeping. Alan had his head in his hands. Joseph left

The closing notices were put up the next day and he booked himself a flight home. In the cab back from the airport, he was reading the paper and saw a piece about his father: it was his seventieth birthday and there was a concert that night at the Festival Hall. Joseph booked a ticket.

The audience was quite different to the ones he was used to, not a First Night kind of crowd. A lot of beards, and grey hair worn unwisely long, sometimes even ponytails – the Old Testament prophet look that Iz Herzl seemed to favour in the photos Joseph had seen. But there were a surprising amount of young people, earnest couples holding hands, who probably wanted to make the world a better place and believed that it might still be possible. A lot of badges and T-shirts with slogans. Very few AIDS ribbons, Joseph was glad to see. They tended to be the accessory of choice at the kind of shows he was involved with.

He had presumed the show would be rather shambling, but from the beginning he was surprised at how well put together it was. A good set, simple: a patchwork quilt backdrop with a seemingly random mix of posters and photographs – Joseph recognised the miners' strike and the riots at Sharpeville. There were drops right and left, mirror images, with the same giant photo of the man himself. The sound mix was balanced well and they had clearly got someone good to do the lighting. There's a proper producer on this, Joseph thought.

And the crowd there: Joseph wanted to organise buses to Heathrow, charter a plane and fly them to New York as quickly as possible to see *Monte Cristo* before it closed. They would certainly cheer. The audience in New York hadn't. The count could let them see his scars. Political prisoners, jails and escape from oppression. What more could they want?

What his father had that night was what Joseph always prayed for: an audience show. No us and them; no division between stage and audience. They connect. They rhyme. Although the Festival Hall was full, there was a kind of intimacy there. It helped that the crowd knew the material – they cheered at the first strum of most of the songs – but Joseph had seen shows with familiar songs fall as flat as a pancake.

It was billed as 'Iz Herzl and Friends' but his father did not actually come on until the end of the first half. There were a lot of friends. For the first number a very young girl sang a folk song unaccompanied in Hebrew. Joseph remembered that Israel was where his father had first become famous. That was where he began collecting folk songs when he wasn't freedom fighting.

After the girl, a whole variety of people came on. Some spoke and some sang. He didn't know who most of them were. There was a lot of talk about inspiration from people who'd been with Isaac Herzl in South Africa or Guatemala or on the Aldermaston March. Joseph knew that before too long someone was going to come on and talk about the famous demonstration outside the US Embassy. He kept thinking, how long can they keep this going without the star appearing? You'd never have got away with it in a musical.

Then about an hour in, the stage lights went off and stayed off for what seemed like an agonisingly long time. People began shouting his name. Someone screamed 'Happy Birthday!' and everyone laughed and clapped. Then there was movement on the stage. All Joseph could see were little beams of light pointing horizontally out and moving downstage. Slowly a group of men assembled – they were miners with lighted helmets. A follow spot suddenly lit up a figure at the back and Iz Herzl walked forward to the front of the stage. The audience went wild. He didn't acknowledge them at all. If he hadn't started playing his guitar, Joseph thought they would go on cheering for ever, but when he began singing the words *If they take you from the light, And force you into darkest night*, everyone fell into an awed silence. When the miners began singing the chorus, Joseph could see tears rolling down the face of the man next to him.

At the end of the song, the miners stood there impassively facing the audience as his father walked off. Then, one by one, they turned the lights in their helmets off until the stage was in darkness once again. That's how you stage a number, that's how you do it, Joseph thought in awe.

Iz Herzl did not talk much, but he was a strangely charismatic figure, big and bearded with a powerful tenor voice, wearing a leather cap and a baggy suit that looked as if it was made from old hessian sacks. Joseph imagined that if you hugged him, he might smell of tobacco and mustiness. The greatest performers, he thought, give you an intense feeling that they are quite different from you, on some other plane completely, but the strength of their personality can pull you into their world. That was what Iz Herzl was like.

The moment the audience loved most was the most intimate. Joseph thought it was a bit of a cheap trick. Who he guessed to be Iz Herzl's children were brought onstage. They clearly did not know what they were meant to be doing – the boy was tiny, maybe four or five, the girl a few years older. They looked terrified. Iz Herzl began to sing and the little boy started crying. Bizarrely, people seemed to love that and they began to clap. Joseph did not understand much about children – the only child he had ever really known, certainly the only child he had loved, was Shirley's daughter, Sally – but he thought that what Iz Herzl was doing was cruel. The girl put her arms round the boy and glared at the audience. She had an angry, sulky look on her face. Joseph liked the look of her; he liked her spirit.

The final song he did, the last of several encores, was the oddest moment for Joseph. Iz Herzl sang 'I Dreamed I Saw Joe Hill Last Night'. It was a fairly predictable choice at a concert like that, a song about an activist who had been wrongly executed, but he felt something move in his stomach: a hard little ball of lead. It's my name, he thought, the name my father gave me at birth – Joe Hill Herzl – the name I have never used.

Iz Herzl's voice filled the hall, so powerful and loud that Joseph thought the sound system might not be up to it, that the speakers might begin to throb. The applause went on and on. He just stood there for a while, then he laid his guitar gently on the floor of the stage, gave the tiniest bow and walked off. When the lights came up and people began filing out, Joseph stayed in his seat for a while. He was thinking. He was rewriting the song Isaac Herzl was singing:

> *Iz dreamed he saw Joe Hill tonight*
> *Unseen for thirty years*
> *Said he, 'But Joe – I cut you out,'*
> *'Oh no,' Joe cried, 'I'm here!'*
>
> *'Oh no,' Joe cried, 'I'm here!'*
> *'Betrayal knifed my heart,' Iz cried,*
> *'You were like a canker.'*
> *Said Joe, 'It wasn't me, but you*
> *Although I hold no rancour*
> *Although I hold no rancour'*

He was almost the last person to leave the hall. There was an old lady walking slowly up the aisle closest to him, leaning on a stick. She looked at him and smiled. Joseph wondered if she thought he was so overwhelmed by the concert that he was unable to get out of his seat.

'Very moving,' she said. 'So much to do in the world, so much bloodshed. Extraordinary man, isn't he? He's held us all in place.'

'Yes,' Joseph said, 'Like an anchor.'

Rose

The problem with Huddie was that his limbs were wasted. I felt that was an ambiguous description because it could imply that he might have wasted them by his own doing, like a talent that he had been careless with. The talents in question were walking and moving and breathing and he had not been careless with them: he had Duchenne which was in the muscular dystrophy family, one of the forty or so versions of the disease and the most deadly, not that anyone was listing them by speed of death in *Guinness World Records*.

I don't really remember the beginning of the disease, but Carla told me. Huddie was about five. He had begun to have a kind of waddling walk that people thought was cute and funny. In fact, he was compensating because his leg muscles were wasting. Doctors came to the house. Sometimes the things the doctors did made us laugh. Once, one of them knelt by Huddie and kept gently hitting his knee with a little steel hammer. I was on the other side of the room watching them and I did it to myself with the edge of my hand. The difference was that my leg bounced upwards while Huddie's did not. Even a reflex needs muscles.

It was very gradual. A year or so later, he seemed unable to run. Then, by the time he was nine or so, he began falling over all the time and could not get up. There were hushed conversations behind closed doors. Iz seemed be around more, which was unusual in itself. Huddie kept going into hospital and I was not allowed to go with him. I knew things were being hidden from me. They should have told me what was happening, I don't believe you should shield children from anything, even the worst things.

What I remember most vividly was a van pulling up outside the house. I followed Carla and Iz outside and watched two men open the doors at the back and lower a wheelchair out. They pushed it through the front door and into the study.

Huddie came in, slowly manoeuvring himself on the crutches he had been using for a while and stood in the corner. The wheelchair sat in the middle of the room and we all watched it warily for what seemed like a very long time, as if it was a strange animal that might attack at any moment if we moved. I knew there would be no going back from this.

I was intrigued by the things that were handed down from parent to child. We came from a family of songwriters, but clearly that particular gene had not passed down to me and Huddie because we had no talent in that direction whatsoever. It must have been passed down to our mysterious half-brother Joseph, though, because almost the only thing we knew about him was that he wrote songs.

The gene that had been handed down from parent to child in Huddie's case caused his disease. Muscular dystrophy comes through the female line, but it is boys who are affected. The problem was a mutation of our mother's X chromosome so that was one more thing we had to blame her for.

I had read that sometimes, when there was a disease in the family, people often felt that they should become experts on it, as if understanding the disease could help fight it. Nobody else in our family had tried to learn much: they did not travel the world looking for the radical doctor with the unconventional treatment. They did not trawl the Internet for glimmers of hope from other sufferers. They did not have coffee mornings or car-boot sales to raise money for research. Iz had never given a benefit concert for muscular dystrophy, although he would give one for the victims of oppressive regimes. As regimes went, I thought, Duchenne was a pretty oppressive one.

Despite the research I had done, all you really needed to know about the disease was that there was no cure and it killed you. It was not one of those conditions like multiple sclerosis where you could survive for many years. I knew that the chances of Huddie living beyond his teens were slim. I did not have much faith in hope. Hope did not alter the course of events. People sometimes said things to me like, 'He's strong. He can beat this,' but as far as I was concerned, muscular dystrophy was not an arm-wrestling competition. Anyway, Huddie was not strong, he never had been.

Over the years, many people had asked me what the symptoms of the disease were. I explained it like this: there are more muscles in the body than you might think and muscular dystrophy makes them gradually deteriorate. The heart is a muscle. Chest muscles make your lungs work. Even eyelids have muscles. What happens is that finally you are unable to use the organs that your muscles control. There is an inexorable logic to muscular dystrophy: one muscle after another fails, like fuses tripping, and then you die.

Maybe I painted too bleak a picture sometimes, but I did not want people to be unrealistic about Huddie's chances. He was in a wheelchair because his leg muscles were completely gone. He did not have much power in his hands, but there was still a little in his fingers. If I placed them on the computer keyboard, he could type a little, but that, too, seemed to be getting harder for him now. For the time being, Huddie still had some power in his chest muscles to get rid of the fluid on his lungs, but his throat muscles were not in good shape and he found it difficult to swallow his saliva. When I was with him, I kept a hanky to wipe his mouth. He would pause while he was talking and I would lean over so he could dribble into the hanky. Spitting requires muscles.

I was surprised that Huddie could be as cheerful as he was. When we played Monopoly, even though I had to move the pieces for him, he laughed gleefully if he was the first one to get a hotel on his property. If he lost the game he sulked. Someone once said that they hoped Huddie was 'hanging in there', I presumed that one of the things they were asking was if he still had the ability to move up and down the spectrum of feelings from happiness to sadness, from laugh to sulk, rather than just flat-lining into depression. Yes, I said, for what it's worth, he is hanging in there but that will not extend his life. I did not want people to underestimate the logic in the disease. I did not want them to talk about the power of positive thought.

It would be unfair to say that nobody in our house apart from me took much notice of Huddie, but it sometimes felt like that. Maybe Iz would have done stuff with him if he hadn't been old and ill, but maybe not. He certainly hadn't spent much time with us when we were children. There were several different carers who came in every day and did the practical stuff like the loo and washing him and putting him on the respirator, which he often needed, and the doctor came about every ten days to examine him.

It wasn't really much of a life for Huddie but together we got as close to creating one as we could. I didn't have much of a life either and he did as much for me as I did for him. He wanted to hear about what I had been doing at school and what I did when I wasn't with him. I had to exaggerate a little because if you have to live vicariously you want to live through someone who at least has some good stories to tell. I made out to Huddie that I lived a life full of teenage activity – gossip with friends, boys I fancied, school trips I took. But I didn't really gossip and there weren't any boys I fancied much. School trips were to places like the Science Museum where I had been far more often and knew far more than any of my teachers. I found a lot of them rather limited. I liked learning on my own – my pace was faster than theirs.

I was not solitary by choice. At school I tried to be friendly. There were girls I could pass the time of day with but I knew they would have preferred someone else to sit next to them at lunch. They did not invite me to their birthday parties or to go outside the school gates to smoke with them. It was lucky I had Huddie. He was all I really needed. He was so bright and funny even though nobody except me really got his sense of humour. He knew so much about so many things. If he had not been dying, I think he could have achieved anything.

The school holidays had begun, so I could spend more time with Huddie. On that day, as usual, I gave him his breakfast – mostly liquid – which always took a while to do. Then it was time for his teeth. I bent his fingers around the toothbrush and helped him raise his hand to his mouth. He was not going to win any teeth-cleaning competitions, but what did it matter if he needed a few fillings?

I helped him with deodorant. He used a roll-on one because he could not press the button on a spray so I put it in his hand and then raised his arm so he could rub it on. I wanted him to do as many things as he could, while he still could. Next, even though he did not need to shave every day, he jerkily raised his chin and I sprayed a little aftershave on his neck. We had almost finished the bottle of CK One and we had talked about moving on to something else so I had got him some little sample bottles to choose from. Then we did his trousers. Huddie was very particular about cleanliness: because of the food stains he liked his loose tracksuit bottoms to be changed several times a day. That was easier said than done because it was hard to pull them off without him raising his backside. He had perfected a little squirm, which normally helped get the job done. Our morning routine was easy and unselfconscious. We were like a couple who did ballroom dancing: we knew each other's moves by heart.

After we had finished all the early morning stuff, I pushed Huddie to his desk and turned the computer on for him. Just then, the door opened abruptly. It was Joan.

'Could I have a word?' she said.

I exchanged a glance with Huddie and went out into the kitchen with her.

Neither Huddie nor I had really taken to Joan. For one thing, we thought she looked like a witch. She always took her shoes off and glided silently round the house. You never knew when she might appear. I was cross with her now.

'You know, Joan, maybe you should knock when you come into Huddie's room.'

Joan looked taken aback. 'Well, I'm sorry,' she said in an insincere voice.

'I'd knock if I came into Carla's study.'

'Well, we're working. We don't want our concentration broken.'

'Huddie's working.'

'Oh, I thought he was just listening to music on his iPod.'

'Actually, I download talking books on to it for him,' I said coldly. 'He's listening to Thomas Hardy. I'm the only person who reads to him now, but I can't do it all the time. Everybody else is too busy these days.'

Joan ignored that. 'Oh, Thomas Hardy,' she said scornfully. 'All those downtrodden women up to their knees in Wessex mud.'

I did not want to go on with this. 'Was there something you wanted?' I said as politely as I could manage.

'Carla and I need the kitchen and dining room tonight from about six. Our group is coming round and we've got to do food for them.'

'What group?'

'Carla and I are planning a concert at the Magpie's Nest. We've got an advisory group together. We're calling it "An Evening of Sister Songs".'

'I didn't know you sang.'

'I don't,' Joan said. 'I'm Carla's manager.'

'Since when? She's never needed a manager before.'

'That's because she's had to be a housewife up to now. Her singing career is going up a notch or two. It's her turn.'

I laughed. 'Carla's never been a housewife! She's never done any cleaning. The only thing she can cook apart from toast is Boston baked beans.'

'And why should she cook, young lady?'

'I'm not saying she *should*. I'm just saying she *doesn't*.'

'Anyway, maybe it's time you looked after yourselves.'

'Huddie can't look after himself. Nor can Iz.'

'Actually, we're thinking about getting a professional carer for Iz. It's too much for Carla.'

'Lally does most of the caring for Iz.'

'A medically trained carer.'

'Huddie has a carer. Now Iz is going to have one, too? Are we going to have one each?'

'Very funny.'

'Why are you involved?' I said.

'Carla's got so much on her plate. I'm just trying to help.'

'I can't just not use the kitchen tonight. I need to do Huddie's food at eight.'

'Can't he eat earlier?'

'He has to eat at regular times.'

'You know, Rose – of course Huddie's got problems but maybe it would give him more self-respect if everyone didn't treat him like an invalid.'

'He doesn't need lessons in self-respect from you, Joan. Or anyone.' I left the kitchen and went up to my room and slammed the door.

Within few minutes, I could hear Carla come downstairs. I knew that Joan had sneaked on me. 'Rose?' she called. 'Where are you?'

I came out of my room and stood in the doorway with my arms folded. Carla came forward and took me in her arms.

'Oh, Rose,' she said. 'Please help me.'

Carla was still attractive. She had a lovely voice, still American but softened by her years in England. Her hair was hardly grey at all. She pinned it up so loosely that it gradually fell down as the day went on. Her skin was unlined and she never wore make-up, which everybody else her age seemed to do.

She did not sound cross, but then she was never cross. She seemed to glide through life unaware of other people. Obviously, Joan was an exception.

'Joan can be awkward, Rose. Things don't always come out the right way,' she said.

'No,' I said.

'People sometimes hide their vulnerabilities.'

I did not understand why someone would want to hide their vulnerability under a layer of rudeness and aggression. It might be better to do it the other way round.

'She doesn't care about Huddie.'

'We all care about Huddie, Rose.'

'But nobody spends any time with him.'

Carla gave a sigh. 'You know, if anyone had asked me when I was twenty what it would be like in my forties, I would have said they would be the serene years, but they're not. There's so little time – everything is so difficult.'

'If someone had asked Huddie when he was twelve what it would be like when he was fifteen, I don't think he would have said anything about serenity.'

'Oh Rose, everything's so black and white for you. You'll—'

'Please don't tell me I'll understand when I'm older.'

Carla took my hand. 'All I want to do is to sing again, do some little concerts. I think I'm owed that, aren't I?'

'When you used to do them, Iz would come on and sing at the end with you. That's not going to happen any more.'

'Rose – I loved singing with Iz. He taught me everything. But when I did concerts on my own I knew
everyone was waiting for him to come on at the end. I
was like the salad course. That didn't feel so great.'

I hadn't thought of that. 'Of course you should do some
concerts. But why does Joan say she's your manager?'

'Oh, Joan – she just wants to be involved.' Carla smiled
as if it was an amusing little quirk.

'Why can't she be involved in her own life?'

'She's my friend, Rose. I'd be welcoming to any of your
friends who came over.'

'But none of my friends do come over,' I said. I didn't
want to say that I had no real friends to invite over.

'There are so many rare songs that my father collected
on his trips. People haven't heard them. Joan's helping me
sort them out. The concert's a kind of tribute to him.'

'Then why don't you call it "An Evening of Father
Songs" instead of "Sister Songs"?' I instantly wished I
hadn't said that.

Carla looked hurt. 'Our work is important to me, Rose.
I don't want everyone to just think of me as Iz Herzl's wife.
Joan is very dear to me. She helps me in so many ways.'

'With folk songs?' I said doubtfully.

'She's an historian. She's finding linking passages to put
between the songs so they're in some kind of historical
context.'

'If she wants to come here all the time, she should have
some consideration for Huddie.'

'I know,' she said. 'And I should do more.'

'Why don't you spend some time with him this afternoon? I've got to go to the library.'

She sighed, 'Oh, Rose – I just can't today. Joan and I
have got an action group.'

'For what?'

'We're trying to force the council to do an Eco-Audit.'

I just looked at her. 'Is that it? An Eco-Audit?'

'It's important,' she said.

'Maybe I'll understand when I'm older. Maybe I'll understand everything then.'

Shirley

Shirley tried to have as much faith as she could when she thought about Sally, but it might have been easier if she had a different faith than the Jewish one, in which life after death or reincarnation were mired in endless theological disputes. In their version, after all that agony, Jesus did not even get resurrected.

Alan had no faith at all. She was sad that he had closed off Sally in his mind. To him, she was simply dead. His family were from Hampstead, more assimilated than Shirley's, intellectual Jews who scorned any traditions or sentimentality. Alan's parents were the first people she had met who were prepared to express some small doubt about the State of Israel, to enter into the kind of debate, which, in their house, with the smart Italian furniture and abstract art, could turn terrifyingly lively.

Down the hill, in the less rarefied climes of the Garden Suburb, there seemed to be no scepticism at all. Unlike Alan's family, hers certainly believed in Israel. During the Six-Day War and the 1973 one, she remembered her mother listening to the radio for hours. When Shirley's father returned from work she would bring him up to speed after they had stopped arguing with each other about their interpretation of key events on the front line as if they even knew one end of the Golan Heights from the other.

As a child, her parents had often played Iz Herzl's children's songs and now from some distant recess of a cupboard one of his old albums, *The Hope – And Other Songs of Zion*, was dredged out to scratch its way round the turntable. The song they listened to most was 'The Hope', a slowed-down version of 'Hatikva', the Israeli national anthem, which Iz Herzl had translated into English. He was a hero to her parents and their friends. They went to his concerts. He was a big figure then but Shirley had always felt rather ambivalent about him. Although he did not generally talk about it, Joseph had told her and Alan years ago that Iz Herzl was his father. She could not believe a father would want to have no contact with his son. What else was there in your life other than your children?

Shirley was going to Manchester later in the week for the first previews of the show. She knew that Alan and Joseph would need protection. The rehearsals in London had been a vipers' nest and it would be worse up there. They were clueless together. They knew how people were in musicals, just not how they were in real life. She was glad she could fit in one more meeting with the Group before she left.

She had grown to rely on the Group. She still hoped it would help her. Everything else had failed: the spiritual advisers, clairvoyants, psychics, whatever you wanted to call them, that she seen over the years. They had failed to deliver. You can't really ask for your money back, she thought. They don't offer a guarantee. But just because a coin comes up heads a thousand times in a row, it could just as easily come up tails the next time. All she knew was that Sally was too strong and vital a person not to be somewhere. She had glimpsed her once a long time ago and she knew that she might be able to do it again. She had not gone into any detail with the Group. Sally was hers and she did not want to pass her around like a box of chocolates.

It annoyed Shirley that some members of the group always arrived late. She had raised it on more than one occasion. A meeting was not like a cocktail party where you could turn up when you felt like it. While they were waiting around for everyone to arrive, it meant that there was some awkward small talk. It was not like talking to friends. You knew both too much about the people in the group and not enough. It was irrelevant what their holiday plans were or what colour they were going to paint their kitchen.

The Group was a collective, but somebody had to step forward to make some of the decisions and it tended to be Shirley – she took the subscriptions and organised the bank account from which the rent was paid and circulated the little newsletter to everyone. She had got used to the people in the group. It was not that she did not want new members, it was just a question of getting used to each other's energies. It was important to have an air of calm in the room and strangers tended to jangle that up. A few months before, she had suggested that they should close the membership, but Ella, a rather aggressive Welsh woman who Shirley had not taken to, got rather upset and said it was cruel to turn people away. Everybody seemed to agree and Ella said rather rudely,

'After all, Shirley, you were a new member once and we took you in, didn't we?'

The hall was pleasant in the summer. Then they had the big windows open, even though the curtains suddenly billowing out as if there was someone behind them could make the less experienced of the group overexcited. It was cold in the winter and they sometimes discussed moving somewhere else but Shirley worried that a new location might dissipate any ground they had gained. It could take months to get back up to speed.

There were more women in the group than men. Alan did not come. He had never come. People say that men are more sceptical and less emotional than women, but Shirley was not convinced. The men who were regulars often seemed very vulnerable. One of them, David, who was the informal leader of the group and the only person she had got to know a little, had broken down and wept in front of them more than once. He was a structural engineer. His wife had been a chronic invalid for twenty years before she died. He had told Shirley that he felt he hadn't done enough for her. That was why he wanted to get in touch with her. A lot of people came to the group looking for forgiveness.

Once, soon after Shirley had started coming to the group, he had asked her out for a drink after a meeting. After some small talk he had said that, owing to his wife's illness, they had not been able to have marital relations for many years and now she had passed on he felt he should rectify this gap in his life. He said he had the feeling that Shirley might possibly be unfulfilled in that area, too, and wondered whether there might be an arrangement they could make together, possibly in the afternoons, if that suited her. He said it so politely and diffidently that she did not take offence. If you don't ask, you don't get, she thought. But she said, thank you, no, that was not really the kind of thing she was looking for from the group.

She sometimes wondered exactly what it was she was looking for. They did not do anything silly like Ouija boards or séances but they did talk a lot about psychic energy. Everyone, in their own way, wanted to find the person they had loved, although what each one of them meant by 'find' was different. They mostly talked about their experiences. She found it reassuring to be with people who might understand something of what she had gone through with Sally.

She worried sometimes that there might only be a finite amount of psychic energy in the room, and if it was used it to try and contact someone like Ella's mother, who had died a perfectly ordinary death at ninety-seven from natural causes having led a perfectly ordinary life, it might get diluted. There were expected deaths and there were unexpected deaths. Shirley's mother had had a heart attack at eighty-four and she could think of no circumstances in which she would have tried to contact her unless it was to get her recipe for chocolate rugelach.

But she found some people's stories very moving. Fraser had told them about his wife's death: he had been driving while he was drunk and she had gone through the windscreen when he drove into a motorway bridge. Maybe he had had enough punishment, Shirley thought. One of his legs had been amputated and he was in a wheelchair. Aaron's daughter had lived in Hastings and she had committed suicide by walking into the sea. He had bought a little hut on the beach and spent his weekends there watching the tide come in and out.

There was often a lot of talk about coincidence and whether it was significant – seeing people in the street who reminded them of their loved one, strange phone calls on birthdays when there was silence on the line. Tonight someone was talking about a supermarket bill.

'I don't normally even look at the receipt but in the last couple of weeks I've had two bills that came to sixteen pounds and five pence. Sixteenth of May – that was my husband's birthday. He always did the shopping. Could that mean anything?'

Ella was always the one who was sceptical. She said it was important to be rigorous, to try and sort out the false alarms from the real glimmers to avoid disappointment, although there never seemed to be any false alarms where her mother was concerned.

She was dismissive. 'I don't know,' she said. 'I wouldn't set too much store by it if I were you.'

The woman looked crestfallen, and Shirley felt rather sorry for her.

'We're not in the business of certainties, are we Ella?' she said curtly. 'It's all about belief. If she believes it means something, it probably does mean something.'

Then someone else spoke up. 'I wanted to ask a question – is it easier to get in touch with someone who died a natural death or someone who died before their time?'

Ella, of course, jumped in before anyone else could speak. 'I think it's less to do with timing than guilt,' she said. 'I think if guilt is involved it can be very hard.'

'Why do you think that?' David said

'Well, if it's been a simple loving relationship both sides want the connection to continue, don't they? I've glimpsed my mother quite often, actually. There was so much love there,' she said smugly.

'I don't think that's specific to you,' Shirley said crossly. 'I think you'll find that there's love in all the relationships we had.'

'Of course there's love,' Ella said sharply, 'but for some people here there's a lot of guilt, too. I think that puts up barriers. With my mother I just felt sadness when she died. There was no guilt there.'

'That's very lucky for you.'

Ella ploughed on. Irony was not her strong suit. 'I'm not saying there's any stigma about guilt. Not at all. Everybody here has been very open about it. Look how brave Fraser was when he told us about his guilt over his wife's death in the crash.'

'But I still don't know what you mean,' Shirley said. 'What's your point?'

'I mean that if there's blame involved, the person who's died may not want to be contacted.'

'Oh that's ridiculous.'

Ella ignored her. 'And there are areas of blame that are not clear cut.'

'How do you mean?'

'I know that Aaron would be the first to admit that there might be family factors in his daughter's suicide. And what about a child addicted to drugs who takes an overdose? Or anorexia…'

The word hung in the air for a moment. Shirley felt herself turning cold.

'What about it?' She could not stop her voice trembling a little.

'I read an article about it recently. Sometimes there can be social issues connected with anorexia, family pressures—'

Shirley was on her feet. 'You are an extraordinarily foolish woman,' she said. She could feel her eyes filling with tears. 'You don't know the first thing about my daughter.'

David got up and put his hand gently on her shoulder. 'Shirley …'

She pulled away from him. Everyone in the group was staring at her.

'People don't know what causes anorexia, but I can tell you one thing, Ella: there were no pressures in my family. I do not have one iota of guilt about Sally. You're not the only person who ever had a perfect relationship with someone who's died. Sally and I had more bonds of love than you could ever know.'

The tears were streaming down her face. She wiped her eyes. 'I have to go now, I'm sorry. I'll see you next week,' and she walked out of the room with as much dignity as she could muster.

By the time she got home she was feeling calmer. She wished she had not got so upset. Still, she could apologise next week. The Group was all about forgiveness, wasn't it? What was odd was that Alan wasn't at home. He was always there with an open bottle of wine and something simple like sandwiches when she got back. Then she realised: she had only been out for forty-five minutes. The Tuesday night group normally lasted at least two hours so he must have thought he had time to go out and do whatever he was doing before she got back.

She went to the bathroom to redo her face. Her eyes looked like a panda's. As she looked into the mirror she saw a scrunched-up ball of paper in the corner that had obviously missed the waste paper bin. She reached down and picked it up. Without unfolding it, she knew it was one of those small-print leaflets about side-effects you get in a box of pills. She was a doctor's daughter, she could spot anything medical from five hundred paces. She had heard about Viagra, of course: you could hardly pick up a magazine these days without some article about how it had changed people's lives.

She sat down on the lavatory and felt tears come into her eyes again. She dabbed them with some loo paper. She didn't want to have to do her make-up again. There were so many things going through her head. It was like finding a secret message in a bottle and it made her want to take Alan in her arms and hold him close. She wanted to say, 'Oh my darling, I don't mind, I never minded. You gave me – you still give me – so much.' She could understand his reasoning in getting the pills – 'out of practice' hardly covered it – but why after all these years? What was the tectonic shift in Alan that made him choose today to bring it back into their lives? It wasn't that she felt unfulfilled exactly, but she felt less soft – dried-up and less giving than she once did. Despite what David said to her the night they had had coffee she hoped that there wasn't some aura of discontent flowing out of her, some cry for comfort pitched at dog-whistle frequency that only a middle-aged engineer with sharp hearing could pick up.

She rarely thought about that side of their marriage, but if she did she would say that it had not precisely vanished but that they had put it in a Swiss bank vault and somehow the combination had gone missing. Now Alan was trying to find it again and she loved him for it, even though she was not sure that she could just flick that switch after all this time. It was like a surprise party being given for her and she didn't know if she could conjure up the requisite wide-eyed amazement, but if it meant that much to Alan she would try.

They had shared so much. You could not take that away or diminish it. She had heard that the death of a child could break a marriage. She understood that. You recover and you don't recover. A shared pool of grief could drown you both, could have you fighting against each other to get to the surface. Maybe it was easier not to share it. Maybe that was why they had survived. But there was a price to be paid: not everything could go on as it had before.

She knew that people were meant to think about sex all the time. She didn't. She wasn't sure she ever had. It was never really like that with Alan and her. Of course he was attractive, or at least she found him so. He was the first person she had slept with. She had done other things with other people, quite a lot of things with quite a lot of other people, but he had got the prize. That was how people looked at it then.

You would never know it from reading the papers but there were other bonds that held people together. It was not all rumpled sheets. She and Alan were so close that you could scarcely fit a sheet of paper between them. They had grown up together – from the age of thirteen they were at school together with Joseph. Alan was shy and didn't have a lot of friends apart from him, and Shirley had dragged them out of their shell. She was still doing it.

Normally, when she got back from the Group, she and Alan sat and talked for a while. She liked to wind down: the group could be very intense sometimes. The one thing she and Alan had always done was talk. That was something that never stopped after Sally died, although they never talked about her. She wondered what they would say tonight.

Alan got back just before ten. He looked surprised to see her. He said he had been round at Joseph's trying to fix the last song, despite having worked on it all day. It hadn't gone well, apparently, and Alan seemed down. There was a lot of pressure: they were heading to Manchester next week.

Alan seemed distracted. She had to ask him twice if he wanted some wine. To her surprise they did not sit and talk. He said he was going straight to bed. As he passed behind her chair he put his hand on her shoulder and gave it a little squeeze.

She did not normally have a bath in the evening but she thought it would be a good idea to have one tonight just to be on the safe side. She was feeling rather tense, anyway. Maybe she took too long because by the time she came out of the bathroom, Alan was asleep in his bed.

She woke early, before it was light, and went downstairs to make herself some coffee. There was a white envelope on the mat, no stamp. It had been delivered by hand.

Dear Shirley,

This is rather awkward, I'm afraid. After you left tonight, we had an informal chat and the general consensus was that the Group feels that you should have a break from our Tuesday sessions for a while. Some people feel that the kind of positive energy we need so badly has been compromised and that it will be some time before we can get back on track. I hope you will understand.

> *Yours very sincerely*
> *David Arbuthnot*

She felt her eyes welling up. She had to reply to the letter, and she was going to do it gracefully. She sat down at her computer.

To: All members of the Tuesday Night Group
From: Shirley Isaacs

I don't think it is beyond the powers of our Group to extend the same courtesy and respect we employ when trying to reach those we have loved and lost to our deal-ings with the living.

> *My daughter Sally and I could not have been closer*
> *and more bonded. All I've ever wanted is to let her know*
> *that I love her as much as I did from the day she was*
> *born to the day when the brutal disease of anorexia came*
> *out of nowhere and extinguished her like a candle. While*
> *the Group has been helpful on occasion, I can just as*
> *easily do my own work in moments of quiet reflection.*
> *I wish you all the very best of luck.*

They would need it. They were a sorry lot, really. Maybe leaving the Group was meant to be, and she wasn't going to weep for it. Anyway, by the time she and Alan and Joseph got to Manchester, there was more than that to worry about.

Maurice

A year before, in the freezing winter of 1946, a bus had
skidded off the road on an icy patch and ploughed into
the wall of the school, its nose going right into one of
the storerooms by the porter's lodge. Maurice liked to
think of the runaway bus as an attack on the school by
the forces of real life. If only it had crashed all the way
through to the cloisters and lain there like a great beached
whale blocking the path to the school chapel: that would
have been a symbol nobody could ignore.

Because of the wartime shortage of building materials,
the roadside wall had not been repaired, simply patched
up and boarded, but Maurice knew how to ease himself
in, which one of the planks had some give to it. Although
he had never found anyone else in there, he was clearly
not the only person to use it. The rubble-strewn floor was
dotted with cigarette butts, and old newspapers crackled
underfoot. Once he had trodden on a used rubber. Of
course the place was out of bounds – some feeble punishment would be meted out to him if he was caught – but
what was not out of bounds at King George, what trans-
gression did not go unpunished? This was his secret

place. This was where he had worked out his plan for the Communist Society.

Some weeks after the choir debacle he was sitting there on a dirty concrete block smoking a cigarette he had stolen from his father's silver case. It was almost time to head to the assembly hall. Today was Open Day, always held at the end of the summer term, when the next term's intake of new boys was brought by their parents to tour the school. Among the other activities of the day – a lecture by the headmaster, a gymnastics display in the quadrangle, a march-past by the school corps – the school societies all set up stands in the hall to entice the new boys to join.

When Maurice put in his application for his society to the committee, headed by Mr Costello, they began putting up obstacles immediately. First, they rejected it because they said there should be two proposers, not one. Several people he asked to help him laughed in his face. Finally, he had to twist Arthur's arm to get him to co-sign the form, waving away his objection that he already had his hands full with the Rowing Society.

Then, even with two proposers, the committee rejected the application on the grounds that societies were meant to promote hobbies and interests, not to encourage political affiliation. When he pointed out that there was already a Conservative Society, Mr Costello said that it was because of the special circumstances of the head boy being the son of Godalming's MP. He knew there was nothing to be gained by arguing the point. He resubmitted the application calling it the Russian Society and, on the basis that it was going to concentrate on literature and music, it was grudgingly allowed.

It was going to be a big day for him. He felt nervous and unsure, but there was something he always did to calm himself down. He took the pencil case out of his satchel and removed the dull, silver dividers. He rolled up his sleeve and ran the points along the skin of his inner arm. They left thin white lines, and a pleasant, itchy feeling. This was just the preliminary, he was just drawing the map. His favoured pattern was the shape of a noughts and crosses board. He pressed harder now, and the skin broke, like the meniscus on a glass of water. The pleasure was in the precision of the angles, the way the lines slowly bubbled up with red. This time, there was not a lot of blood. Maybe his system was sluggish and tired. Maybe his body was conserving its strength for what might happen later. He mopped his wrist with some tissue paper, pulled down the sleeve of his shirt and buttoned it up. There would be a stain, but it would be hidden by his jacket and he could scrub it later so that his mother would not see the blood when she did the wash.

When he got to the hall, there was a lot of activity. People were milling around, setting up trestle tables and pinning posters to the wall. His stand was between the Fencing Society and the Model Soldier Society. He unrolled the huge red banner he had painted on a big square of canvas with 'Russian Society' stencilled in black letters at the top, stood on a chair and painstakingly nailed it to the wall. He placed his old gramophone on the table in front of the stand and laid the 'Internationale' on the turntable. The music began and he waited.

The hall was beginning to fill up but the new boys, shepherded by their parents, seemed to be giving him a wide berth. Some of his classmates pointed and sniggered at him. After five minutes, even though it was not particularly loud, Mr Costello strode over aggressively and told him to turn the music off because it was interfering with the military marches the Corps Band were playing a few stands away. To be silenced by 'Colonel Bogey' and a medley of Imperialist Souza marches was a metaphor in itself. There was a lot of noise in the hall anyway, and Mr Costello had certainly not asked the choir to sing more softly. They were processing round the hall in full regalia, their dark-green cassocks matching the school colours, holding candles aloft and singing a selection of their standards: the *Nunc Dimittis*, the *Magnificat* and Psalm 81, for which Mr Costello had done a special setting. Maurice knew the music backwards: at last year's Open Day he had been part of the choir.

On the first circuit round the hall, Arthur had given Maurice a wave, but when the choir came round a second time, he stopped by the stand. Although they were in some of the same classes, Maurice did not see much of him now. When Arthur wasn't singing, he spent most of his time with the rowers. He had a sleekness about him these days, an easy way of moving through a room that Maurice, despite himself, rather envied.

Arthur gave an awkward little grin. 'Any takers?' he said, gesturing at the big red banner.

Maurice closed the notebook in front of him so Arthur could not see the blank page on which he had hoped to fill in some names. 'People are just nervous,' he said. 'I'm not offering any easy options.'

Arthur laughed. 'Like the Ramblers' Society.'

Maurice couldn't work out if that was a joke or not. 'In this place, people would be more interested in a Fascist Society.'

Arthur smiled as if Maurice had just said something witty, then he said, 'It's my birthday on Saturday. I'm having a party. Will you come?'

'I'll be going to London on Saturday. I'm there a lot these days,' Maurice said grandly.

The last birthday party of Arthur's he had been to must have been two years ago. Arthur's father had organised a treasure hunt. It would probably be different now, but he was a bit out of touch with that kind of thing. People had stopped inviting him to their birthdays.

'Why don't you go to London on Sunday instead? It would be nice if you came.'

Arthur did have a curious sweetness about him, and for a moment Maurice was touched. He hadn't actually planned to go to London at all.

'We're going to go rowing,' Arthur said. 'There'll be a race. With prizes.'

'I don't think I'd be very popular with your rowing friends.'

'Oh, they won't mind,' Arthur said.

'Well, they should mind,' Maurice answered, rather more aggressively than he had meant.

If Arthur looked crestfallen, that was too bad. You had to make sacrifices, discard people if they distracted you from your purpose. Too much singing to the glory of God had rotted the boy's brain, even if he did have a lovely voice.

But then Maurice softened. He wanted to say something else to Arthur, to let him know that despite the vast chasm between them he still considered him to be a friend. But it was too late: Arthur was scuttling up the hall to catch the other choristers who were still droning their *Nunc Dimittis*. He had left his candle behind, but Maurice wasn't going to go chasing after him.

A great sense of desolation came over him. Of course you weren't meant to dwell on the sacrifices you had made, you were meant to concentrate on the things you had achieved and were going to achieve. But what were they? It wasn't just that he was ignored, it was as if he had become invisible – not the kind of invisible that you might find in a fable, that would let you sit unnoticed in the girls' changing room, but the kind that had you screaming for recognition in an unseeing world. It was as if everyone was colour-blind. Did his huge red banner read as grey to those smirking, self-satisfied boys, their colour spectrum as limited as a dog's? They ran in packs, anyway, sniffing one another's rancid arses, trying to get their pathetic merit badges and silver cups and arguing over which was the smartest college at Oxford or Cambridge to apply for.

Had a war been fought just for everything to continue in the same way? He felt ashamed that he personally had sacrificed so little, but it was hard to know what to contribute when you were not in control of your own destiny and lived in a house where complacency enveloped everything like a blanket of snow. Maurice's father was not even prepared to enter into a debate about the new people's health scheme that the government was talking about bringing in. And he was a doctor! Weren't they meant to want to make people well? All his father would say was that he did not believe people should get something for nothing. But most people had nothing to start with – why couldn't they get an injection for typhus or cholera for nothing as well?

Everybody seemed to think that now the war was over the struggle had ended, but that was demonstrably not so. 'Permanent Revolution' – that's what Trotsky had called it. It was lucky he had never set foot in Godalming. If he had, he might have given up the struggle in despair and put the ice pick into his skull himself.

Maurice suddenly realised that what he was doing was too small to register with anyone. He had to go further, make them all understand how serious he was. He reached under the table and picked up the can of black paint with which he had stencilled the society's name on the banner. He stood on the chair and, with his arm stretched out, began to paint a hammer and sickle as large as he possibly could. It did not matter that the paint dripped down. It did not matter that it was crude – so much revolutionary art was.

The headmaster was beginning to make his welcome speech at the far end of the hall and tea and cakes were being served. It was grotesque how the well-fed burghers of Godalming would go anywhere for free food when the people that really needed it were starving. They weren't offering Victoria sponge in the displaced persons' camps in Germany.

Afterwards, he could not quite remember the exact sequence of events. He did know that it was then he had switched the gramophone back on and turned the 'Internationale' up as high as it could go. But what happened with the candle? Did it fall off the table and roll to the wall on which the banner hung down? Did he kick it there? It didn't really matter.

It wasn't that the music was loud enough to drown out everything else in the hall but there was something about the mass of deep voices singing the song in Russian that made the other music sound tinny and superficial.

Heads began turning towards him. He saw Mr Costello up near the stage cocking his head like an animal sensing danger and doing a double-take, first outraged by the level of the music and then seeing the smoke beginning to rise from the bottom of the banner. It was interesting watching panic start. He saw a woman do a double-take when she noticed the smoke rising up from behind him, but all she did was grab her scrawny kid to her bosom and tug on her husband's arm who was facing in the other direction. He glanced over at Maurice's stand, looked startled and then conferred with his silly wife, as if the subject needed some discussion before they could come up with a solution. Then someone shouted '*Look!*' in a horrified voice and a certain amount of cautious pandemonium broke out as Mr Costello began running in Maurice's direction like a demented bull. The other sounds in the hall were dying out as people began to realise that something was up. The choir stopped in their tracks and the Corps Band petered out except for some straggling tuba notes. The fencers seemed to have had some fairy-tale curse put on them that turned them into statues.

Now, without much to compete with it, the 'Internationale' sounded as it was meant to sound – rousing and strong and defiant – even if it was only for a moment: the first thing Mr Costello did was to kick over the table on which the gramophone sat and it clattered to the floor and the music screeched to a halt. Heads were turning this way and that to spot the disturbance, but finally, as if by general consensus, they began to turn in Maurice's direction. Mr Costello was standing in front of him, breathing hard – in fact, almost frothing at the mouth. His hands were flailing around and he pushed Maurice out of the way to get to the flaming banner behind him. He kicked at it in rather a feeble way, as if he didn't want to get his shoes dirty. '*Water!*' he shouted. '*Get some water!*'

The fire alarm began ringing loudly which caused an instant panic. Someone had opened the big double doors that led to the quad and some of the masters were pushing people through. Maurice was no expert, but he had read somewhere that the last thing you should do in the case of fire was to open doors and let oxygen in, but the masters were clueless as ever. Now the noxious black smoke and the flames spreading up the banner were sending Mr Costello crazy. He was trying to pull it away from the wall, making jerky little lunges as if he was frightened it was going to fight back.

A boy from the fourth form arrived with two buckets of water and Mr Costello grabbed them off him and doused the banner, then screamed at him to get more. It was typical behaviour from someone in authority – keep the people who were just following orders as downtrodden as possible.

The fire alarm suddenly stopped, but it had been so loud that the reverberations continued in Maurice's ears. Gradually the sound levelled out and all that was left was the echoing footsteps of the few people left in the hall and Mr Costello breathing heavily at him through clenched teeth. Maurice wondered if he was going to hit him. The water had put out the flames but there was still a lot of smoke. In as cool a voice as he could muster, he said, 'Sorry, sir. Bit of an accident.'

Mr Costello gave him a look of pure hatred. Almost whispering he said, 'You have no idea what trouble you're in.'

The elation Maurice had felt briefly began to ebb away, but he was not going to let it show on his face. Mr Costello bent down and picked something up from the charred debris on the floor. He thrust it in Maurice's face.

'What's this?'

'It's a church candle, sir.'

'Yes, that's precisely what it is,' he said, and stalked off across the hall with the white stub grasped in his fist.

The candle that had started the fire appeared to acquire some totemic significance. Even his parents, who were waiting for him when he got home with the curtains drawn even though it was only mid-afternoon – presumably so that nobody would be able to see their shame – mentioned it.

'And you did this with a candle?' his father said.

Maurice nodded.

'A church candle?'

'Yes.'

His father shook his head slowly, unable to comprehend so transgressive an act. 'How could this have happened?' he moaned.

Maurice wondered himself. Was it just chance or was it was it the kind of historic inevitability that led Martin Luther to post his edicts on the church door or Joan of Arc to hear voices or Lenin on the Sealed Train going to the Finland Station?

He was suspended until further notice. The sad thing was that it meant he was not at school to hear what was being said. His father told him he was not to go out: apparently he was meant to spend all day in his bedroom. There was lots of reading he could do – he was working his way through a Sartre story but found it hard to concentrate – but there were only so many times you could have a wank. Anyway, he needed to conserve his energy for what was going to come, whatever that might be.

When the summons came from the headmaster to present himself, along with his parents, a few days after the event, it came as something of a relief from the boredom, although a small feeling of apprehension began to build in him as they walked silently up the main staircase to the headmaster's study. The school had always seemed an alien place, but now it seemed so strange to him that it was as if he had never set foot there before. In a way that didn't surprise him – the landscape was obviously going to look different after you had fought your way out of your cocoon or pupa, or whatever it was that caterpillars did before they took flight and became butterflies.

But when they got to the headmaster's study and were told to wait outside, Maurice could not have felt more earth-bound. And there was something odd: Arthur was sitting there quietly with his father. He looked briefly up at Maurice and then quickly looked at the floor. Dr Mayall and Maurice's father nodded curtly to each other and then they sat in awkward silence until they were called in.

As they entered the room, he saw that the furniture had been rearranged. Four chairs had been put at the back for the parents and Arthur and there was one in front of the headmaster's desk, presumably for him. This was not what Maurice was expecting. It was going to be a Show Trial.

The head was sitting at his desk like a judge and Mr Costello was standing behind him. He was going to be the prosecutor, of course. During his opening address, Maurice began to count how many times Mr Costello used the word 'shame'. It was liberally distributed: on himself, his parents, his friends, the town of Godalming, but mostly, of course, on the reputation of the school. There had already been a piece in the local paper titled 'Fire Dampens King George Open Day'.

Then Mr Costello moved on to a different tack and his delivery became less declamatory and more quizzical.

'Now,' he said silkily, 'this society of yours and Mayall's…'

For a moment Maurice was confused. 'It wasn't Mayall's society,' he said. 'It had nothing to do with him.'

Mr Costello turned to the desk and picked up a piece of paper. 'On the application form for the society, your seconder was Mayall, was it not?'

Before he had a chance to say anything, Arthur suddenly blurted out from behind him, 'He made me!'

Maurice turned round in amazement. Arthur was looking away.

'I understand there was a lot of pressure,' Dr Mayall said.

Maurice's voice rose in indignation: 'No!'

'I'll thank you to keep quiet,' Mr Costello barked at him. 'You'll have your turn soon enough. Would you say, Mayall, that there are other people involved in this society? Not at King George necessarily, but behind the scenes? Other influences that might have encouraged a stunt like this?'

Arthur looked confused. 'I'm not sure, sir.'

'Don't play the naïf with me, Mayall. There are factions all over this country of one hue or another that encourage subversion. Sometimes it's bombing and violence like those Yids who tried to hit the Foreign Office in London a few months ago. Sometimes it's covert activity. Have you seen Gifford with people you don't recognise? Maybe people in the town? Older people?'

'He goes to London a lot,' Arthur said breathlessly.

'London?' Mr Costello said, in a voice of wonder.

'He goes to the British Museum,' Maurice's mother said in a whispery little voice.

'Would that be for the Middle Eastern antiquities? The Elgin Marbles, perhaps? Does he share these interests with you, Mayall?'

'No, sir.'

'Several people saw you by the so-called Russian Society before the fire was started. What were you discussing?'

'I just asked if anyone had signed up for the society.'

'I see. Had you talked beforehand about how many people you hoped would join?'

Arthur shook his head.

Mr Costello leaned over and took the candle from off the headmaster's desk. 'And this, Mayall. Is this yours?'

His face began to crumple. 'He took it from me, he made me give it to him,' Arthur mumbled tearfully.

'No!' Maurice said again, suddenly on his feet.

Mr Costello was in his face in an instant. 'You sit down this minute or the consequences will be very serious indeed.'

Maurice sat down. He tried to block out the awful disintegration going on in front of him. Arthur was allowing himself to be destroyed. He was so terrified by the prospect of being implicated that he was prepared to lie and make everything worse. If Maurice had had the chance to speak first, he would have made sure that everyone realised that the idea of any involvement on Arthur's part was laughable. But it was typical of totalitarian regimes to see plots where there were none, to see predetermination where there was only accident. That was the system: rule by fear and division, make people lie and betray their friends, squeeze out of them any modicum of will they might possess. If you were to visualise Arthur's will now, it would look like a small pile of ash under his chair, so weightless that a gust of air would blow it away, so fine that it would only register in the brightest shaft of sunlight.

Arthur was being led out of the room now, weeping, his father's manly arm around his shoulder. He would be taken home and given tea and a slice of cake, gruff re-assurances that he had done the right thing: he had been brave, he had told the truth, he had had the courage to stand up and be counted.

At that moment, Maurice felt a kind of love for him, the tenderness and pity you might feel for a wounded animal. He found it hard to see the future for himself, but he could see it clearly for Arthur: his voice would still soar to the roof of the chapel in Morning Service, his arms would become taut and sinewy with rowing, he would move easily among that indistinguishable pack of the bright and the promising who did credit to themselves and their school. Soon Arthur would forget that he had ever been in a line of choristers that walked through the school hall on Open Day in their dark-green cassocks singing the *Nunc Dimittis* and that he had stopped for a moment to speak to a friend and forgot to pick up his candle when he left.

In the silence that followed Arthur's departure, Maurice stared straight ahead. He would give them nothing now.

'So,' Mr Costello said. 'What do have to say for yourself?'

'It could have been a box of matches,' Maurice said.

'And what's that supposed to mean?'

Maurice raised his hands and mimed striking a match against a box. 'It didn't matter to me how it all started.'

'I suppose it was more symbolic for you using a church candle.'

He shrugged his shoulders. 'No. I just didn't have any matches. We're not allowed to bring them into school. It's a rule.'

The headmaster suddenly looked up from his desk mournfully, and he uttered his first words since they had come into the room: 'Why? Why did you do this thing?'

Mr Costello looked startled by the interruption.

'It was an accident,' his father said from the back of the room.

'Yes,' Mr Costello said contemptuously. 'That's what he said to me too. That was his story.'

'Maurice – tell them!' his mother wailed from behind him.

'Are you shielding the people who put you up to this?' Mr Costello said. 'Because, I assure you, we will find them. Even if we have to get the police involved.'

'Let the boy speak,' the headmaster said. 'Was it an accident?'

'There are no accidents,' Maurice said.

'If you think that mumbo-jumbo's going to get you off the hook—' Mr Costello exploded.

The head put his hand up to stop him. 'You leave us no option,' he said.

His mother had her hand over her mouth, trying to stifle her weeping. His father put an arm round her. It was almost touching how the weak were protected in the middle classes. They were not so generous to the proletariat.

There was a difficult moment when it was all finished. Nobody knew what to say and, on their feet by this time, they all stood around awkwardly. Finally, as if he could think of nothing else to do, the head cleared his throat and walked round shaking everyone's hand. As he was going through the door, trailed by his apparatchik, Mr Costello, Maurice said in a surprisingly clear voice, 'Please don't punish Mayall by stopping him singing, sir. He will do credit to the school. He has the voice of an angel.'

Mr Costello turned round, his face a nasty scowl. 'I don't think you're in any position to—' but before he could go further, the head put a restraining arm out. He seemed unexpectedly moved and Maurice thought he could detect a glistening in the man's eyes. 'I wish you the very best of luck,' he said in a low voice.

'Thank you, sir.'

'May God be with you.'

Although that was unlikely, Maurice was touched none-theless. The head was the old regime, corrupt but benign, now being replaced by the new breed of *gauleiters* – a word he had got from one of the war comics that boys passed around at school – like Mr Costello, who would send people to Death Camps for preferring jam to marmalade.

His parents seemed worn out by it all. In the car on the way home, his mother sat slumped in the front seat. Whenever his father glanced in the rear-view mirror he caught Maurice's eye in the back seat and finally he moved to the side of the car to avoid his look.

Once home, he went straight up to his room and closed the door. He lay on his bed. In a while he was asleep. When he awoke, it was dark and the room was stiflingly hot. The alarm clock by his bed said 1.30 a.m. The house was silent. He opened his door and on the floor outside was a tray with a bowl of soup and a hunk of bread, cold now. It was like being in jail, only the soup was not fish heads and watery broth, but one of his mother's hearty vegetable soups, thick with leek and parsnip and potato pulled up from the garden.

On the tray was a folded-up piece of paper with his name written on it. Maurice opened it. It was written in his father's handwriting on lined paper.

Dear Maurice,

You will go and stay with your uncle Jack on the farm and work there for the summer until we decide what is to be done with you. You will take the train tomorrow. Please pack some hard-wearing clothes. You

have disappointed your mother and I beyond measure
although you will always be our son.

Your father

If he lay down on his bed and wept, it was not out of regret
or disappointment or shame, but because it was not easy
shedding your skin like a snake. He was something different now, but there was a small part of him that could still
see the boy who had once sung 'Blow the Wind Southerly'.

Breakfast the next morning was awkward, his parents
bustling around, trying to pretend this was a normal
day. They weren't bad people; he knew he was too hard
on them. It wasn't their fault they couldn't see beyond
all the things that had been drummed into them by
their parents and all the people who went before, beliefs
contained within beliefs like those Russian dolls which
you unscrewed to find smaller, but identical ones, inside.
The one with his face on it was not identical: it was carved
from some other wood, hard and unyielding and dark,
like teak. No wonder they were sending him away.

Yet deformed and ugly though he must have seemed
to them, some parenting instinct sat alongside their blin-
kered perspective and complacent beliefs. While they
ate toast and margarine with a little smear of jam that
his mother had made from last year's rosehips, he was
presented with what must have been the last of the bacon
ration – two fatty strips – and a rather undercooked fried
egg. In other circumstances it might have been regarded
as an unexpected treat, but he was obviously not meant
to construe it as a reward of any kind or a lessening of his
parents' anger. It was just the last meal before the noose
was placed around his neck and the trapdoor sprung.

He wished he had been hungrier, but he was obviously not one of those condemned men who were able to eat a hearty breakfast. In fact, as he chewed each mouthful he found it was an effort of will to keep the food down and as he broke the egg yolk and it spilled across the plate like a ruptured dam, he jumped up from the table, ran into the bathroom in the front hall, put his head in the lavatory and vomited.

When he returned, his parents were sitting in silence. 'Are you all right, Maurice?' his mother said, the first words that had been spoken that morning.

He nodded, and they all stared at the half-finished food for a moment before his mother got up and put it by the sink. He could see his father eyeing it wistfully. It had already become a metaphor on a plate – the latest rejection of all they had tried to give him over the years. Anyway, bourgeois thrift being what it was, there was no likelihood of it going to waste. The remains of the bacon would probably reappear chopped into little pieces in one of his mother's potato bakes, but as Maurice waited alone on the front steps with his suitcase, he heard his mother angrily exclaim from inside, '*Trevor!*' When his father came out he was looking sheepish, licking the grease from around his mouth and wiping his fingers on his trousers. Once, they might have exchanged a conspiratorial glance in response to his mother's rigidity but too much damage had been done for that now, and they walked silently to the car.

His mother stood stiffly on the doorstep, and as the car turned out of the drive she raised her arm in a spastic flutter of a wave, like a wounded bird. At the station it was awkward, too. His father was obviously weighing up whether to wait for the train or just to leave Maurice there.

His father tapped his watch. 'Ten minutes.'

Maurice nodded his head. 'Right.'

'Well…'

Maurice put him out of his misery. 'Don't wait, Dad.'

His father glanced at his watch again as if he hoped time might have sped on since he had looked thirty seconds before. Maurice put his hand out to his father. It was time he took control.

'Goodbye, Dad,' Maurice said, then he turned and walked away. Just as he was going into the ticket office, he thought he heard his father call his name, but he kept on walking.

He would never see his father or mother again, but even if he had known it at that moment he would not have turned back. When he had bought his ticket, he went out on to the platform and walked along to the end where he could see the car park. He thought his father might have waited in the car, but he had gone. He was on his own now.

Although the train was quite crowded, he managed to find an empty carriage. He put his case on the luggage rack and settled down by the window. The door opened and a middle-aged woman came in. She sat down opposite him and gave him a friendly smile.

'Are you travelling far?' she said.

He thought for a moment. 'I hope so,' he said, and the train started to grind into movement and Maurice began the long journey that would take him to Isaac Herzl.

Joseph

At the show that night Kevin was sitting a few rows in front of them with some of the investors. 'Why have they got better seats than us?' Shirley said to nobody in particular.

Sometimes there can be a sense of anticipation, a buzz of excited conversation as people take their seats, a discernible feeling that they are in for something special. Joseph did not feel it tonight.

The first act was very shaky. The sound kept cutting out. There was a problem with the radio mikes. But when it moved to the daughter's bedsit, and the mother came on, Michelle got a big hand. Then the revolve jammed. Toni's parents and about twenty family members were down the row cheering whenever she opened her mouth. They were behaving as if they were still in the audience of the talent show she had won. They were probably planning to phone in and vote, Joseph thought.

The 'Taste of Honey' number at the end of Act 1 was still the best thing in the show, so at least the curtain came down on a bit of clapping, but at the end the reception was frostier. A few people got to their feet, but not enough people.

Joseph had been disciplined for the last few days, but now he went to the lavatory, locked himself in a cubicle and allowed himself a medium-sized line. Before he could snort it, he could hear people come in and the sound of someone urinating. He was good at reading the runes by listening to people's comments. Rarely – however good the show is – are they raving about it. It takes a while for a show to become a whole in people's minds, often not until they have read the reviews so they know what to think. What they tend to discuss are moments: this song or that scene or which characters they liked. Joseph often thought that the best sign was a passionate argument because the really good shows tend to polarise opinion. This was the worst scenario of all: they weren't discussing the show at all.

'Tenerife any day. Honestly.'

'Diane says Marbella. She thinks it's smarter.'

'Well, you can't do better than that posh hotel, what's it called?'

'Yeah, but isn't everybody on their bus pass there? I want to see someone by the pool whose tits aren't scraping the ground.'

'Get full board. Food's fabulous. Paella, anything you want. Lobster. Five courses at dinner.'

'With my cholesterol?'

'There's a gym.'

'It's meant to be a fucking holiday, mate, not boot camp.'

After they left, Joseph looked at his line on the loo seat. It was going to be a long night. He chopped out another one. He did not want to keep nipping out during dinner: the loos in pizza places were only one step up from the ones in Chinese restaurants. I have some standards, he thought.

Kevin had booked a table in a side room. When Joseph got there everybody was standing around chatting in an ominously low-key way. Kevin wasn't there yet. They gave a little clap when Joseph came in. There was a lot of kissing and the masculine bear hugs that everyone seemed to go in for now.

Someone was laughing about Michelle catching her dress on a chair in Act 2 and it falling over as she moved away from it. There was a general consensus that the mother's lover was going to need a better wig. None of this was an uncommon experience during previews – everyone dwelling on the little but repairable things that have gone wrong to avoid talking about the wholesale disaster onstage. The only question was how long this meniscus of good will was going to last. Not long, judging by the expression on Shirley's face as she and Alan arrived.

A small, synthetic cheer was given up when Kevin came in. He positioned himself at the head of the table and there was an awkward moment while everyone else was working out where to sit. The other end of the table from Kevin filled up first.

'What we all need is a stiff drink,' Kevin said jovially and clicked his fingers for the waiter. He made a show of looking through the wine list and then said in a low voice, 'House wine will be fine. And some water.' Then he added aggressively, 'Tap.'

When their glasses were filled, Kevin got to his feet. 'That's what I call a team effort, guys!' he said expansively. 'There's a production meeting at nine tomorrow so we don't need to go into detail now. All I want to say is' – he put his hand on his heart and tapped it – 'this feels very good. I don't think there's anything standing between us and London!'

A valiant little cheer went round the table. Then, in the silence that followed, a voice said quietly, 'The money?'

Kevin looked round the table as if he didn't know who had spoken. 'Excuse me?' he said.

'The money,' Shirley said again. 'The money's in place for us to transfer the show to London, I presume. You don't want to raise everyone's hopes, Kevin.'

'Of course, we need great reviews here, but this whole business is built on hope, Shirley, as you know. And sound financial underpinning, of course. I have no worries about the money,' he said witheringly. 'Not after tonight.'

'That's great,' Shirley said. 'So all the money's there. All in place. Good.'

'I don't think this is the time or the—'

'Why not? Everybody's here.'

'As you know, there has been a significant overspend. Unavoidable. And yes, we are in an overcall situation. But I have no worries.'

'After tonight's performance?' she said incredulously.

There was a long silence.

'I don't think I need remind you, Shirley, that you have no official function on this show.' He let out a strange yelp. 'Alan – will you please control your wife?'

Joseph's head was buzzing. He wanted to be somewhere far away. There was a big plate-glass window opposite his side of the table and he tried to concentrate on the blackness outside. He thought he might have to go to the loo again. He forced himself to zone out of Shirley's and Kevin's rising voices but the noise clamoured back into his head.

Something odd happened then. As if a pebble had been thrown into a dark lake, the blackness of the window opposite Joseph began to dissolve and, as if coming up from underwater, Gaz's face loomed slowly into view. In a second he was gone. It could have been a dream, but Joseph stood up. Kevin had moved away from his seat and was standing over Shirley. 'Do you know what I've gone through to get the show this far?' he was shouting. 'Do you? *Do you?*'

As Joseph slipped out of the room he ran into a phalanx of waiters heading in, each balancing three or four pizzas on their arms. He eased himself round them and went into the main part of the restaurant. The few people eating there had their heads turned listening to Kevin shouting, but he was out in the street in a second.

It was cold and rainy. Through the window he could see Kevin waving his arms around. Shirley had got to her feet and was facing him, her hands on her hips. He did not care about inside. Inside was another country.

He looked around. The street was deserted. A few yards away there was an alley that went down the side of the restaurant. He stood at the top of it for a moment. 'Gaz!' he shouted. 'Are you there?'

After a few seconds there was a movement like an animal stirring by the restaurant's wheelie bins. He walked towards it. Gaz was leaning against the wall behind the bins with a cigarette in his hand. He didn't look at Joseph.

'Gaz,' he said. 'What are you doing here?'

Gaz took a puff of his cigarette. He still didn't look up.

'Go back to your friends,' Gaz said.

'They're not my friends. Not many of them anyway.' Joseph put his hand out and touched his arm. 'You're soaked. How did you get here?'

'Hitched. Some cunt in a BMW.'

'You should have called.'

Gaz did not answer.

'Are you hungry?'

'I don't want to go in there with those dickheads.'

'We don't have to do that.'

'You got any gear?'

Since being with Gaz Joseph's vocabulary had grown by leaps and bounds. 'Yes, I've got some gear.'

'I thought you wanted me to see your play,' Gaz said aggressively.

'It's over for tonight, thank God. You can see it to-morrow.'

'I can't stay.'

'What? You're going to hitch back tonight?'

'Got to get back to my job.'

'I didn't think you had a job. Aren't you doing a business course?'

'It's part-time.'

'I'll get you a train ticket tomorrow. Come back to the hotel. We can get something from room service.'

'The gear?'

'I don't think the gear is on the room-service menu.' Gaz did not smile. Irony was not his strong suit. Joseph tapped his pocket. 'It's here.'

'I'm tired. I need something to get me going.' Gaz's face was very close to Joseph's. He could smell him. He was sweaty and unshaven. He reeked of cigarettes. He looked like a sulky little boy.

Why was Gaz like this? He could be nice when he wanted to be, when he wasn't filled with self-loathing. Everybody has to cope with that, Joseph thought. Nobody made Gaz go to the club where they had found each other any more than they made him go. There is such a thing as free will, even if you're a Christian Fundamentalist.

The hotel was only a few minutes away. As they walked through the lobby, someone called Joseph's name. He looked round. Michelle was gesturing at him from the bar. His heart sank.

Gaz said, 'Is that…?'

'Yes. Come and meet her.'

'I don't know what to say.'

'Don't worry, she's not very frightening.' Gaz reluctantly followed behind him, pulling his hood down and tidying his hair.

Michelle jumped up and hugged Joseph. She had changed out of her curtain-call dress into a pink tracksuit.

'Sorry I didn't come to dinner. I'm really knackered, love,' she said in her throaty voice.

'I bet you are. You were great. Really.'

She put her hand on his cheek and made a little clucking sound. They were observing the niceties.

'This is Gaz,' Joseph said.

Her meeting-the-public voice clicked into place. 'Hello, Gaz, how are you, love?' She gave him a big hug.

Gaz looked stunned. 'Can I have your autograph?' he blurted out.

'You are *very* sweet,' Michelle said. 'Isn't he sweet? Do you want a photograph, too?'

Gaz nodded. She reached into her handbag and produced a pile of pictures and signed one of them. Gaz gave her an inarticulate thank-you grunt.

'We should go,' Joseph said. 'Let you get some rest.'

'Thanks, love. Couldn't have done it without you. Fingers crossed!' Then she gave both of them a big hug.

When they got out into the lobby, Gaz whined, 'You shouldn't have told her my name, man. She'll know.'

'She'll know what?'

'She'll know,' he repeated.

'And what if she does know? Who will she tell? I don't suppose she's got a direct line to your family, Gaz. Or the Almighty.'

Gaz was in a funk when they got up to the room. He slumped on a chair and put his hood up. He turned the television on.

'Are you hungry?' Joseph said. Gaz didn't answer. The minibar cheered him up. Joseph guessed he had never seen one before. With a look of wonder on his face, Gaz said, 'This is so cool. Are these, like, free?' Joseph didn't know why he wanted to know. All drinks were free for Gaz. He took all the miniatures out, arranged them on the table and drank several of the little vodkas one after the other. It was nice to see him happy.

They had some coke. They had quite a lot of coke. The miniatures weren't going to last. Room service brought a bottle of vodka up and some sandwiches. They started on the vodka. The sandwiches were not going to be eaten. Gaz had taken his trousers off and was bouncing on the bed in his socks singing 'Like a Virgin'. He was using the vodka bottle as a microphone. Then he found the bathroom. He loved that. Joseph found him surreptitiously putting little bottles of shampoo in the pocket of his hoodie.

'You're allowed to take them,' Joseph said. 'It doesn't count as stealing.'

'What do you mean?' Gaz said angrily.

'You can have them. Take the soap. Take the shower gel. You can have the bathrobe, too.'

Gaz looked at him. 'Maybe I'll have a shower,' he said.

'Don't have a shower,' Joseph said. 'I like you the way you are.'

'I'm not doing it,' Gaz said.

'What?'

'All that stuff you make me do.'

'I don't make you do anything, Gaz.'

'I'm going. I need to get back for my job.'

'Oh Gaz, do have really have a job?' Joseph said wearily.

'I'm working with my uncle.'

Gaz seemed to have a varying number of uncles. 'Is this the uncle who's the fashion photographer? Or the one who was a stunt man on *Casino Royale*?'

Gaz grabbed his arm hard and twisted it behind him. 'You don't trust me! You don't believe me!' he shouted, slurring his words. He pushed Joseph roughly against the bathroom wall, his cheek against the tiles. Joseph twisted round out of his grip. They looked at each other. Gaz was breathing hard. He grabbed Joseph's wrists. Joseph pulled him towards him and kissed him. Gaz pushed him down to the floor roughly and went out of the bathroom. Joseph could hear him chopping up a line in the other room.

Gaz came unsteadily back into the bathroom. He had brought the vodka bottle. Joseph was still on the floor. He looked up at him. Joseph's heart was beating fast.

'Sing some more.' Joseph gestured to the bottle. He laughed: 'With your microphone.'

Gaz wasn't looking at him. He stood very still. His mouth was open, but he did not start singing. The sound in the bathroom cut out for a moment, like it did in the show when the radio mikes had gone down. Then it came back and Joseph heard something – a guttural kind of cry. At first he thought it came from Gaz, but then he realised it came from him. He felt blood streaming down his face and into his eyes.

It was all much clearer now. The sound of the bottle breaking on the tiles was pin-sharp and Gaz's strange wail and the click of his knees as he bent over Joseph and hit him again. The shirt that Shirley had bought him for the opening would be torn and bloody. But now Joseph had gone somewhere else. He had gone to his country. The boundaries had begun to break down, everything was running into everything else, like a row of dominos knocking each other over.

Who is Joe Hill? he thought. Am I him? Says I, says he, says who? Maybe Gaz was Joe Hill. Maybe Iz was Joe Hill. Maybe everybody was Joe Hill. It didn't seem to matter much. Joseph was just thinking about the songs. They were all he had now and suddenly they all joined together into a single song:

> *I dreamed I saw Joe Hill last night*
> *At a zoo with chimpanzees.*
> *Says I, 'Oh let them see my scars,*
> *Speak to me father, please'*

Shirley

The hell of out-of-town: she had been on more try-outs with Alan and Joseph than she could count: more hotel rooms, more cold theatres, more late-night crisis sessions. Shirley knew that the good thing about her was that she was objective. She did not have an axe to grind like everyone else.

At least in London there had been some vestige of civility between her and Kevin, although she could see the look of hostility in his eyes whenever she came to a meeting with Alan and Joseph. She was always polite despite his pathetic attempts to get rid of her. But after a day in Manchester, it was open warfare. It's not healthy to be in a bubble of delusion, she thought, let's be realistic about the problems. That's why she said what she did in that awful pizza place.

When they got back to the hotel after the dinner, everybody was subdued. Shirley could understand that it was not pleasant for everyone to see their producer, if you could call him that, practically getting into a fist fight with the composer's wife. Everyone was tired and nobody wanted to have a drink with her in the hotel bar. Well, it had been a long night. Alan was in an odd mood, too, and Joseph had simply vanished. He had left the pizza place early and nobody knew where he had gone.

As for her, she was fizzing with energy with nowhere for it to go. Maybe that's why she didn't sleep. Normally she was out like a light. The moment of serenity that would be needed for Alan's Viagra plan to happen was clearly not going to be found in Manchester. He had been distracted and grumpy, huddling together with Joseph trying to do the new songs. Anyway, she wasn't feeling very serene herself.

She could not tell whether she had not gone to sleep at all or whether she had slept fitfully and woken up. Whichever it was she was wide-awake now. The last time she had seen Alan he was nursing a glass of minibar Scotch at the mean little desk that the hotel had given them when she complained there was nowhere for him to work. But now he wasn't in the room at all, nor did he seem to have got into his bed – the covers were untouched.

She got out of bed, but then instantly felt shaky. She leaned on the bedside table to steady herself. Little flashes of light were going on and off in her head, odd little pops of noise. Although it was not exactly like what had happened at the shiva all those years before, it was similar enough for her to know that something was happening. She could feel – almost hear – her heart beating faster.

Then the noise in her head was overlaid by a different sound. It was coming from the bathroom. She could see the light on under the door. Alan was talking in there, not so distinctly that she could hear what he was saying but his low tone seemed to have a strange kind of urgency. She felt like she was sleepwalking, but she was conscious enough to put a dressing gown on over the new nightdress, ridiculously silky and low-cut, that she had bought in a giddy moment after her discovery back in London.

She pushed the door open slowly. Alan was standing with his back to her by the shower holding his phone. 'I know. I know,' he was saying softly. 'I know you do. I do, too, but—'

He turned round and clicked his phone off quickly. She looked at him. She could not imagine what expression was on her face.

'I was just going to the loo,' he said. 'Go back to bed.'

'Who were you talking to?'

'Talking?'

'On the phone.'

'Joseph,' he said. 'I was talking to Joseph. About the song.'

'Why are you sitting in the bathroom talking on the phone to someone who's five doors down the corridor? Why don't you just go to his room?'

'I didn't want to wake him up.'

'But you have woken him up if you phoned him.'

'*Get* him up,' Alan said, 'I didn't want to *get* him up.'

'You're not talking to Joseph,' she said in a whisper.

There was silence, then tears began coming down Alan's face. Shirley had not seen him cry since the shiva. He moved forward and tried to take her in his arms, but he was irrelevant now. Something bigger was happening, something awful, but she knew it was nothing to do with Alan. The strange popping noise came back into her head, like a vacuum being released. There were little glimmers of light but they were not consistent enough or long enough to tell what was being lit up, what was waiting to be seen. It was muddled and messy and crackling like bad reception on a radio channel, but as she ran out of the bathroom she saw two bright flashes, the first murky but the second as clear as a photo taken on the brightest, brightest day. The first was Sally and the second was Joseph. He was looking at her with a terrible look on his face. She said his name out loud and repeated it again.

Alan tried to grab her arm as she ran to the door but she was out in the corridor in a second. She was so disorientated that she couldn't remember whether Joseph's room was left or right, in the direction of the lift or the other way. All she knew was that she had to get there as fast as she could. She didn't care that the room-service tray that someone had left on the floor went flying, a wine glass shattering against the wall and then a sharp pain on the sole of her foot as she ran over the pieces.

A door was open, Joseph's door. It was bright in there, glaring after the dimness of the corridor. It was hot and fetid, a mouldy sweet smell permeating everything. And messy: bedclothes on the floor, a tray of sandwiches overturned, only one curtain left on the rail. As she went into the bathroom, identical to the one where she had just been with Alan, she felt something wet on the floor, something warm and sticky. Some of it might have been the blood from her foot, but there was too much for it to be only her blood.

The other curtain from the bedroom was covering a large bundle by the bathtub and as she bent down to pull it off, she suddenly saw Sally again. Before everything went mad, before she uncovered the bundle on the floor, she thought, Oh Sally, thank you – you've let me glimpse you again.

The first time she had seen Sally was after her funeral. Shirley's mother had taken everything over. She and Alan would not have done the funeral that way. She hated the cemetery at Golders Green. She hated that there were no flowers, no roses for Sally. She tried never to think about the funeral but when she did, the thing she remembered most clearly was Joseph. Her and Alan's grief was compulsory – they were her parents – but Joseph did not have to feel so deeply. His grief was voluntary. Sally had loved him. He was the only person apart from them she allowed to come to the hospital at the end.

It was announced at the service that they would sit shiva from 8 p.m., but as the funeral was over by 5 p.m., a lot of the non-Jews came straight over to the house. These were Alan's work friends: actors and music people. The one thing they had in the house was drink and a lot of it was drunk before the Jewish contingent arrived.

By then, Shirley's mother was organising the food, barking out orders to the caterers who had brought little salt-beef-on-rye sandwiches and mini bagels and cakes. Her mother had wanted to do Sally's favourite foods, but that was a hard act to pull off with someone who was anorexic. Shirley told her that one radish sliced into thin pieces and four apple segments would not hit the spot.

As the non-Jews got more raucous her mother found it difficult to hide that look of disapproval Shirley knew so well. Her mother's best friend, Bonnie, had set up a non-alcoholic bar at the other end of the room and was offering exotic cocktails made with ginger ale and pomegranate or mango juice. She had prepared a tray full of bits of fruit and she threw some of them into each drink, then added a candy-striped straw for good measure as if she was presiding over a children's birthday party. Her husband Phil was running the coffee next to her from a huge steel urn that was steaming all over the place.

Her mother expected her and Alan to sit on low stools. Shirley had no idea why the bereaved were meant to sit low. It was bad enough having her hand endlessly grasped as she moved around the room and people saying, 'I feel for you,' without being pinned down like a target on a stool at floor level. She knew she looked awful but luckily her mother had covered up the mirrors – another of the bizarre things you were meant to do at a shiva – with a selection of horrible shawls.

By now there must have been seventy people in the house. Shirley didn't even know some of them: her mother's imports. She was glad to see a lot of Sally's schoolfriends there. They had visited her in hospital for a while, but then they had gradually stopped. Shirley didn't blame them: Sally did not want to see people towards the end anyway.

Shirley's strategy was to keep moving around the room so she did not really have to talk to anyone. She kept doing circuits, trying to hold a distracted look on her face as if she was on her way to do some hostessly duty that urgently required her presence somewhere else. It meant that she only had to stay for a moment with whoever had hugged her or threw some platitude stolen from a greetings card at her. She felt dizzy with the effort, and finally after the fifth or sixth circuit, like a child jumping off a roundabout, she left the room and headed for the kitchen to escape.

They'd had it remodelled a while ago. New cabinets, new double oven, new marble tops. An island in the middle that doubled as a breakfast bar. Shirley had no idea why kitchens were so expensive. It was a waste of money with an anorexic in the house.

Jews always brought food to a shiva – the bereaved are not meant to do any cooking while in mourning – but this was unbelievable: big Tupperware boxes of stews and salads, giant casserole dishes, tureens of soup and trays of brownies and cakes on the marble counters. There was enough food to last for weeks. It would have been Sally's worst nightmare, a house heaving with food. The smell alone would have ensured that she stayed in her room for days.

Her mother had delegated the task of organising the kitchen to her friend Naomi. She jumped when Shirley came in and her hand was instantly over her heart in shock when she realised who it was.

'Oh my dear, you shouldn't be in here!' Naomi said. 'You sit down, Shirley. I don't know what you're even doing in here! Now…' she said, shuffling dishes of food around, '…I'm going to put together a little plate of things for you. And a strong cup of tea.'

'I'm fine, Naomi. Really.'

'I'm just sorting things out. I'll put some stuff in the freezer, just to be on the safe side.'

'Oh, Naomi, please stop fussing.' Being on the safe side was not high on Shirley's list of priorities at that moment.

Naomi suddenly turned all mock stern and waved her finger at her: 'You need to eat, my girl.'

'I'm not hungry.'

Later, her mother – predictably – called it a breakdown. Shirley didn't see it that way. As Naomi was fiddling with the cling film that covered the turkey, she thought she was going to faint. She leant on the counter so she would not fall. There was a strange flash of light in her eyes that flickered like a malfunctioning neon sign. She knew she was going to throw up: not the kind of throwing up that you can circumnavigate with a little discipline and positive thought, but the kind that you know is inevitable.

Naomi gave a little scream as Shirley lunged towards her in order to get to the sink. She got her head there in time and out it all came. When she brought her head up from the sink, Naomi was in shock. Her hands were holding her cheeks and her mouth was open like that Munch painting. It goes against everything Jews hold sacred to throw up in a kitchen, Shirley thought.

'I'll get your mother,' Naomi whispered, not the first port of call a rational person would have gone to in an emergency, but it gave Shirley a bit of time alone to do what she needed to do.

A few minutes later, there was a clattering down the corridor and Naomi, her mother and a gaggle of her friends burst into the kitchen. They stood in the doorway and looked at her in stunned silence.

'What are you doing?' her mother screamed.

'I'm clearing up,' Shirley said calmly. 'Go back to the living room. I'm fine.'

The vats of soup were halfway down the sink and she had left the tap running so the drain would not get blocked. The room looked a mess. It was hard to keep the black garbage bags open with one hand and put food in them with the other. Some of the seams had split and gloopy bits of stew were leaking out. Shirley would clear it up later. She didn't want her new kitchen to look like a tip after they had spent all that money on it.

'Excuse me,' she said to the ladies as she manoeuvred herself past them into the corridor. She was holding two bags and she moved quickly so that they would not leak on the carpet. The front door was ajar. She pushed it open with her foot and then she went outside and put the bags in the little wooden shed where the dustbins were.

When she got back to the kitchen, Dr Gestetner was there. He had retired recently, but he had always been their family doctor. They had taken Sally to him for a while, but then had to move on to more specialised care.

'Shirley,' he said in a soft, putting-her-at-her-ease voice, 'what are you up to, you silly old thing?'

'I'm clearing up.'

'In the middle of Sally's shiva?'

'Yes,' she said. 'In the middle of Sally's shiva.'

'I think you need to take it easy.'

'Naomi – you've just stepped on a bit of food,' Shirley said, pointing at her foot. Naomi yelped and everyone turned to her. Shirley used that as an opportunity go out to the bins again. Then she went back to the throng in the living room carrying a big roll of garbage bags.

It was bustling in there. She tried to be unobtrusive, she knew it must look odd for the bereaved mother to be wondering around holding a large bin liner. Still, nobody seemed to take much notice until one of the waiters offered her a mini smoked-salmon bagel from a large silver tray. Instead of taking one of them with the napkin he offered her, she took the whole tray out of his hands and tipped it into the bag. The next to go were the devilled eggs – her mother's favourite – then the herring on rye bread. She handed back the empty trays politely. The waiters' mouths were frozen open. They kept glancing at each other for help.

'Why don't you offer some drinks around?' she said. 'People probably need a refill.'

The next thing she did was go over to Bonnie and Phil's table. Bonnie grasped her hand from across the makeshift bar and said, 'Let me do you a cocktail, darling. You must be exhausted. I've got apple, mango, orange—'

'I'm fine, Bonnie.'

'Or coffee,' Phil chipped in. 'Remember how Sally loved a frothy cappuccino?'

She did remember. Coffee was all Sally drank by the end, not cappuccino, of course, which had too many calories, just black. But she wasn't really listening to Phil. She had squatted down and was sweeping the brownies and fairy cakes and flapjacks into the bag. That was when she realised that the room had begun to fall silent, with the only buzz of conversation coming from the other end, the non-Jewish end, where they had probably had enough drink not to notice much.

Her mother was suddenly standing above her, and with surprising strength pulled Shirley up on to her feet and snatched the garbage bag out of her hands.

'Shirley, I want you to stop this now,' she whispered in her ear. 'I want you to come upstairs with me and lie down.' Then she tried to pull her by the arm, but Shirley was having none of it.

She had some sympathy for her mother who would hate everyone staring at them. The most important people at a shiva were the bereaved: they were meant to be cosseted and pampered. What they were not meant to be was manhandled out of the room trailing an overflowing garbage bag into which they had deposited the food so kindly brought by the mourners.

Shirley resisted her mother's pull, so the next move was to call for help. 'Does anyone know where Alan is?' she said, hoping a sing-song quality to her voice might mask her desperation. Then she shouted, 'Alan! Alan! We need you.'

People began turning round to see where he was. Gradually, a little gap began to appear that ran all the way through to the other end of the room as people moved apart, and Alan came into view. He was staring down the room at Shirley, a deranged woman with her hair coming down and her mascara running and food stains on her clothes, trying to wrest a black garbage bag from the hands of her mother. He began to weep in great, soundless hiccups until, finally, he bowed his head as if in shame.

The person who saved the day was Joseph. He walked slowly down to where they were standing and simply took charge. He put his arm round her mother and gently moved her towards Bonnie and Phil.

'I think Mrs Levy needs a drink,' he said. 'Can you make her one of those nice cocktails you've been doing?' Then he came back to Shirley.

'You can't do this on your own,' he said softly. 'Tell me what I should do. Is it the drink you don't want, or the food? Do you want everyone to go?'

'No, they can stay and drink. Just the food,' she whispered.

He nodded briskly. 'Okay. Leave it to me. You sit down.' He gently pushed her on to one of the low stools that her mother had wanted her to sit on all along. He took the full garbage bag out of her hand, tied the top of it and put it under Bonnie's make-shift bar. Then he grabbed a breadstick from the table and made a little chime on the side of his glass to get everyone's attention. He didn't need to do that really: the whole room was staring at him in silence already

He spoke in a light, clear voice, as if he was announcing no more than where the coats were meant to go. 'Please have some more drinks, but there's been a little problem with the food,' he said. 'If you don't mind, I'll be going round clearing it up.'

A woman, about to pop one of the little bagels into her mouth, looked down at it closely and quickly put it back on the tray as if it had salmonella.

Joseph knelt down beside Shirley. 'Are you okay?'

She nodded and hugged him. 'Thank you,' she said. 'I think I saw Sally. She told me what she wanted.'

She had seemed so clear that day to Shirley. It wasn't that she was less clear now, it was just that she had become two-dimensional, like a photograph rather than a sculpture. There had been no more visions of Sally in the fifteen years since her shiva. No wonder the vividness had faded. But it had come back tonight.

At three in the morning Shirley was sitting in the lobby of the hotel in her dressing gown talking to the police. The paramedics were upstairs in Joseph's room and they would be bringing him down soon. It was hard for her to concentrate. She could not keep everything that had happened tonight in her head at the same time: Alan, then Joseph and, most perplexing of all, Sally. That was the only positive thing that had come out of tonight. She was going to store it away like a present and open it later.

She had already done some crying. She did not know whether it was for Alan or Joseph. Now she was just in shock. Before the police arrived she had been to the bathroom behind the reception desk and thrown up. There was quite a mess, but what did it matter in this place? It was filthy anyway. Now she looked terrible. She did not like being seen without make-up but it was all in her and Alan's room and she had not gone back there after discovering Joseph's body.

She felt fuzzy and her stomach ached. She was trying to focus on what the policeman was saying.

'Is Mr Carter a relative, Shirley?' She was not sure why they were on first-name terms.

'No.'

'But you know him?'

'Yes. He is a friend.' She was trying to hold herself together, but she could not stop her voice shaking.

'And you were in his room? You were both in there?' Then he added in a softer voice, 'Together?'

She said coldly, 'We were not together in his room when whatever happened to him happened. I only went to his room afterwards.'

'Because you heard cries?'

'No.'

'Then why did you go to his room?'

She paused for a moment and thought about how to answer that. She could hardly mention Sally. 'I wanted to talk to him.'

The detective nodded. 'I see. At two in the morning?'

'He is a great friend of mine. There's no reason why I shouldn't go and see him even if it is two in the morning.'

The man sounded contrite. 'I'm sorry, Shirley. We have to ask painful questions. Do you know what happened to Mr Carter?'

'Of course I don't know what happened to him. I just saw his body,' she said.

'Do you know who was in his room with him?

'No, I don't.'

'We'll be examining the closed circuit footage from the corridor and the lobby.'

'Well, I hope you find him.'

'Him? You know it was a man?'

'I don't *know* it was a man, but I *presume* it was a man.' She was trying hard not to cry. Oh Joe, she thought, what have you been doing?

She was tired now. 'I've told you what I know, which is really nothing. All I did was find the body and call an ambulance. Anyone would have done that, wouldn't they? May I go now? Please.'

'Yes,' he said. 'Thank you. We may want to talk to you later, Shirley.'

She stood up. She did not want to go back to her room, but she had to get dressed if she was going to go to the hospital when Joseph went. She took the lift back up. The door to the room was open and all the lights were on but Alan wasn't there. She was relieved. She felt sick at the thought of seeing him, sick at the thought of what he had done. She dressed and slapped some make-up on. When she came out into the corridor the paramedics were bringing Joseph out of his room on a stretcher trolley. She followed them.

'How is he?' she asked. 'I was the one who found him.'

'We'll have to wait until we get to the hospital, until the doctors can examine him.'

'All I'm asking is if he's still alive,' she said.

'Yes, but he's unconscious.'

'I'll be coming to the hospital.'

'Are you a relative?'

'Yes,' she said thinking quickly. 'He's my brother.'

The stretcher trolley was too big to fit in the lift so the men had to manoeuvre it down the stairs, trying to keep it level. When they came into the lobby, she saw Kevin and Alan talking to the police. She felt her heart plummet.

'This is Shirley,' the policeman said. 'She was the one who discovered Mr Carter.'

'They know who I am.'

Alan was not looking at her. Kevin stood up and moved a few yards away. 'Shirley – can I have a little word with you?'

Reluctantly, she followed him to the corner of the lobby. He pulled Shirley into his arms and gave her a great hug. Their row seemed a long time ago.

'Oh Shirley,' he said. 'My heart goes out to you. What you've been through…'

'It's not me who's been through anything, Kevin.'

'Don't think for a minute I'm not grieving. In my whole career nothing as awful as this has ever happened.' She did not say that his whole career did not encompass very much. She was going to be polite.

'I need to ask you something. I need you to do something for me.' She waited for him to continue. 'This is a very delicate situation.'

'That's one way of putting it, yes.'

'I know we've had our differences but let's not argue, Shirley. Let's be friends. I know how much you've done for the show. I know how much it means to you.'

She sighed. 'What is it you want, Kevin?'

'How we handle this is absolutely crucial. The show was shaky tonight, I know that. We both know that. There are press people coming up from London for the matinee this afternoon. I would cancel them if I could, but can you imagine how that would look? I don't want anyone to think the show's in trouble. Which it isn't. I'll give the cast a pep talk before the matinee; tell them they've got to up their game. They have to give the performance of a lifetime today. It's got to be brilliant, Shirley. It's make or break.'

He was so transparent. 'And you don't want anyone to know about Joseph yet. Is that it?'

He nodded. 'Please. Not till after the show. What kind of performance would they give? Nearly everybody's staying in those service apartments so they're not going to hear for a while. It's only a few hours till the matinee. I'll organise a quiet meeting after the show to tell everyone. I want to do it sensitively. I want to tell the cast and crew when they're on their own. You know how important this was to him. It's what Joseph would want.'

Shirley thought about it for a moment. Reluctantly, she conceded that it probably was what he would want.

'All right, Kevin, I won't say anything.'

'Thank you, Shirley, thank you. We're doing this for Joseph.'

Shirley hoped he was not going to say, 'The show must go on.'

He gave her another hug. 'The show must go on.'

She walked back past Alan and the policemen. She did not look at Alan. At the reception desk she said, 'I want you to organise another room for me. Preferably not on the same floor as I'm on now. And will you call me a taxi? I'll be waiting outside.' Then she walked out of the lobby. She heard Alan call her name.

Of course it was chaos at the hospital. She had to insist that they moved Joseph's gurney out of the corridor while they were waiting for the doctors to arrive. Under the bright fluorescent lights, his face looked terrible. It was the colour of putty where it wasn't bruised and bloody. She was holding his hand, clammy and cold.

They would not let her go with him when the doctors took him away. She had to sit in a scruffy waiting room where there weren't even any magazines, just a pile of pamphlets about sexually transmitted diseases. People do go to hospital for other kinds of illnesses, she thought.

She had to wait for three hours before she saw anyone. Finally a young doctor came and sat beside her.

'Your brother is in a very serious condition,' he said.

'Yes, I realise that. I did discover his body, you know.'

'He's unconscious. His injuries are very extensive.'

'Yes, I know that. My father was a doctor. Our father.'

'Well then, you'll know how crucial the next twenty-four hours are.'

She began to cry.

'Would you like a cup of tea?'

'No, I would not like a cup of tea. I would like to see him.'

'I'm afraid that's not possible at the moment.'

'Well, when will it be possible?'

'We'll let you know.'

Finally, around lunchtime, they let her see him, but they made it very clear that she could not stay for long. She asked them to leave her alone with him for a moment, but they said no: they wanted to monitor him constantly. On balance, she did not think that saying she was a doctor's daughter again was going to alter the situation.

She decided to walk back to the hotel. As she passed the theatre she realised that the matinee must have already begun. She went in and stood at the back. They were halfway through the first act and it did not seem to be going too badly. The revolve was working properly again and there were no sound problems. It seemed to be more focused than the night before. At the end of the first act, after Joseph and Alan's song, there was a lot of applause, much more than last night.

Even though it was only mid-afternoon, she felt she needed a drink, but when she walked into the bar she saw Alan. She turned round to go, but in a second he was by her holding her arm to stop her leaving. She wrenched her arm away and said, 'Please don't say: "We have to talk."'

He pulled her over to the corner of the bar. 'I'm sorry,' he said.

'What about? About what's happened to Joseph? About what you've done?'

'This and Joseph all at once – it's like the perfect storm,' he said in an agonised voice.

'Oh please – don't resort to clichés. There are enough clichés in this situation as it is. And what exactly do you mean by "this"?'

'I'm sorry,' he said again.

'Is "this" a fling? Isn't that what middle-aged men have?'

'I was trying to end it.'

'Who is she?'

'Nobody you know.'

'Who is she?'

Alan looked down. 'Someone I met online.'

Shirley thought she was going to be sick. 'Was she the first?'

There was a silence. Finally Alan said, 'I didn't know what I was doing.'

'What? You were trying to buy a book on Amazon and strayed on to some sex website by mistake?'

'I didn't know what I was looking for.'

'But you found it anyway.'

'We can work through this. We can make it all right.'

Then she began to cry, which was the last thing she wanted to do at this moment.

'It can never be all right. You've betrayed me!' she shouted. 'You've betrayed Sally.'

His voice was shaking. 'I would never betray Sally. I loved Sally. You weren't the only one to suffer.'

'It's not a competition, Alan. There's no first place.'

'You suffered so much there was no room for me.'

'Oh please,' she said, 'tell that to some agony aunt.'

'We were so unhappy.'

'Of course we were unhappy! Sally died.'

'Before then.'

'I don't know what you mean.'

'Even before she got ill Sally wasn't happy. She was so withdrawn.'

'She was a teenager, for God's sake!'

'She hated that school. We should never have sent her there.'

'It was a better school! If she was going to be a doctor—'

'She didn't want to be a doctor.'

'She could have done anything she wanted!'

'She didn't have a chance to do anything she wanted.' Alan closed his eyes. 'I feel guilty every moment of the day.'

'Even when you're with your online woman? I bet that distracts you.'

'Yes. Maybe it does,' Alan said quietly.

'You are beneath contempt. Nothing distracts me from Sally. Nothing. And the one thing – *the one thing!* – that's kept me going through these long, hopeless years without her is that I don't feel guilt. If I did, I couldn't go on living. How dare you use her as some kind of excuse!' she shouted. 'It's nothing to do with her. It's all you. You've destroyed us.'

She turned and walked out of the bar and into the theatre as the lights were coming down.

She was shaking so hard that she had to steady herself by holding the rail at the back as the second act started. She tried to concentrate on the ridiculous things that were happening onstage. When it ended, to Shirley's surprise, people were getting to their feet and clapping.

She was trying not to think about Alan. Every betrayed wife seemed to stay with their husband. She had seen politicians who had been caught in some tawdry scandal standing with their arms round their frumpy wives in a pathetic display of solidarity as flashbulbs popped. She had more dignity than that. She would cut Alan from her life. He would be dead to her. He would be more dead to her than Sally was.

After the curtain call, as the lights came up, she turned round to leave when suddenly a sepulchral voice boomed over the loudspeakers: 'Ladies and gentlemen, Mr Kevin Lever.'

And there was Kevin, walking slowly out on to the stage. There was another round of applause, as if this was part of the show. He held his hand up and the clapping began to die out.

'I'm Kevin Lever,' he said. 'I am the producer of this show, our wonderful *Taste of Honey*. I have to tell you something that will break your hearts.'

Shirley gasped in shock. She knew what Kevin was going to do.

'Our friend, Joseph Carter, the writer of the extraordinary book and lyrics for our show, has been the victim of a shocking attack. His head injuries are very serious indeed and he is being monitored around the clock but our brave friend is hanging on. I know that quite a few journalists are here from London today. Please treat what has happened sensitively. Just concentrate on the show. It meant everything to Joseph.'

As the news sank in, everyone onstage looked confused for a moment. Then Michelle's hand went up to her mouth, and she gave a little scream. The cast, which had been in a perfectly composed line behind her for the curtain call, began to dissolve into chaos. People began to weep. Gasps spread through the auditorium.

Kevin put his hand up again. 'Ladies and gentlemen, keep him in your thoughts. *A Taste of Honey* is like our child. We want it to go to London; we want everyone to see the brilliance that is Joseph Carter.'

Then he bowed his head and put his hands together as if in prayer. Michelle threw herself into his arms as the cast circled them. The audience were staring open-mouthed as if this was the climax of the show.

Kevin stepped down from the stage and walked slowly up the aisle followed by the cast. A few people sitting on the edge clasped his hand as he passed. Nobody appeared to want to leave the theatre. Kevin stood in the middle of the lobby with a throng of people around him – not just the cast, but other people who were staring at him in awe. She pushed through the crowd until she reached Kevin's back. She grabbed his shoulder and he turned round.

'Shirley…' he said nervously.

She could hardly move. Her legs felt like concrete. First Joseph and then Alan, and now this cheap publicity stunt. It was as if someone had swept their arm across a mantelpiece and a lifetime of ornaments had crashed to the floor. She was trying to contain her fury so hard that her voice came out as little more than a whisper.

'You are disgusting, Kevin,' she said, and then she did something she could never have believed she would do in a million years: she spat in his face.

Rose

I was always interested in etymology. The Latin word *evitabilis* means 'evitable', capable of being avoided: obviously adding the prefix 'in' – meaning 'not' – turns it into the antonym: inevitable. I liked Latin: it had such a logic to it. Even though I had every reason to be, I was not particularly pessimistic but I thought it significant that the word 'evitable' was almost never used when 'inevitable' was used all the time. Did that imply that more things in life were evitable than inevitable? Certainly Huddie's death was not going to be evitable. I didn't know whether what had happened to Joseph was or not.

I normally only read the political and scientific articles in the newspaper because I didn't want to waste time on the other things: I was not interested in celebrities and show business and sport. That day, I looked at the paper while I was having breakfast before I went into Huddie's room to get him going for the day, not that his day involved much going.

When I saw the article, I initially passed over it, but for some reason I went back. It was headed 'West End Songwriter Assault – Man Arrested'. Although I knew our half-brother was called Joseph, I could not remember his last name so when I saw the reference to him being Isaac Herzl's son I almost gasped.

'Huddie!' I shouted.

The sun was streaming into his room. He never wanted the curtains closed and he left the lights on. I couldn't have slept like that, but he said that if he woke up in the night, it was easier if the lights were on because he could find the glass of water by the bed. The truth was, I left the glass of water there, filled with fresh water every night, more for old time's sake than for anything else: he was beyond stretching his arm out for it now. I thought I knew the real reason for leaving the lights on. The drugs he had to take made him groggy and he slept very deeply: he could not bear slowly rising to the surface of a silent, dark room and not know whether he was alive or dead.

I touched him gently to wake him up. I didn't want to shake him too aggressively because he might wake up in a panic and think something awful had happened like the house being on fire and we would not be able to get him out of his room before the place burned down.

He opened his eyes slowly. 'I was dreaming,' he said. Someone else might not have been able to understand what he was saying, but I had got used to it. It was like a language I had learnt. It's hard to talk without being able to move your mouth and tongue much and all conversations with him took a long time.

'What about?' I asked him.

'I was dreaming about a cat. A big ginger one. It was climbing up me and I was worried it would lie on my face and suffocate me. But then Placido Domingo pulled it off and brought me a plate of curry.'

Someone more conventional who had Huddie's disease would have been dreaming about running or climbing a mountain. Huddie was too original for that.

'We need Dr Freud,' he said, and made the little noise he did in his throat when he was trying to laugh.

'You have to see this,' I said, holding the newspaper up.

'What is it?'

'It's about Joseph.'

'Joseph?'

'Yes. Someone attacked him. He's in hospital and they've arrested someone.'

'What does it say?'

I skimmed through it for him: 'He was in Manchester doing some musical... he came back from the theatre... went to his room... then got beaten up.'

'Was it a robbery?'

'I don't know. Did you know he was fifty-six?'

'What? I knew he was older than us.'

'That's old enough to be our grandfather!'

'Well, Iz is old enough to be our great-grandfather.'

'Someone called Gavriel O'Donnell has been arrested.'

'What sort of name is Gavriel?' Huddie said.

'Maybe it's a misprint for Gabriel.'

'People called Gabriel don't beat people up. It's the name of an angel. Go on.'

'He was unemployed from Walthamstow. Everything in the article is "alleged".'

'What do you mean?'

'"It is alleged that unmarried Joseph Carter knew his alleged attacker... it is alleged that Mr Carter and his alleged attacker had been seen together in the hotel before the alleged attack in Mr Carter's hotel room." And it keeps going on about their ages: Joseph Carter, fifty-six; Gavriel O'Donnell, twenty-two.'

'I think that's called subtext,' Huddie said. 'It's silly grown-up code. They're gay but the paper doesn't want to come out and say it.'

We let it sink in for a moment and then I said, 'Joseph doesn't sound much like the kind of child Iz would have had.'

'Are we like Iz? Anyway, Joseph writes songs, doesn't he? That sort of runs in the family.'

'Yes, but he writes musicals. Iz hates that kind of thing. Didn't he refuse to let us go and see *Mamma Mia* because he said it would rot our brains?'

'I suppose being gay is different from Iz. He's had three wives. Maybe four if he was married to Joseph's mother.'

'Do you think Iz knows about him being beaten up?' We looked at each other.

I heard Carla in the hallway, and I went out to see her. She was with Joan, of course.

'Have you seen this?' I asked her, holding up the paper.

'Yes, what a shocking story,' she said in her cool way. 'I saw it a few days ago. I've made sure Lally keeps the papers away from Iz, not that he ever reads them these days.'

Joan shook her head as if the whole thing was too distasteful. That seemed to be all the discussion I was going to get out of them because they were getting their coats.

'Sorry, Rose, we're late for the demonstration,' Carla said.

'What demonstration?' I asked, not that I was very interested.

'To get the council to do more rubbish collections,' Joan said.

'Rubbish collections?' I said. 'Aren't there any totalitarian regimes to demonstrate about today?'

Joan gave me an icy stare and then they were out of the door.

When Lally came in to see us later, I asked her if she knew. She looked rather shifty.

'Well, yes, I did see it actually. What a horrible story.'

'Does Iz know?' Huddie said.

'I'm sorry, dear, I can't hear what you're saying. I'm a bit deaf this morning.'

Lally tended to be deaf when she wanted to be.

'He's saying, Does Iz know?'

Lally looked amazed that we might be asking. 'No, Rosie, I haven't told him. We've still got a long way to go with the archive. I don't want him to be distracted.'

My voice rose in indignation: 'Lally – "distracted" isn't what someone might feel if their son was badly injured. He'd be upset, wouldn't he?'

'Well then, I'm certainly not going to tell him,' Lally said. 'If he heard about it, he would think back to what happened with him and Joseph all those years ago.'

'I thought he didn't look into the past. He ought to know what's happened.'

'Maybe if the man was dead, but he isn't. Of course it's upsetting, but it would be just as upsetting if it was a stranger. Which he was in a way, really. I don't mean I'm not sympathetic, of course, but the stories about him... he's obviously one of the gay ones.'

'So what? Anyway, you don't know anything about being gay.'

'No, you're right, I don't, Rosie. There are so few of them in the folk world.'

'The folk world is not representative of the whole world, Lally!'

'And all the better for it. He was obviously having some kind of relationship with that boy. So young! What do you think about that?'

'What about Iz with Molly and Carla? He was thirty years older than both of them!'

'There's really no comparison,' Lally said primly. 'He has so much to teach a young person. The boy certainly didn't learn anything from Iz when we met him.'

'You've met him?'

'Well, only once.'

'When?'

'Oh, years ago. He must have been fifteen or so. You know, I didn't entirely take to him, though I suppose he was just trying to do his best. He was a bit stuck-up, to be honest. The name Iz had given him when he was born was Joe Hill Herzl – such a distinguished name! – but he said he preferred to be called Joseph, which I thought was a bit rude to Iz. And, what's more, he used his mother's surname, Carter.'

'Who was his mother?'

'Well, it was before my time, dear, but I think she was a bit of a middle-class girl pretending to be a radical. She just wanted a piece of Iz, like so many people did. I think she might have tricked him into getting her pregnant. Anyway, Iz never saw her after the baby was born. I think she died later. Her parents brought him up. Iz tried to see the boy, but they refused to let him. They thought he was a communist activist, which of course he was in a way. The grandparents obviously poisoned the child. And the boy did something horrible to Iz later, a sort of betrayal, really.'

'What did he do?' I asked, intrigued.

'You'll have to ask Iz. He doesn't like to talk about it.'

'Well then, there's no point asking him, is there?'

'Of course children always find fault with their parents,' Lally went on. 'Iz did – but he had a very bourgeois upbringing and he was right to rebel against it. It's different for you and Huddie. Don't stray from Iz like that boy, Joe, did. Writing songs for musicals – what a waste of Iz's legacy. Don't you two waste it as well. You must celebrate Iz and everything he is.'

Maurice

Maurice first saw Isaac Herzl on the lane that ran round the back of his uncle's farm a few weeks after he had arrived in Kent. A boy roughly Maurice's own age was trying to ride an old nag that was resolutely refusing to move. There were some others who were cheering him on, sprawled in the back of the cart the horse was meant to be pulling. The boy on the horse was the one who seemed to be the leader and he was the one Maurice watched, even though the two girls on the cart might have drawn his eye more, particularly the one who had short curly hair and breasts you could see beneath her baggy dungarees and T-shirt.

The boy was leaning forward and slapping the horse's neck with his hands, but it just stared ahead, motionless. Trying to stay upright without a saddle, gripping the horse's sides with his thighs, he kept slipping off to one side and when someone in the cart suddenly jiggled the reins and one of the others shouted 'Get a move on, Iz!', the horse was startled into a jerky canter that dislodged the boy and left him doing the splits, one leg over the horse and the other dragging along the ground. When he finally came off and hauled himself to his feet, he was almost weeping with laughter, bent over holding his sides and trying to catch his breath.

Watching from the other side of the gate at the corner of the field, Maurice had been very still but as he edged forward to get a better view, his movement caused one of the girls in the cart to catch sight of him. In an instant, like an animal sensing danger, she shot a warning glance over to the others and they suddenly fell silent. Iz took a moment to pick up the signal but then his eyes found Maurice. He stared warily and then did something strange: he winked at him and burst into laughter. Maurice, suddenly embarrassed, spun on his heels and hurried up the track even though that was not where he planned to go, and he had to pass through the boggy mess where the stream had overflowed.

Later, when he asked his uncle Jack who they were, he called them 'The Jew-boys next door' even though the farm they were on, apparently owned by a Jewish organ-isation, was at least a mile away. With a look of distaste on his face his uncle said he hoped the police were keeping an eye on them, they were up to no good.

It was like that in the country, Maurice thought, people were suspicious of anyone different, although these ones just seemed to be getting on with their work like everyone else – the deadly slog of farming that seemed grimmer to him every day. It was not like this on Levin's farm in *Anna Karenina* or in *Far from the Madding Crowd* where work-ers, although poor and exploited, found some measure of dignity through their labour. Of course, they might have had more if exploitative land barons had not owned the land they worked on. His uncle had three hundred acres, but Maurice found it hard to think of him as a land baron and, if the truth was told, was a little disappointed that he did not fit more obviously into that category. His uncle seemed just as downcast as the workers: none of the swagger you might have expected from a grandee, no sable coats or stove-pipe hats or silver-tipped canes.

After a few days on his farm, Maurice realised why his parents did not see his uncle very often. For his mother, her brother must have been a grim reminder of all the reasons she had left this shabby farm in Kent to reinvent herself as a Godalming matron. She would not have liked to host their elegant summer parties or one of her animal charity fundraisers in the filthy, damp farmhouse with the stained ceilings that she had grown up in. Nor would a marquee have looked good in the yard with its cracked concrete and broken fences and cow shit everywhere.

Her brother was clearly much better for her in the abstract where her description of him as the local squire would not be contradicted by his grubby appearance. More than that, he was not very pleasant to be with. He was a silent, gaunt figure who limped around the farm because there was something wrong with his leg. Whatever it was, it looked painful. Sometimes Maurice would find him in the kitchen taking soiled bandages off his leg and putting new ones on – there seemed to be a lot of pus and blood. It must be hard to be a crippled farmer, Maurice thought. He suspected that his uncle had been swayed by the idea of free labour rather than any desire to forge links with his nephew.

Every evening, when the light began to go, Maurice came back to the farmhouse and his uncle would give a little grunt and nod that was probably a greeting. There was food on the table for him – bread and soup from vegetables that had been grown on the farm, sometimes a little fatty meat or scrawny chicken. It was always the bony bits. What happened to the breast? Maybe his uncle kept it for himself – it was typical of a landowner to give the workers the worst rations and eat the best – but Maurice never saw him eat. He did see him drink, though: when he went upstairs after supper his uncle was usually sitting in a tattered armchair in the kitchen with a bottle of gin beside him listening to the radio.

Maybe his uncle stayed up all night floating dreamily like people did in opium dens in China: Maurice hardly ever heard him come up to bed, nor did he ever hear him use the squalid bathroom either. A faint smell came off him – a mixture of old sweat and cow shit.

Several times a week his uncle sharpened his knives on a strap with fevered intensity. They were his meat knives, and he used them to cut up great haunches of flesh on the kitchen table, most of it to be sold but the scraggy bits kept for them to eat. There were gashes on the table stained with dark blood, which his uncle never seemed to clean. You could probably catch some horrible disease, but Maurice did not give it much thought: he was always too hungry to worry. Sometimes he found his uncle counting his money, the earnings from selling farm produce for cash, and he would hurriedly turn his back if Maurice came in unexpectedly. He thought that Maurice had not seen him stuffing the notes in a saucepan, putting the lid on and pushing it to the back of the cupboard under the sink.

In the mornings, his uncle told him what he had to do that day, not that the tasks varied very much. At this time of year it was mostly haymaking. His uncle had taught him how to saddle up the horse and attach the finger-bar mower to the harness. She was a mangy old nag with matted hair, not the kind of sleek beast with a shiny coat that might be ridden by a proper member of the landed gentry. Maurice had never ridden before but his uncle seemed to think that no lessons were needed. After an awkward start, he found that it was not that difficult. Anyway, with the heavy mower behind it, the horse moved so slowly across the fields that it was unlikely that any harm would come to him.

After Maurice had cut the grass and it had been left to dry for a few days, he would attach a trailer to the horse and pick it all up, which took several days, and then unload it into the barn. There were the cows to be milked, but his uncle tended to do that – presumably because he could sit on a stool and not use his damaged leg. Maurice was left to muck out the stables, which was a back-breaking job that left his trousers and shoes covered in shit. When he first went to the farm, unused to physical labour, his muscles ached so badly by the end of the day that he could hardly move, but after a week or two his body had begun to get used to it.

All in all, Maurice thought, it could have been worse. It was a hot summer and he liked being outside most of the day. He didn't know how long he was going to be there for, or what awful plan his parents were concocting for his future. There had been no communication from them yet.

A couple of weeks after Maurice had seen Isaac Herzl for the first time he encountered him again, this time alone. Maurice was walking up the lane away from the farm, and saw a figure heading towards him. Even though the boy was far away, he recognised him instantly. As they got closer to each other, Maurice did not know whether to look at him or keep his eyes averted. The boy obviously had no such dilemma: his gaze was firmly fixed in the other direction. As they passed, Maurice smiled at him, but the boy did not even look at him. A few yards further on, Maurice halted and turned.

'Excuse me,' he said.

The boy did not stop. Maybe he had not heard him so Maurice repeated it more loudly. The boy finally turned round and looked at him with a blank expression on his face. He was carrying a satchel and he moved it nervously from one shoulder to the other.

'Hello,' Maurice said and walked towards him. He had no idea what to say next. He was out of practice talking to people. Arthur would have had the boy engaged in friendly conversation in a second.

'Do you live around here?'

The boy spoke curtly: 'Why?'

'I just wondered,' he said feebly.

'Yes, I live up the road.'

He spoke in a very precise way, separating out the words so there were little spaces between them. Maurice could tell he was not English – he had the remnant of some foreign accent.

'Are you farming?' he asked. The boy did not speak. He pushed on: 'I'm working for my uncle on his farm over there,' and he pointed.

'Yes, I think I asked him for some directions once. He is a very rude man.'

Maurice gave a little laugh. 'He's very suspicious of strangers.' Then he added quickly, 'I'm not.'

The boy nodded. 'Well,' he said. 'I must go,' but he did not move off immediately.

'Where are you from?'

The boy clearly did not want to answer. Finally he said, 'I am German.'

Maurice could not help a look of surprise on his face. Weren't they meant to be in Internment Camps, or had they all been let out after the war?

The boy suddenly laughed. 'Don't worry, I am not a German spy. That's what people around here think. I'm a Jewish refugee. I've lived in England for a long time. I am a citizen. I have a British passport.'

What now? 'My name is Maurice,' he said desperately.

'Isaac,' the boy said after a moment. 'Well, Iz. That is what people call me.' Now they had been introduced, Maurice put his hand out. The boy looked down as if he did not know what to do with it. Finally he shook it.

'Well, goodbye,' he said.

Maurice followed him. 'I saw you with your horse the other day.'

'Yes.'

'Do you mind if I walk with you?'

'You seemed to be going the other way.'

'I've got to go back to the farm. I've forgotten something,' he said. It did not sound entirely convincing. Iz shrugged his shoulders and they walked in silence for a while.

Then Iz said something unexpected. 'I have an uncle in Germany with your name. Well, I had an uncle in Germany. I think it's spelled differently though: M-O-R-I-T-Z.'

'I'm M-A-U-R.'

'Well, that's the posh English way, isn't it?'

'I'm not posh. My parents think they are, but really they're just bourgeois. Actually, we come from peasant stock,' he said with a hint of pride in his voice. They had reached the fork in the lane that led to the farm.

'This is where I live,' Maurice said.

'I'm going up there,' Iz said, pointing in the other direction. 'We live at the Kurtz Farm.' He raised his hand in a gesture of farewell. 'Well, goodbye.'

Iz had gone about twenty yards when he turned round and shouted something that made Maurice smile: 'My parents were members of the bourgeoisie, too! There are a lot of them around.' Then he gave a little laugh and vanished round the corner of the lane.

When Maurice saw Isaac Herzl for the third time, it did not go so well. He was in the field picking up the dry grass and putting it on the trailer when he heard the sound of hooves clacking on the road. He turned round. Like the first time he had seen Iz, he and his friends were sitting in a cart pulled by their horse. Iz was at the front holding the reins. He was wearing the kind of cap that Maurice had seen Lenin wearing in photographs. He walked to the edge of the field and raised his hand, but the cart passed him. Nobody answered his wave. In fact, nobody even looked at him, not even Iz.

It was a week before they met again. Sitting on the wall that ran along the lane having his lunch – two thick slices of bread filled with spam – Maurice could see Iz coming down the lane towards him walking beside the horse and guiding it with the reins.

There was an awkward look on Iz's face when he saw him. Maurice decided not to say anything. After the other day, he did not feel very friendly. To his surprise Iz walked over to him.

'Hello,' he said.

Maurice nodded at him. Iz tied the horse's reins to the gate. There was silence for a moment. Maurice was not going to make it easy for him. Isaac Herzl was the one who should make amends.

Charles Elton

'What are you doing today?' Iz said. 'It's hot, isn't it?'

'The hay. That's what I'm doing today,' Maurice said curtly.

'I saw you the other day. When we were on the cart.'

'Yes,' he said. 'I saw you too.'

'People are suspicious of us,' Iz said in a rush. 'They're not friendly. Someone put a brick through the window once. Our cart has been overturned. The others are nervous. We have to keep ourselves to ourselves. I'm sorry. It must have seemed rude to you.'

Maurice nodded. 'Oh, I see,' he said. He felt better now. 'I can imagine it must be difficult for you living in a place like this. The people have no vision.' Then, as a peace offering, he added, 'If you're hungry you could have some of my sandwich.'

'That is very kind, but no thank you. We keep kosher.' Maurice was a bit hazy about exactly what that involved, but he was not going to ask.

'What about an apple?'

'Yes, I will have one. Thank you. I like fruit.'

He took his satchel off and sat down on the wall beside Maurice. He took a big bite out of the apple.

'Can I ask you – why are you here? I mean, in Kent,' Maurice said.

Iz did not immediately reply and Maurice could tell that he was deciding whether to brush him off with an evasive answer.

'I'm here to train. I'm in Habonim. It's the Jewish youth organisation. Like your Boy Scouts, except we do more important things than learn how to tie knots. Your Scouts are just a totalitarian organisation.'

What a wonderful phrase that was! 'Well, yes, of course they are,' Maurice said loftily. 'I was never a Scout.' That was not entirely true: he had been a Cub for a while when he was younger.

'We're training to be farmers. I will be going to Israel soon.'

Maurice was impressed. 'But aren't they stopping people going?' He had read that somewhere.

'Yes. The British have fucked us.'

He was thrilled by that. Maurice had never used the word himself.

'You blockade the ships. There are millions of Jews trying to go there and you only let a tiny amount of people in every month.'

Maurice gave a nervous laugh. 'Well, it's not me exactly. I don't agree with it at all. It's the army, the *gauleiters*. Isn't that what you call them in German?' Iz looked rather impressed.

'So how are you going to get there?' Maurice asked.

'It is difficult but not impossible. There are ways,' Iz said.

Maurice knew that was an evasive answer if he had ever heard one, but he decided not pursue it. 'How long have you been in England?'

'I came over when I was eight. On a boat with other children. They managed to get some of us out. It was called the *Kindertransport*. My parents stayed behind. And my brother, Abram. They thought he was too young to go. Then I was in a Jewish children's home in Liverpool. I came to the farm last year. It's a kind of commune.'

A proper commune – how exciting that sounded! 'You're all equal then? No bosses? Group decisions and all that?'

'Well,' Iz said, 'it's more like sharing the cooking. And we're all meant to repair the machinery as well, but of course the girls don't help.'

'Oh, I see,' Maurice said. 'And your parents and brother? Will they be coming here now that the war is over?'

'No, they're all dead,' he said. 'I should think they're just a great pile of ashes in some camp.'

Maurice tried not to look shocked, but Iz saw it on his face. 'It's difficult, but you have to cut sentimentality out of your life,' he said. 'It's the future not the past we must concentrate on.'

Maurice was impressed by that. 'My parents aren't brave enough to die for their beliefs. They wouldn't ever be martyrs.'

'I don't think my parents were being brave,' Iz said. 'Being murdered is not necessarily dying for your beliefs, you know,' he said.

Maurice could feel his face turning red. He looked away from Iz, embarrassed. He changed the subject. 'So – how is your training going? Do you like farming?'

'It's a skill. I am acquiring other ones, too. I'm learning to shoot. Only rabbits at the moment. I'm going to need that in Israel.'

'Are there a lot of rabbits there?' Maurice said.

Iz laughed. 'I won't be shooting rabbits! Don't you know what's happening there? It's a battlefield! Everyone's against us – the Arabs, the British. We're fighting every day!'

Maurice had never felt more ignorant. Here they were: two boys of the same age. One was almost a revolutionary and the other was… what?

'Isn't fighting against your religion?' Maurice asked uncertainly. He wished he had his father's *Encyclopædia Britannica* to look 'Jewish' up in.

Iz laughed. 'We are not Quakers! We are not religious. We're a political group. We don't do things like observe the Sabbath. I suppose we might go to the synagogue if there was one close to here but there isn't.'

'Of course, I'm not religious myself. Not at all,' Maurice said.

'Anyway, the Sabbath is really rather foolish,' Iz said. 'From sunset on Friday night you are not meant to do anything – not cook or read or turn a light on. It would mean we couldn't work on Saturdays. Anyway, Friday's our night off. That's when we have fun. We go swimming in the quarry if it's hot. We cook something good. Some of us are musical so we play chamber music. And we're learning to dance. Someone comes to teach us.'

'Like the waltz?' Maurice's mother had tried to make him take ballroom dancing lessons.

Iz laughed. 'No! Things like the *hora*. It would probably look like Scottish dancing to you. Sometimes there's a bottle or two. We're not meant to drink, but you have to break the rules sometimes, don't you think?'

Maurice nodded vigorously. 'Yes, I do. One absolutely must.'

Today was Friday. A vain hope came into his mind: maybe Iz would invite him for the evening. He could get to know them all. Maybe he could become friendly with the girl he had seen on the cart. But he knew it would not happen.

'Do you get on with everyone at your farm?' he asked. 'Are they your friends?'

Iz shrugged. 'I like some of them. They are very juvenile though. I think it's because they are all sexually frustrated. Maybe there's bromide in the water. The girls never go all the way. You might get a kiss if you're lucky. The boys are all desperate. They have competitions: they jizz on matzo biscuits and the last one to shoot has to eat his up.'

Maurice's jaw dropped in amazement. Then they began to laugh. 'That's why I'm going to Palestine,' Iz snorted.

'Girls always let you do it to them. Don't think there isn't a lot of *shmushka* over there!'

After supper that night, he told his uncle he was going for a walk – an unlikely thing to do – but his uncle just said, 'Lock the door when you come back. I don't want thieves.'

He walked down the track to the lane and headed in the direction Iz had gone the other day. After a mile or so he came to a set of iron gates padlocked together with a thick chain. About a hundred yards away he could see the silhouette of a house with two smaller buildings on either side, maybe barns or cottages. There was light coming through the downstairs windows of the big house. He climbed over the gate and moved cautiously towards it. There was the sound of music. He went as close to the windows as he dared and looked in. He could see a big room, like a hall. The tables had been pushed to one side to create a space in the middle and about fifteen people were dancing clumsily. Maurice could see Iz.

Music was blaring out from a gramophone and then it stopped. An older woman came from the side of the room waving her hands. 'No! No! No!' she shouted. 'Are you complete dunces? You have feet like blocks of concrete!'

She moved among the dancers and rearranged them in a circle. They stood there awkwardly and she sighed in exasperation. She went up to a couple standing next to each other and thrust them together. The others followed suit and took each other's hands. The woman turned on the gramophone again, and the dancers began to move slowly round in a circle. They got faster as the music speeded up and the woman began clapping her hands in time. 'Yes!' she shouted. 'That's more like it. Yes!' Then, as they were still going round, they all moved a few steps forward into the centre of the circle, then moved back. Some of them began laughing with pleasure. They were getting into the swing of it.

Maurice was enthralled. These were people with a sense of purpose. They were working to change the world. They deserved to let their hair down sometimes. This was not like Arthur and his friends having a treasure hunt at a middle-class birthday party.

After a while they took a break and came outside. Maurice moved back to the cover of the trees. He stood very still, but he knew that it was too dark for anyone to really see him. They were talking and laughing and he thought he could hear Iz's voice, but whether it was him or not, what he said was lost on the evening breeze.

When they had gone back in, he turned and walked back to the gate. He suddenly felt very lonely. He wished he could be part of them. But then, as he went down the lane, an idea came into his head. Tomorrow was Saturday. It was his day off, and he would hitch-hike into Ashford. He had a plan.

A week later, Maurice was working in the field when he saw Iz walking towards him. He felt pleased: Iz had been looking for him. It was hot, and Iz had taken his shirt off. The top of his dungarees was hanging down over his trousers and his satchel was over his bare shoulders. He was holding his Lenin cap in his hand. Maurice was surprised at how thin Iz was. He thought he would be tanned and muscular from working in the fields, but he was rather like Maurice: pale and scrawny. Of course, fighting for a cause was a mental discipline as well as physical, Maurice thought. You didn't have to be Charles Atlas.

Iz raised his hand in greeting. 'Hello there!' he said cheerfully.

'Good morning,' Maurice said and shook Iz's hand rather formally. 'How are you?'

'I'm very well, thank you. It is a lovely day.'

'Yes, isn't it?'

'I think it may rain tomorrow.'

Maurice hoped it was not going to go on like this for too long: they were being shy with each other. He sat down on the wall and Iz sat beside him. He put the satchel on his knees.

'You're always carrying that satchel,' Maurice said. 'What do you keep in it?'

Iz shrugged. 'There is a lot of pilfering at the farm. Things are always going missing.'

That didn't sound very communal. 'Oh, I see,' Maurice said.

Iz looked away. 'I never had many things. I could hardly bring anything when I came from Germany. I do not want to lose what I have.'

To have nothing – what could that be like? Maurice hated himself for being so insensitive. It was the way he had been conditioned: to assume that everyone was like himself, used to warm houses and food and the kind of deadening security that the middle classes aspired to. He wanted to imagine how life was for other people, for people like Iz who had lived on the edge and knew what they wanted to fight for.

'When will you go to Israel?' he asked.

'I don't know. I have not been informed yet. I hope it will be soon.'

Maurice felt a pang. He had not had a friend for a long time, and he did not want to lose him.

Now it was time to put his plan into action: 'Will you be joining the Haganah or the Irgun?' he asked. 'They were responsible for bombing the King David Hotel last year, weren't they? And isn't there another group? Palmach, is it?'

Iz looked surprised. 'Oh,' he said, 'I didn't know anyone outside Israel knew about such things.'

Maurice knew about such things. He had spent the day at the library in Ashford learning about such things.

'The Irgun are a bit more aggressive, aren't they?' he asked confidently.

'Well, they are certainly prepared to take more risks, I think.'

'I suppose everyone in Israel hates the British?'

Iz thought for a moment. 'Well, we certainly hate what they are doing to us. All we want is our country back.'

'Yes – didn't we promise it to you thirty years ago? It was rotten of us to renege on that. There was some declaration, wasn't there? What was it called? The Balfour Declaration? Or maybe it was the Sykes–Picot one, I can't remember.' He didn't want to sound too much of a know-all.

Iz looked unsure. 'Yes, I think it was something like that.'

Maurice clearly knew more about it than he did.

'I'd love to see the old city in Jerusalem,' he said. 'All that history! They say the Wailing Wall is extraordinary. The Dome of the Rock, too. And I would do anything to see Masada. That was where you made that incredible stand against the Romans, wasn't it?' Then he paused. 'You know, not all the British are bad. Some of us want you to have your own country, to go back to Israel.'

'You don't take the British side?' Iz said, surprised.

'Well, patriotism's a state of mind, isn't it?' Maurice said airily. 'I don't feel very British. You've got to be objective about your country, weigh up the pros and cons. Anyway, we should be grateful to you. There have been so many great Jews: Einstein, Sigmund Freud, Trotsky. Even Houdini was Jewish!'

In the library encyclopædia there had been a list of the fifty most influential Jews, but Maurice could not remember any more. Anyway, it was time to stop. He did not want to overplay his hand.

They sat in silence for a moment. Then Iz said, 'Do you know a Great Russell Street in London?'

'I don't really know London very well, I'm afraid. Of course, I want to live there one day. I think it's very exciting. There's so much political activity. Why do you ask?'

'The Jewish Agency is in that street. I've never been there. That is where I will start the journey to Israel. When they call you, you must drop everything and go.' He laughed. 'How foolish it would look if I got lost.'

'I think my uncle has a map of London,' Maurice said. 'I could look it up for you, if you wanted.'

'Thank you. You know, you're different to people around here. I have not met someone like you before. You're my only friend who is not Jewish.'

And you're my only friend, Maurice thought.

Then Iz did something strange. He leaned over and gently took Maurice's wrist in his hand. He ran his fingers lightly over the thin pink ridges. 'These scars, I saw them the other day. How did you get them?'

Maurice felt himself turning red. Now it was his turn to give Iz an evasive answer: my hand went through a glass window; I was caught on some barbed wire; a dog attacked me.

He took his hand back from Iz. He took a big breath. 'Sometimes I cut myself. A razor blade, maybe a pin, anything sharp, really. If I get angry, if I get frustrated by something, it calms me down. I don't know why. I mostly did it at school – it was so awful there. I don't think I will cut myself again, though. I haven't done it for a while, not since I've been here.'

Iz smiled sadly. 'I am sorry for your frustration,' he said. 'I know what that is like: when you want to change things and you can't. I hope it will be easier for me to do it in Israel. But I think you are brave and strong, Maurice. You will bring about change. You will achieve great things in this country.'

Maurice felt tears come into his eyes. He looked away from Iz. He wanted to say: But I don't want to stay if you're not here. Let me go with you, we are comrades.

Instead he said, 'I think we could achieve great things together.'

'Yes,' Iz said. 'If only that were possible. But I should go now, go back to work.'

'Well, goodbye Isaac.' Maurice had never called him by his name before. He would not call him Iz: that was for everyone else.

'Yes,' Iz said, and they stood up. 'We will see each other again soon, I hope.'

Rose

Because one of the many things Huddie did not do any more was go to school, the local education authority made periodic checks on him. He was in a category that was called 'student with additional needs'.

Until six months before he had gone most days. The school provided a van with a hydraulic tailgate that could raise his wheelchair and get it into the back. He had begun to find school increasingly difficult. The problem was that everyone was so polite. They were helpful and kind, but there was a formality in their behaviour that made him feel awkward. Nobody ever told him a joke. If a group of pupils were heading towards him in the corridor laughing, their laughter would have wound down by the time they got to him. They would stop and talk to him, even though none of them, including Huddie, really knew what to talk about. What he needed was some friends. What he wanted was a girlfriend.

When Huddie could still see some possibilities at school, he had asked a girl out, although he admitted he was slightly unsure what they would do and where they would go. He told me he liked her so much that he would be her stalker if it was possible to stalk someone in a wheelchair. When he summoned up the courage to ask her, she said that she couldn't because her boyfriend would be so jealous. It had made him smile for a moment to think that he might be a threat to someone's relationship but he knew she did not have a boyfriend. That was why he had asked her out in the first place.

After that, he had said that did not feel strong enough to go to school any more. I knew that this was not entirely true – he could have gone on going, at least for a while longer if he had wanted to. It was not a failure of strength; it was a failure of hope.

After lunch, I cleaned Huddie up in preparation for the meeting with the education person. I didn't want anyone to think he was neglected. We put a clean pair of trackies on him and the T-shirt that I'd had printed for him that said: 'You don't have to be dying to live here, but it helps'.

Huddie looked tired. He had got so thin and his skin seemed transparent.

'Couldn't we just cancel it?' he asked wearily.

'It's better just to get it over with. If we say they can't come they'll think you've been chained up in the attic covered in shit and eating out of a dog bowl. Then they'll take you into care.'

'Don't raise my hopes,' Huddie said.

The special needs facilitator hardly looked any older than us. He bounced into the room over to Huddie and put out his hand, which was awkward because Huddie could not raise his hand to shake his. The man withdrew his hand rather awkwardly.

'You're looking good,' he said cheerfully.

Huddie didn't look good. He hadn't looked good for a while now, but I presumed that being cheerful was one of the skills the man needed for his job.

He sat down on the chair next to Huddie, then turned to me. 'Will a parent be joining us?'

'No, I'm afraid a parent has had to go out,' I said.

'Oh. Right. Well, that's fine. So… Huddie.'

'Yes?'

'I've got a bit of a checklist to go through. We want to cover the waterfront.'

'Okay.'

The man looked down at the clipboard on his lap. 'Number one: Your additional educational needs – are they being delivered on a consistent basis? I know you have a tutor who comes in, but we can offer extra tuition if you need it.'

'I don't think Huddie really needs anything extra,' I said. 'He's probably further ahead than anyone else in his year. I should think he could do his A levels now.'

'If I could use a pen,' Huddie laughed.

'We would provide someone who takes dictation.'

'I think it would be hard to write an essay that way,' Huddie said. 'You couldn't go back and correct anything, could you?'

'Well, the service is there if you change your mind,' the man said briskly. 'Number two: We offer career guidance in Year 10. Would that be appropriate?'

'What kind of career are you thinking of?' I asked.

'Let's not be negative,' he said cheerfully. 'Let's keep an open mind.'

'The power of positive thought,' Huddie said.

'Exactly. Just have a think about it. Number three: Your social interaction needs. Are they being met?'

'I don't really get out that much.'

'There are all sorts of activities. Haringey provides wheelchair basketball training. Would that be of interest?'

'It doesn't sound like my kind of thing.'

'There are organisations, lots of clubs.'

'Duchenne Anonymous?' Huddie said.

The man roared with laughter. 'What a wonderful idea! At least there's nothing wrong with your sense of humour. Number four—'

'I'm sorry,' I said, 'but can you not number everything? It makes Huddie seem like a shopping list.'

'Point taken. It's all bullet points these days, isn't it? Okay, let's move on. Are your access needs being fulfilled on a consistent basis?'

I was so tired of all this. 'Why don't you ask about Huddie's access *wants* instead? They're not the same as his access needs. He *needs* to have his wheelchair pushed but he doesn't *want* to have his wheelchair pushed. He needs to be taken to the loo but he doesn't want to be taken to the loo. He doesn't want four people to carry him up the stairs in his wheelchair and he doesn't want to wait alone at the bottom of the stairs for five minutes while the four people are summoned to carry him up the stairs. But what he mostly doesn't want is for people to look at him in the way they look at people like him when they're fulfilling their access needs.'

The man nodded his head. 'Right,' he said, and wrote down something on his clipboard then looked up. 'Well, we're here to help. Anything we can do.'

After he had gone, we sat in silence. That was unusual for us, but recently Huddie had begun to talk less and less. It felt like the air was gradually being squeezed out of the things we talked about.

I finally said, 'I'm sorry, Huddie. I don't know why I did so much talking.'

'That's okay. We know what we want to say, so it doesn't matter which one of us says it.'

'Do you want to do anything now? Do you want me to read to you?'

'Actually, I'm tired. Do you mind leaving me alone for a while?'

'Sure,' I said as brightly as I could. In the little rowboat of Huddie's life, now springing more and more leaks, the feet of clumsy strangers stepping in made the boat rock dangerously and it took a while for it to right itself.

I left Huddie for a couple of hours. When I went into his room it was almost dark. You could easily forget that Huddie couldn't switch on the lights himself. Maybe I had come in too quietly. It wasn't exactly that he jumped in surprise but I knew the little twitch his body gave was as close as he got to it.

'Hold on,' he said abruptly, but I had reached him too soon. His fingers were on the keyboard of his computer and he was trying to move them quickly, which was hard for him. He was trying to turn off the computer and I could see why: on the screen there was a naked man and woman. She had his penis in her mouth and was pushing what I thought must be a dildo in and out of her. The sound was turned off and it looked strange that they were doing whatever they were doing in complete silence. It must have taken Huddie a long time to make all the keystrokes to get to the site.

I tried to compute the different ways I could handle the situation. I wondered whether I should turn the computer off, but I would not normally have done that and I knew I should behave normally. What I did was to move behind the desk his computer was on so I would not be looking at the screen.

Huddie's face was in shadow, but the light from the screen lit up the rest of him. I could see the problem: his tracksuit bottoms were made of thick material and he could not touch himself properly unless they came off, and that was impossible for him to do. There was almost nothing that hadn't been taken away from Huddie, but this seemed to me the cruellest thing of all in Huddie's world, already bursting to the seams with cruelties.

I thought about what to do for a moment, then I came to his side of the computer but kept my back to the screen. I pushed the wheelchair away from the desk and Huddie's hands came away from the keyboard and fell by gravity into his lap.

'You spend too much time on that computer,' I said breezily. 'You're going to get that repetitive strain thing. Do you need to change? Did your lunch get down your throat or is it all over your trackies? Huddie, they're so gross! Anyway, black's not your colour.' I gave a little laugh. 'Grey's better – it doesn't show up the food so much.' That was the kind of joke we normally enjoyed.

I bent down on my knees in front of him and began to pull on the legs of the tracksuit. 'I can't do this all on my own, Huddie,' I laughed. 'You'll have to move a bit.'

He did his little squirm and, with difficulty, the track-suit bottoms came off. I kept my eyes closed. I did not want to look at his penis, but I hoped it was a good size because I knew that boys always wanted that. It was fortunate that it was not a muscle: it was blood pressure that controlled it. I hoped that everything would work: luckily his fingers still had some grip in them.

'Have a nap,' I said as I was leaving. 'You didn't sleep well last night. I'll make sure nobody disturbs you. I'll keep watch.'

I waited an hour – I wasn't entirely sure how long something like that took for boys – and then went back. Huddie had fallen asleep. He wasn't used to so much exertion, I supposed. His head lolled over sideways and I raised it so that it was straight. It was important to keep the airways open.

Another man had joined the couple on the screen. They looked as if they were having a good time. I switched the computer off. I knew I would not be able to get Huddie's tracksuit bottoms on without waking him, so I went to the bathroom and brought out a clean towel which I laid over his lap and then wrapped a blanket round him. I would help him to go to bed later, and listen to some music with him while he fell asleep.

When Huddie woke up he would be embarrassed even though, really, there was nothing to be embarrassed about. I knew that we would never talk about it, but I would have liked to be able to tell him that I would help him again if he wanted.

Joseph

Seeming like a dream was not the same as actually being a dream. That much Joseph understood. On the other hand, for all he knew, it could perfectly well be one. Anyway, it didn't matter much.

He went through the possibilities of where he might be and what might have happened to him to put him in whatever place he was. In the end, he thought it must be a hospital. He could dimly feel prodding and poking sometimes which could well be doctors. Anyway, he was comfortable, but maybe if he was in hospital he was being pumped with morphine.

He used to spend a lot of time thinking about what songs to write or what to eat or where to go. Because he had no need to do any of those things now he had time to just think, but he was not sure how enjoyable an experience that was. He was like a jazz musician riffing on the piano, moving up and down the keyboard trying to find some notes he remembered.

Maybe he had a kind of Alzheimer's thing on top of everything else. Didn't that make you forget whether you had put the kettle on but give you total recall of what happened at your fifth birthday party? Well, he certainly remembered that. It was when he had gone to live with his grandparents after his mother had died. It was clearly a long time since they had given a birthday party: they did not seem to know that you were meant to invite other children. There were certainly no magicians or clowns like Shirley and Alan had hired for Sally's parties in the days when Marmite sandwiches and potato crisps and pink cake might be tempting for her.

He thought his mother had died of breast cancer, but he was not sure: he supposed that in those days people did not talk about either breasts or cancer. Now people talked of little else. His grandparents were long dead and he did not miss them. He sometimes said that they were kind people, but what he really meant was that they attended to his needs without complaint – that was on the same wavelength as 'kind' but not precisely the same thing. But he would never speak ill of them. They could not have wanted to take in a five-year-old boy. Particularly one whose mother had rejected everything they stood for and gone off to London to join the Communist Party – that was a first for a girl from St Albans in those days – then took up with a bearded radical with subversive intent, not only a Jew but one who did not keep it quiet and broadcast it by singing his Jew songs. It was no surprise to them that he had impregnated and abandoned her practically the moment she had the baby. They said that it was typical of 'that world'. Joseph thought it might have been worse for them if he had not abandoned her. Would they have really wanted him to come and have a family Christmas with them? Joseph had no idea how observant a Jew Isaac Herzl was, but he did not think that cooking kosher turkey would have played to his grandmother's strengths.

She would often say, 'Enough about that man!' but they never seemed to get enough of him. At breakfast, reading the newspaper, his grandfather would sometimes pass it to his wife. She would take a quick glance and give it back to him, letting out a sigh that sounded like the last breath of a dying woman. There was a review of a concert, or some quote from Isaac Herzl about an atrocity that had been committed in a far-off country that his grandparents had never heard of. Joseph thought that they would have preferred an atrocity in a familiar place, like the Isle of Wight or Tenerife. And when they read that Isaac Herzl had been arrested at a demonstration, they looked pityingly at Joseph: on top of everything else, he was now the child of a jailbird.

As he grew older, he had some opinions of his own. Obviously he did not think that abandoning your girlfriend the moment she had given birth to your child without even marrying her was a nice thing to do, but he wondered what the other side of the story was. His grandparents were certainly not very complimentary about their daughter either, so maybe some of the fault was hers.

He was not proud of his father. How could he be with his grandparents' inexhaustible catalogue of transgressions? – but he did take a little secret pleasure in the fact that he was so well known, even if it was for the wrong reasons. Except for Alan and Shirley, he did not tell any of his schoolfriends – not that there were very many of them to tell – about his father. He had inherited enough of his grandparents' genes to feel a little embarrassed about being illegitimate.

He was thinking about Alan and Shirley now. Did he dream that Shirley was in the room with him sometimes? Did he imagine he heard her voice? It was she who had helped with the letter he wrote to his father. He had first thought about doing it when he was a child, but then it had seemed like an impossibility. When he was fifteen, he realised that all it would take was a piece of paper and a stamp. But what would he say? Where would he send it?

Shirley knew. Shirley always knew those things. Isaac Herzl was giving a concert and she said they could send it to him c/o The Festival Hall, South Bank, London. That would get to him: they would think it was fan mail. They had decided that Alan's suggestion of 'Dear Dad' was out of the question, but Shirley thought that 'Dear Father' would do the trick.

'That's a bit presumptuous, isn't it?'

'It isn't a presumption, Joseph, he *is* your father.'

Joseph could see the logic in that, but he still couldn't do it. In the end, he insisted on 'Dear Mr Isaac Herzl', even though Shirley shook her head in exasperation.

They spent the entire evening thinking about what to say, but it wasn't until they were on the school bus the next morning that they finalised it.

Dear Mr Isaac Herzl,

You may remember my mother, Susan Carter, who I believe you knew 16 years ago. This is just to let you know she died some time ago and I live with my grand-parents. As I say, she was my mother and you will know that this means I am your son. I am sorry to bother you, but I thought it might be mutually beneficial if we could meet up at some time in the near future. Obviously, you are the only father I have and it is possible that I am the only son you have, unless you have some other children but I do not know if you do. If you do, it would be nice to meet them, because I have always thought that I was an only child and would welcome some siblings, even if they are only half-siblings.

If you would care to agree to this plan, you could get in touch with me at the above address. My discretion is assured. I very much hope to hear from you soon even though I know you are a very busy person. I have heard some of your music on the radio and think it is very good.

Yours faithfully
Joseph Carter (15 years old)

Shirley and Joseph had a last spat about whether you were meant to say 'yours faithfully' or 'yours sincerely', but Joseph prevailed. They were pleased with the letter – it seemed to tread the line between formality and sincerity rather well – and that night, he took a sheet of his grandparents' blue Basildon Bond paper with the address embossed in a darker blue at the top and carefully wrote the letter in the best handwriting he could manage.

He thought it would take two days to get to London. Isaac Herzl might take two days to answer it and it would be another two days for his letter to come back. In fact, Joseph's timescale was way off the mark. Months passed. The letter had been sent while he was revising for O levels, and a response did not arrive until after the results had come in.

Joseph did not get many letters, so his grandmother looked intrigued when she handed it to him one morning. Later, although she was not a nosy person, she could not resist asking him who it was from. A schoolfriend, Joseph said, which seemed to satisfy her even though it did not seem very convincing that someone he saw every day at school would be writing him a letter. He was nervous about opening it. He wanted to do it with Alan and Shirley.

Shirley didn't come to the canteen because she was on a diet – she had taken to wearing miniskirts and someone had made a comment about her legs looking fat – so Alan and Joseph had to go and look for her after lunch. Joseph held up the letter.

'Oh my God,' Shirley gasped. 'Well, open it!'

Joseph did not want to just tear the envelope so he used a pencil to slit the top of it. He gave it to Shirley. 'You read it,' he said.

Alan leaned over her shoulder to look as well. It didn't take very long to read.

'Well…' Shirley said. 'It isn't actually from him.'

'Oh,' Joseph said.

'But that's not bad – I think it must be from his wife. She's called Herzl, too. Unless he has a sister.'

Joseph shrugged his shoulders – he had no idea. Shirley handed the letter to him.

Dear Joseph Carter,

Thank you for your recent letter. Mr Herzl is currently in the United States singing in a memorial concert for Dr Martin Luther King, who, as you will know, was murdered last year. However, he will be back in this country next week and would be able to meet you, even though I am afraid it cannot be a long meeting because of existing commitments.

I presume you are at school and therefore will not be free on a weekday so I suggest Saturday the 20th of September. I very much hope that you will be free on that date. The best time for Mr Herzl would be 3 p.m. at the Bar Italia, 22 Frith St, London W1. You will find that easy to find. Please confirm that this arrangement will be convenient to you.

Yours sincerely
Lally Herzl

'Well,' Joseph said, looking up at Shirley and Alan. There was a brief silence. 'Lally? What sort of name is that?'

'I've never heard of it,' Shirley said. 'It certainly isn't Jewish.'

'I don't think the letter's too bad,' Alan said in a conciliatory voice.

'Oh *Alan* – I think it's awful! The man can't even be bothered to answer himself! This is his son we're talking about!'

Joseph could not have felt less like anyone's son at that moment.

'Not that I'm surprised, as he's made no effort to contact Joseph for fifteen years. It's absolutely—'

'Shirley, calm down,' Alan said.

'My parents think Iz Herzl is some kind of hero. They listen to his records! I'm going to tell them what he's really like.'

'Please don't, Shirley.'

'Are you going to go?' Alan said.

'I don't know.'

But he did know. Of course he was going to go.

The first problem was what to wear. He was not sure what would be suitable for this kind of meeting. What he normally wore on a weekend was corduroy trousers, an open-necked shirt and maybe a V-neck sweater if it was cold, but that seemed too casual. The only other alternative was his school uniform, with its blue blazer and crest on the breast pocket. He tried it both with and without a tie and decided the tie might be better. It wasn't perfect, but at least it looked smart and implied that he was a good student. That might please a parent. He just hoped that nobody he knew would see him walking to the station wearing his school uniform on a Saturday. He told his grandparents that he was going to the British Museum.

Joseph did not know London well, but he had looked Frith Street up on a map. He was early. He looked through the window of the bar but he did not see Isaac Herzl – there were sometimes photographs of him in the newspaper so he roughly knew what he looked like. He didn't really want to sit on his own, but there was nothing for it but to go in. He found a table at the back and sat down. There was a radio playing music very loudly. By 3.30, nobody had come. He wasn't sure what to do next. How long was he meant to wait? But then someone arrived: a woman of indeterminate age with slightly greying hair done up in braids and a dress that looked as if it was made from a sack. She spotted Joseph immediately – not difficult as he was the only schoolboy in the place.

'Hello, I'm Lally,' she said.

He got to his feet and shook her hand. 'I'm Joseph.'

'Well,' she said. 'Good. Right.'

He felt his stomach tighten with nerves.

'I expect Iz will be here soon. Who knows? Always rushing around.'

'Is he doing a concert?' Joseph asked cautiously.

'Oh yes – there's always something in the pipeline.' Then her voice changed tone. 'I must apologise,' she said. 'My letter to you must have seemed rather cautious. The thing is, the whole world seems to want something from Iz and we have to be careful.' She gave a little laugh. 'I'm thinking of having postcards printed saying, "Isaac Herzl thanks you for your recent communication but regrets that he is unable to provide whatever it is you are seeking from him."'

She suddenly groaned. 'I wish they'd turn this music down,' she said, gesturing towards the radio on the bar which was playing 'Where Do You Go to, My Lovely'. 'I can hardly hear myself think. I really don't like' – she made little quotes with her fingers – 'modern music, pop music like this. The words are so silly: who could sing like Marlene Dietrich and dance like Zizi Jeanmaire at the same time? – Well, who would want to listen to that? Ridiculous!'

'It's number one in the charts,' Joseph said, then added hurriedly, 'I mean, that doesn't make it good.'

'No,' she said. 'I shouldn't think it does.'

Joseph felt a little movement next to him and he looked round. Isaac Herzl was standing beside him. He jumped to his feet so fast that his chair fell over behind him. He knew he was going bright red.

'Here he is,' Lally said.

Isaac Herzl nodded and put his hand out. Then he sat down. He was a tall man. He had an unkempt beard and wore a strange thing on his head like a chauffeur's cap that had been run over by a bus. There was an old satchel over his shoulder and he took it off and put it over the back of his chair.

Lally turned to Iz. 'We've been having a nice talk,' she said.

Isaac Herzl nodded his head and gave a cautious smile. 'Good. We haven't seen each other for a long time, have we?'

'Well, yes… since I was born, I suppose,' Joseph said. That did not quite sound the way he meant it to so he rushed ahead with, 'I mean, I know you're very busy.' That did not sound right either.

There was a silence. 'Well, I'm sorry it's been so long. I'm sorry that was the way it was,' Isaac Herzl said.

'I don't think my grandparents have helped much.'

'No.'

'They're really good people,' he said. Joseph did not want Isaac Herzl to think that he had had an Oliver Twist sort of upbringing.

'Yes, I met them once. I'm not very popular with those sort of people, I'm afraid, and you've been caught in the middle.'

That was not quite how Joseph saw it. To be caught in the middle there had to be some kind of tug of war, and as far as he knew there had not been much tugging from Isaac Herzl's side.

'Well, we're here now, aren't we?'

'Yes,' Joseph said.

'And we must make up for lost time.'

That sounded good. 'Yes.'

'I'm sorry about your mother.'

'I don't really remember her.'

'We weren't good parents. Not in the accepted sense of the word, anyhow.'

Well, Joseph thought, not really in any sense of the word.

'And you're at school, I suppose? I hope they teach you well. If you haven't learnt things properly in the first place, you won't know what you need to throw away later.'

Joseph had absolutely no idea what that meant. 'I'm at Morton College,' he said. 'It's quite well known, I think.'

'That sounds like a public school.'

'Yes, it is.'

Isaac Herzl looked at his watch. 'Oh, I'm really sorry – will you excuse me for a moment? I have to make a phone call.'

He got up and went over to the counter, where there was a telephone.

'Iz uses this place like an office,' Lally said with a little laugh. 'No hiding place.' Then she moved her head towards Joseph's and whispered, as if she did not want anyone to overhear, 'I'm afraid Iz is rather sensitive about private schools.'

'Why?'

'He thinks they're totalitarian institutions. Everybody saying, "Play up, play up and play the game."'

Joseph looked confused. 'But nobody says that at my school.'

'All those elitist sports. Cricket and rowing, that sort of thing.'

'But doesn't everyone play sport at school?' Joseph said desperately.

'Oh, I'm the last person to ask about that kind of thing, dear. Anyway, I hope you come out of it unscathed.'

Isaac Herzl had returned to the table. 'I'm so sorry.'

'We've been having a nice talk about schools,' Lally said.

'Good. And what subjects do you like?'

'I do history. I got an A in my O level.'

Isaac Herzl nodded. 'Of course, it's the future not the past you should concentrate on, but history does have its uses. What's your area?'

'I wrote my main essay on the accession of the Hanovers.'

'But surely you don't just study kings and queens of England?'

'No. We're doing the American War of Independence at the moment.'

'That's all well and good, but I hope your school will teach you about some of the more relevant wars sometime.'

'What's a relevant war?'

'Well, a war that's fought to change people's beliefs. Not just one country trying to steal a bit of land from another. What else do you like at school?'

'German. I thought I should do it because of...' he didn't want to say 'you', so he said, 'the family being

German'. He thought that his learning German might please Isaac Herzl. He went on: 'I know you left Germany when you were young, but you must speak it pretty well. I'm quite good, actually. *Ich mochte in den Scwarzwald zu gehen. Ich bin fifteen. Mein name ist Joseph.'*

If Joseph thought they might have a little conversation in German, he was wrong: Isaac Herzl changed the subject.

'I was interested,' he said, 'you call yourself Joseph.'

'Well, yes. It's my name.'

'Not Joe?'

'Well, everybody calls me Joseph. I mean, no one shortens it to Joe.'

'But Joseph isn't the name you were born with, you know. On your birth certificate you're Joe Hill Herzl.'

'I didn't know,' Joseph said in a panicky voice. 'Nobody told me.' His grandparents had never mentioned it.

'I thought Joe Hill Herzl was rather a fine name for a boy,' Isaac Herzl said thoughtfully, 'But of course Joseph Carter is perfectly good, too. Just not so distinctive.'

'But you know who Joe Hill was, don't you?' Lally said.

'Well… no.'

'Executed in 1915. What a tragedy!'

Joseph was not sure why they would want to name him after someone who had been executed. No wonder his grandparents had stuck to 'Joseph Carter'.

'You should look him up, He's an important figure.' Isaac Herzl said pleasantly. 'Are you musical?'

Joseph nodded. 'I sang in the end-of-term concert. The *St Matthew Passion*. Just in the chorus.'

'Why is it always religious music at schools?' Isaac Herzl laughed. 'It's like brainwashing, isn't it? Do you play an instrument?'

'I'd like to learn the violin,' Joseph said, even though it was not really true. 'Did you start music very young?'

'Yes, I always liked music.'

'Was everyone in your family musical?' he asked cautiously. They might be on safer ground talking about family, although Joseph could not have felt less like a member of it at the moment.

After a moment, Isaac Herzl said, 'My brother played the violin.'

That was interesting, Joseph thought: he had an uncle as well. 'What's his name?' he said.

'Abram,' he said quietly, as if he did not want anyone to hear.

'Where does he live? Is he in England?'

'No. He's dead, I'm afraid. Just a pile of ashes in some camp.'

Just then, there was a shout from the other side of the bar: 'Mr Herzl!' They all turned round. A waiter was holding up a telephone receiver. 'It's for you!' He got up.

Lally moved her head towards Joseph and said quietly, 'Iz had a very painful time when he was young in Germany. His whole family murdered! Can you imagine? He doesn't like to talk about it.'

'But they're my family, too,' Joseph said.

Lally looked taken aback, as if he had said something extraordinary. Then they sat in silence. Isaac Herzl seemed to be having a heated discussion. When he had finished, he came back to the table. 'I have to go. I'm sorry.' He put his hand up in a goodbye gesture. 'Well... that was interesting,' he said. 'Perhaps another time.' Then he turned and walked to the door with long strides and vanished into the street.

'Well,' she said.

'Yes,' Joseph said. He stood up. 'I've got to go, too,' he said. He put his hand out. 'Goodbye, then.'

Lally looked startled by his abruptness. 'But...'

By the time she said 'Goodbye,' he was almost at the door. He could not get out of the place fast enough. Once on to Frith Street, he pulled his tie off roughly and stuffed it in his pocket. What Lally had said was true: whatever it was that anyone was seeking from Isaac Herzl, he was unable to provide.

That was the problem with free-form thinking: it could take you to places you did not want to go, but as he was stuck on this particular train, he might as well go on.

The ironic thing was that it had been Isaac Herzl who helped Alan and Joseph get started, or rather, it was what Lally called Joseph's 'betrayal' of him that did it. When they were at Oxford, they had begun writing songs together, little musical sketches and topical parodies that they performed in pubs and at end-of-term events. Alan played the guitar or the piano and Joseph sang, although his voice was no more than serviceable. They thought that wearing dinner jackets would make them seem sophisti-cated. One of their friends had a father who worked for the BBC. He had seen them perform when he was up in Oxford visiting his son and one day he called Joseph. He was producing a late-night satirical show and a singer had dropped out at the last moment. He was desperate: could Alan and Joseph throw something together?

Joseph did not know where the idea for the song came from. It was only afterwards that he remembered the radio playing it that day in the Bar Italia. The song was a few years old now, but everyone still remembered it. It was their version of 'Where Do You Go to, My Lovely'.

They put it together very quickly. They didn't know whether it was good or not, but it made them laugh. When they read it to the producer over the phone, he liked it, so they went down to London. The show was live which was nerve-racking, but they had time to rehearse it before. The costume designer had kitted them out with camouflage fatigues, big boots and Che Guevara berets. Alan played the guitar and they both sang.

You dance like Angela Davis
And you sing like Herbert Marcuse
You're holding an Uzi machine gun
While you're bemoaning the fate of the Jews, yes you are

You're off to the land that is promised
You're suddenly becoming Kibbutz-y
The girls are simply so stunning
You hope you'll find radical tootsie, yes you do

But where do you go to, my Lefty
When you're alone with your songs?
Will you tell me the hurt that's so painful
When you're thinking of the Viet-Cong, yes please do

Your name is heard in high places
You were a friend of that nice Malcolm X
He sent you a rifle for Christmas
But you wished it had been some Semtex, yes you did

You live in a lovely big mansion
In the leafy hills of Muswell
You talk of the plight of the homeless
But don't they need mansions as well? Yes they do

What really got them the publicity was that some of the reviews picked up the fact that Joseph was Iz Herzl's son. He had not intended for that to happen, but he guessed the producer had leaked it. It did not matter too much to him. People would have guessed that the song was, if not precisely about Iz Herzl, then at least inspired by him. He was all over the place then, singing at demonstrations in Trafalgar Square and being arrested outside the US Embassy and going to South Africa.

It did not take long for the letter to arrive:

Dear Joseph Carter,

I am using the name you prefer because I wonder if you are worthy of the name Isaac Herzl gave you – Joe Hill Herzl. Although you have a biological connection to him, I find it hard to think of you as his son now.

Your song was a shocking act of betrayal towards a man who has used his talents only for the good of other people. You will not find a more distinguished man to demean. If he cut you out of his life like a canker, I would not blame him and I think one day you will bitterly regret it.

Your song is hardly an adequate response to the kindness he showed you when you sought him out some years ago. Despite the evident pride you take in your public school education, good manners have clearly passed you by. I think it would be best if you made no attempt to contact him again.

Lally Herzl

Joseph had not even thought what effect the song might have on Isaac Herzl – their intentions were genuinely more satire than attack – but Lally's letter left him shocked. He was not entirely sure why: it was not as if he had any expectation of a relationship with him. It was not as if being cut out of Isaac Herzl's life was going to make any difference to him. But a thread had been broken, even if it was gossamer thin, even if it would hardly bear the weight of a feather. He shared everything with Alan and Shirley, who were now engaged, but this he did not share.

Still, it meant that when Alan and he were trying to get their first show off the ground some of the producers they spoke to remembered their television appearance: 'Oh yes – you're those guys who…' The show was eventually put on at the King's Head in Islington. The reviews were good. Then the producer of a show that was in trouble out of town called them in to write some new songs for it. The show came into London, was unexpectedly a success and went to Broadway. They were up and running.

Joseph ranged over the shows they had done – the successes, the ones that were labelled 'disappointing' and had a short run, the ones with toxic reviews that closed losing the entire investment, the ones with good reviews that were called 'ahead of their time' and nobody came to see. The screaming, the sackings, the compromises – and, always, the lonely hotel rooms.

Now he felt sad. Maybe he was dead and in limbo, waiting to be admitted to the final hotel room where he would stay for all eternity, the one with the rotting bowl of fruit and the empty minibar. He would only have the Gideon Bible on the bedside table for inspiration, thinking about musicals called *Moses*!

He tried to do a kind of hum in his head, to fill it with white noise so he could block off any more depressing thoughts. He did not want to find himself moving on to Gaz. He had an uneasy feeling that Gaz had something to do with where he was and what had happened to him.

Rose

I did nothing different when I went into Huddie's room on the day he died. It was the normal routine. I turned on his computer first, then I went to the bathroom and put toothpaste on his toothbrush, took the deodorant and aftershave lotion from the cupboard and put them on his bedside table. I put a cloth under the tap and wiped his face and mouth and pressed the button that raised him up in the bed. It was not good to leave him on his back too long because the fluid collected in his lungs.

The only thing that wasn't normal was that he was dead and I had known that from the moment I went into his room. It was not that I was telepathic or could feel that his spirit had left his body and was lurking in a corner or whatever rubbish people think to make themselves feel better. There was just a different kind of silence in the room.

I sat by his bed for a while. I did not touch him or hug him or plant a kiss tenderly on his forehead like people do in films. I would not have done those things when he was alive so why would I do them when he was dead?

I felt quite calm. As I came out of his room, the front door was opening and Lally came in.

'Huddie died in the night,' I said.

'What?' Maybe she had not heard.

Then I went into the kitchen where Carla and Joan were making coffee.

I said it again: 'Huddie died in the night.'

I'm not sure why there was a look of such incomprehension on their faces. It was hardly a surprising piece of news, like the roof being blown off. Anyway, I wasn't going to wait while it sunk in. I wanted to tell Iz. I brushed past Lally standing the hall, looking confused and went upstairs.

'Rosie!' she called. 'What's happening?'

I knocked on Iz's door and went in. As I closed the door I heard a wail from downstairs. The news had sunk in.

The room was dark. Iz was still asleep and I drew the curtains so the light would come in. I hoped that might make him wake up, but it didn't.

'Iz,' I said, then I said it a bit louder. I went to his bed and gently pulled at his arm. I hadn't seen Iz in bed since I was a child.

He opened his eyes.

'Iz – Huddie's dead. He died in the night.'

'Huddie?' he said, as if he couldn't quite remember who Huddie was. Then he looked at me with his eyes wide open.

I repeated it: 'Huddie died.'

After a moment, there was a tiny movement in his face and eyes. If you had filmed it and slowed the film down so you could examine it frame by frame, you might have been able to tell what the look meant, but I couldn't.

Then, the door burst open and the women crowded into the room. Out of all of us, Lally was the only one who was crying. Nobody seemed to know what to say or what to do, but they looked at Iz as if he was going to give us some kind of guidance. All he said was, 'Can I see him?'

When he had dressed, Lally helped him down the stairs and he went into Huddie's room and closed the door behind him. He was in there for about half an hour. We were all waiting outside when he came out.

As he passed us, Lally put her hand on his arm and said, 'Iz…' But he ignored her and walked slowly to the stairs. There was no expression on his face. It looked to me as if it had been carved out of the stone on Mount Rushmore.

There was a lot of hugging from Carla and Lally. I had even had a stiff hug from Joan, which was not pleasant. I wasn't sure what their hugging was meant to achieve. They liked to do things in front of everybody else. I didn't. All the things I was feeling about Huddie were private. They were mine and I was not going to share them with anyone else.

Later in the morning, Huddie's doctor came and examined him. He said there would have to be an autopsy. I was not quite sure why: there were not going to be any surprises, like discovering he had been bitten by a poisonous snake.

We did not know any undertakers so we found one on the Internet and they came surprisingly quickly. Undertakers obviously had a uniform – black suit, white shirt, black tie – but I would not have thought the worse of them if they had been dressed like Huddie in a tracksuit and T-shirt. I suppose most deaths are the same for them so the only glimmer of surprise on their faces was when they asked what kind of coffin the family would like and I said to them, 'It should be the cheapest.' They obviously thought that was disrespectful, but I did not want something in mahogany that had shiny brass handles and a satin lining. Huddie would not have felt comfortable in that. And I supposed Carla would want the cheapest, too, because it would be cardboard or wicker or something and be biodegradable. Then, if anyone gave her an Eco-Audit, she would come out with flying colours.

The undertakers asked whether we would like them to take the body now, or whether we would like it to stay overnight. Of course I knew that when you were dead you were dead – no brain function, no heartbeat, nothing that constituted life – so I said that I did not mind one way or the other, but when the body was taken out on a wheeled stretcher, Huddie covered by a sheet that was too short for him so his feet were sticking out, I knew that what I had said to the undertakers was not really true.

The funeral was at Golders Green crematorium. As there weren't going to be any hymns, we had to fill it out with something. We agreed that the headmaster of his school could say something, and then one of the doctors who had looked after him. I knew they would say nothing of any interest, not to Huddie anyway, so I said I would speak at the beginning. I was a little nervous about doing it and I spent the evening before the funeral preparing it. I wanted to get it right, not so much for Huddie as for myself, just like I got my debating speeches right at school.

The crematorium was very full and we walked slowly – Iz had to use his stick all the time now – to the front pew. I was not sure why Joan was with us, but I made sure I didn't sit next to her.

When everyone had settled down, I walked up to the front and began to speak.

'You probably think Huddie would be pleased that there are so many people here. I shouldn't think so. He would have been the first to point out that statistically you're likely to get a bigger turnout at the funeral of someone young. You're probably mourning the experiences he didn't have and being sorry that he didn't have time to become the person he would have been. Well, don't worry on Huddie's account. He didn't need time to become the person he would have been because he already was and he always had been.

'Huddie knew so many things. He knew that the Bay of Fundy in Nova Scotia has the highest vertical tide range in the world and Ungava Bay in northern Quebec has the second. They make a particular kind of gin there because a rare plant called Labrador tea gives it a special taste and colour. The Labrador dog does not actually come from Labrador but Nova Scotia where the original inhabitants were called "Aboriginal", a word most people think refers only to indigenous Australians. These were the kind of connections Huddie made as he moved across the world. He wrote them down in a notebook and later, when he found it hard to grasp a pen, I wrote them down for him, although he actually remembered them pretty well. He was lucky: the brain doesn't need muscles to work. There was nothing much he could rely on, but he knew that his brain would never betray him like everything else in his body was doing.

'You could ask how relevant these journeys were to Huddie's life, but he could find relevance in everything. On that particular journey I'm talking about, he left the Aborigines in Australia and eventually arrived on an island called Pingelap which is meant to be one of the most beautiful places in the Pacific – clear water and coral reefs and lots of fish – but there is one flaw to the inhabitants' lives: there is a recessive gene particular to that island. Huddie certainly understood that, even though it's a different recessive gene to his. It's called Achromatopsia. The sufferers are called Achromats. I suppose you could call Huddie a Duchenner, like the name of a sports team. The Pingelap gene causes complete colour blindness – they literally only see in black and white. It's found in one in ten people on the island. Duchenne is found in about one in seven thousand people so Huddie's odds against inheriting a recessive gene were better in Muswell Hill than on Pingelap although he said the climate was not so good. He lost almost everything, but at least he could always see and know things in colour.

'You're privileged to have known someone who could start off in the morning at the Bay of Fundy and by the end of the day reach Pingelap without leaving his wheelchair. I don't know much about funerals but I think you're meant to thank people for coming. I'm not going to thank you. You're lucky to be here.'

As I walked down the aisle, I could see some surprised faces when I did not stop at our pew but kept on going to the door at the back. I wasn't going to stay and listen to the headmaster and the doctor give their eulogies: Huddie was snuffed out like a candle, he fought the disease with all the strength he had, he was the bravest person I knew, he bore it stoically, none of us will ever forget him. It would all be white noise to me.

The only thing to come out of the funeral would be an urn of ashes. I was not sure what I would do with them yet but I thought I would probably flush them down the lavatory. That would have made Huddie laugh.

When I got home, I was happy to be the only one there. I didn't want to see anyone and I could begin to sort out my schoolwork. In the days since Huddie had died I had done almost nothing, but soon I planned to pull myself together and get back to all the things I wanted to learn and all the books I had to read to learn them.

Nothing in Huddie's room had been moved and I liked it like that. It was still his room even if he was not there any more. It would always be his room. I was planning to move my stuff into it and sleep there, but I did not want to do that yet although I was happy to spend most of my time there. After all, I had spent most of my time there when Huddie was alive. I would enjoy sleeping in his bed because it was one of those electrical ones that raised your back up when you pressed a button, so I would be able to read in bed without all the hassle of getting the pillows right.

I had tidied his things and had washed his T-shirts and tracksuit bottoms. Huddie liked everything to be clean. I had started to listen to the talking books I had down-loaded for him on to his iPod, all the Thomas Hardy ones he had liked, but I did not really enjoy being read to: just by the way the reader spoke, by the pauses they left and the inflection they gave certain words, they were impos-ing their interpretation on the book and I was not really interested in other people's interpretations.

I sat by his empty bed for a while. Even though, of course, I tried not to look into the past, I did find myself thinking about the last time I had seen Huddie. It was hard to be objective about someone you knew so well. His hair looked as if it had been cut with garden shears. It was greasy, too – getting Huddie's head over the sink to wash it had become harder. One of the arms of his glasses had come off and it was attached by a paperclip, which made the glasses crooked on his face. He had spots on his forehead and by the side of his mouth. His teeth were yellow and snaggled but I did not care what anybody else might think about his appearance. He just looked like Huddie to me, which was to say that he looked as perfect as anyone could be.

Shirley

'Comfortable?' Shirley said. 'What does that even mean?'

The nurse looked nervous. 'Well...'

'Does it mean that he's got his feet up in an easy chair? Is the central heating at the right level? I didn't ask if he was comfortable, I asked how he was. You don't have to treat me with kid gloves. I told you before: I'm a doctor's daughter.'

'I'll get the doctor.'

She had got to know all the doctors in the hospital in Manchester. They finally realised that she knew what she was talking about. Now, in London, where Joseph had been moved when his medical insurance kicked in, she had to start all over again. She had preferred it up there – the hospital was buzzing with activity and there were always doctors and nurses around. Here, on the private, there were deserted corridors and closed doors and muted voices. The food was probably better, but that would not matter to Joseph, who looked like a marionette with the various wires and tubes coming out of him or going into him.

The doctor she had talked to before finally arrived. 'Mrs Isaacs,' he said in a neutral voice, 'What can I do for you?'

'I just want to know what is happening to my brother, what the situation is today.'

'His vital signs are good, but it's difficult to tell how long the recovery process will take. Well, you'll know that. Being a doctor's daughter.'

Presumably that was meant to be sarcastic. Why were these people so hard to charm? Shirley nodded her head.

'Thank you,' she said.

There were still stories about what had happened to Joseph in the news. Thank God that awful boy had been arrested. Oh Joseph, she thought, why couldn't you have found a nice interior decorator? The consistent thing in the articles was that they all eventually came round to *A Taste of Honey*. It was the show that Joseph had waited 'all his life' to write. After an 'uncertain' few years he was back on top form. The show was a 'giant hit' in Manchester. It was reported that the cast dedicated every performance to Joseph, after which there were standing ovations. Shirley had a reflex moment of irritation that Alan was hardly mentioned – all their shows appeared to have been written by Joseph alone – but it passed quickly.

Shirley detected the stench of Kevin Lever in all this. He had probably used the last of the money to hire a phalanx of publicists to shoehorn the show into every available piece about Joseph. And the extraordinary thing was that it had worked. From teetering on the edge of disaster, the show now seemed to be hovering on the brink of success. The show was coming to London. Shirley did not know whether she was pleased or not. If she was pleased, it was only for Joseph.

She did not know where Alan was and she did not care. He had left endless phone messages, begging and pleading. She did not reply. The only contact she had had with him was text messages:

Can we meet? We need to talk.

No.

Can I collect some things?

Out till lunchtime tomorrow. Pick them up then.

It was going to be Alan's last time in the house: she had arranged for the locks to be changed.

She was not going to pretend it was not humiliating. She was not going to pretend she was not lonely. She had read about the plight of dumped wives and it had seemed as relevant to her as the plight of the refugees in Ethiopia. She was going to behave with dignity, though, not like those women who took a pair of scissors to their husband's expensive suits or threw a brick through the windscreen of their flashy car. Nor was she going to comb through their lives and kick herself that she had not spotted the signs earlier. There were no signs: Alan had simply become a different person overnight, a freak event like a tsunami that comes with no warning and washes the village away. Everyone seemed to think that blame for this sort of thing must be shared, but why? She knew that none of it had been her fault.

But a month after everything had happened, she began to realise that having dignity and being able to hold her head up high did not achieve much. It did not help her sleep or fill her days. There were people she could have called, but not many of them, and not any that she wanted to talk to. She thought of going to the synagogue, but she was certainly not about to find religion to get her through. Anyway, she had not set foot in one for years, not since

Sally died. What would she have made of all this? She would be thirty now, maybe married, maybe with children. It was not painful to think of her at thirty because Shirley could not imagine her at thirty. The only Sally was the sixteen-year-old Sally, the one she had glimpsed so briefly in the hotel room in Manchester. She felt like everyone was dead. Even the ones who were alive felt dead to her: Alan and Joseph. Of course, Joseph could come alive to her again when he got better. He was the one person she wanted to be with. She knew she was a powerful person: she was simply going to will him to get better. Maybe Sally would help her do that.

She was unsure precisely why she did it, what she hoped she would get out of it, but she surprised herself: she called David Arbuthnot from the Tuesday group and asked him round for a drink. She could tell he was surprised, but of course he was scrupulously polite. She went to Waitrose and bought some good wine, not the Chenin blanc that Alan liked, but something expensive and South African.

When she opened the door, David was in his usual outfit: grey flannel trousers, a Viyella shirt and tie, and a tweed jacket. His grey hair was neatly combed.

'Shirley,' he said. 'How very nice to see you. It's been a while, hasn't it?'

She did not know whether it was appropriate to kiss him on the cheek. He obviously had the same problem, so they shook hands and she took him into the living room. He turned down her offer of wine and asked for some mineral water instead.

'Is your husband here?' he asked politely. That was such an irritating question. She did have an identity outside her husband. She was capable of having a drink with someone without him.

'No. I'm afraid we've had a small domestic disturbance,' she said coolly.

David looked confused. She was not going to spell it out for him.

'I see,' he said cautiously.

'Yes. We have split up. I'm quite happy about it. At our age we all need a shake-up or else we atrophy and die.' She must have read that somewhere. It did not sound very convincing but she certainly did not want David Arbuthnot pitying her.

'And what have you been up to, David?' she said.

'Did you know I'm doing a PhD?'

'How interesting. That must keep you busy. And what is your subject?'

'Water technology. The history of aqueducts and dams. There's so much fascinating stuff. Amazing stories – you know, when the St Francis Dam in California collapsed in 1928 twelve and a half billion gallons of water poured out? Can you imagine that? Twelve and a half billion gallons!'

'Well, yes, I suppose if it was leaking through your ceiling it could cause a lot of damage. How did you get interested in all that?"

'I studied engineering.'

'At one of those technical colleges?'

David seemed offended. 'No. At a proper university.'

Shirley poured herself another glass of wine. She was trying to think why she had even invited him round.

'I did sociology at university,' she said. 'I thought of going further with it but what would I do with a PhD in it? Anyway I'd learnt everything I needed to know about people by then.' She finished her wine. 'And how is the Tuesday group?'

He looked sheepish. 'I'm sorry about what happened. The letter and all that.'

'Oh, I don't blame you, David,' she said magnanimously. 'I know they put you up to it. Anyway, I don't hold grudges.'

'Yes. I always thought that underneath everything you might be a rather forgiving person.'

She was touched. 'Well, I don't necessarily forget, yes, but I do forgive.' That was not entirely true. She was never going to forgive Alan.

'Actually we miss you. Well, some of us do. The sessions aren't quite as...' – he tried to find the right word – '...*dynamic* as they were when you were with us.'

'Any breakthroughs?'

He laughed. 'You know they come as often as Halley's Comet, Shirley. We do it as much for companionship as anything else, don't we?'

She took another gulp of wine. 'I certainly didn't. I would have chosen my companions more carefully if I was looking for that.'

'Loss is equal opportunity, Shirley. You can't pick and choose,' he said gently.

She poured herself another glass of wine, but then everything went wrong: the glass slipped and it spilled on to her lap all over her beige trousers. 'Oh!' she screamed, leaping to her feet. The sudden action seemed to release something in her because she suddenly found herself saying, 'Actually, my husband left me.'

David got to his feet and pulled her to him. 'Oh my dear,' he said, 'I'm so sorry. How awful.'

She extricated herself from his arms. David poured her another glass of wine.

'You don't have to be embarrassed.'

'I'm not embarrassed,' she said.

'Talking about the pain of loss, that's good, that's what we do in the group.'

'I'm not *in* the group any more, David.'

'But you do think about Sally?'

'Of course I think about Sally. She's always with me.' She paused for a moment, and then said, 'Actually, I did have a bit of a breakthrough. On my own. Without the group.' She didn't mind that it sounded like one-upmanship.

She told him about what had happened in her hotel room in Manchester, how it felt like Sally had led her to Joseph. She left out certain key elements. She did not say she knew him: she simply said that the man in the room down the corridor had had a heart attack.

'That's extraordinary,' David said. 'Well done! I'm so pleased. Sally must have been a very caring person to have guided you.'

Shirley's head was swimming. 'You've been very kind, David. Thank you.'

'I don't have much to offer, but I do understand how hard it is to lose someone whether they're dead or alive. You might be able to find your husband again.'

'He isn't lost, David. He hasn't vanished into the ether like the loved ones you're all looking for. I don't want to be back with him.'

'You'll get through it, Shirley. You're brave. You're strong. You're an attractive woman. You'll be able to move on.'

'Well, I hope so.'

'As I discovered after losing my wife, there's a lot of readjustment. You lose a lot but you can gain a lot. That's the thing you may not know yet.'

Shirley was having some difficulty following what he was saying, but that might have been because he was skating from one inane cliché to another. Or else it might have been the wine. She could see the empty bottle out of the corner of her eye.

David took her hand. 'If there's anything I can do, Shirley.'

She thought that touching her hand would be a brief gesture, but he did not take it away.

'One of the things I found difficult after my wife passed was losing the things we shared together. Though I suppose we really lost them a long time before, when she became ill. The oxygen machine in the bedroom rather cramped our style.'

'Well, yes, not going out together, not having someone to go on holiday with—'

'I really meant more intimate things.'

'Oh,' Shirley said.

'Yes, when that side of things is so fulfilling, it's painful when it's suddenly whisked away. We all have needs. Perhaps you've found that yourself.'

She gave a nervous laugh. 'Well, it wasn't really that kind of thing with my husband.'

He nodded his head meaningfully. 'Then you'll certainly know about need, Shirley. I've always found you very attractive. You know that. I told you once before.'

'I remember.'

'Of course, your circumstances were rather different then. You see, I'm a very sexual person. I sense that you are, too.'

'I don't know about that,' she said nervously, but before she had finished speaking he was on her side of the sofa and his mouth was against her ear, breathing heavily. His jacket smelled a bit musty. Then his tongue was wriggling around inside her ear. She had not liked that much when she was a teenager and it had not improved over the years. She gently pulled herself away.

He took her face in his hands. 'Oh Shirley, we could really have something together. I've always known that. Perhaps now is the right time.'

Before she could speak – not that she had any idea what to say – he was kissing her. I am a fifty-eight-year-old woman whose husband has just left, she thought, and a middle-aged structural engineer who is passionate about dams has his tongue in my mouth. Why not go with it? Maybe it was true: maybe everybody did need a shake-up or they would atrophy and die.

David gently pushed her back on the sofa and lay on top of her. She was surprised how good his weight felt. Soon his hands were inside her blouse. His fingers were scrabbling round the clasp of her bra. How old did a man have to be to finally understand how a bra comes off?

He put his head between her breasts. It was not unpleasant and she put her hands on his head and caressed it, but either his hair was greasy or he had put some kind of lotion on it. She took her hands off and surreptitiously wiped them on the fabric of the sofa, hoping it would not stain.

She was not sure of the etiquette of this kind of thing. 'Should we go somewhere more comfortable?' Her back was beginning to ache.

'Oh yes, please. I want to see you properly,' he said breathlessly. Her heart sank slightly. She realised that was the point of thing, but she was not entirely sure that she wanted anyone to see her properly.

In the bedroom, he said, 'Which one should we use?', gesturing at the twin beds.

'I'm not sure it much matters, David. They're both the same.'

'Is there one that you and your husband…'

'Don't worry: the sheets are clean.'

He pulled the cover back. 'Let me undress you,' he said gently.

'Why don't you go first?' she said nervously.

He was out of his clothes quickly and he faced her naked with his hands on his hips. She resisted the urge to pick up his trousers and put them over the back of a chair.

'Give me a moment, David. I need to go to the bathroom.'

'I'll wait,' he said.

Once in the bathroom, she turned the key very slowly so he would not hear. She could see that locking the door could be misconstrued. She took her clothes off. Well, she didn't look too bad. She was a bit bony and her breasts seemed to have got smaller but she thought she did not look too bad. She put her new negligee on, took a deep breath and opened the door.

David had turned all the lights on and was sitting up in bed, his arms crossed over his chest.

'Do you mind if we turn the lights off?' She gave a nervous laugh. 'I need to ease myself into this gently.' She did not want to ease herself into this at all, but it seemed too late to back out.

She turned the overhead light off, and one of the bedside ones. Then she let the negligee slip to the floor and got into bed as quickly as she could. He was very hot. She thought she better begin stroking his body. She avoided going too low: the top half would have to do for the time being. He began to kiss her again. He put his hand between her legs. To her surprise, she did not find it unpleasant. He rolled on top of her. Was this it? Was this the moment? But he went on kissing her and moving his hands over her body as if he was trying to find something that had gone missing. This seemed to go on for a long time. Her arm had gone to sleep. She wondered if he was being considerate, trying not to go too fast for her. 'David, I'm ready,' she said gently.

'Hold on,' he said, and got out of bed. 'Time for Plan B.' He put his hand into his jacket pocket and pulled something out. 'These are miracle workers,' he said, holding up a box and popping a pill in his mouth. 'Give me fifteen minutes for them to work. I hope we're not in a hurry.'

Outrage surged up in her. First Alan had them, now David. Were those bloody pills going to follow her round for ever? She jumped out of bed and pulled the negligee on.

'Put on your clothes,' she said.

'But—'

'Please.'

'It's nothing to do with you, Shirley, I promise. I haven't been with a woman for a long time. I don't normally need them. Everything works fine at other times.'

'What do you mean?'

'Well, when I… relieve myself.'

She let out a groan of disgust.

'We all have—'

'Please don't say that again,' she said.

'You know, at our age everybody uses Viagra. It's not unusual.'

'So I gather.'

'Shall we forget all this?'

'Yes, I think that's a good idea.'

'No, I meant, forget this conversation. Spool back.'

'I'm all spooled out,' she said, 'Please go, David.'

There had been a small problem at the hospital the next day. The doctor drew her to one side while she was waiting outside Joseph's room. 'A word please, Mrs Isaacs.'

'Yes?'

'Your husband was in this morning.' She had texted Alan to say that she would do afternoons at the hospital, so she did not have to run into him.

'Ex-husband, actually,' Shirley said, not strictly accurately.

'He asked how Mr Carter was doing, and I said that his brother-in-law was doing as well as can be expected, although not entirely out of the woods yet.'

'That's good.'

'Apparently, he is not Mr Carter's brother-in-law.'

'Oh.'

'So that would make you what, precisely, Mrs Isaacs? Not his sister, anyway.'

She did not say anything.

'Look, believe me, whatever silly subterfuge you're indulging in is very low on my list of priorities. We're serious people here. Please treat us seriously. We have a lot to do.'

'Well, I'm sorry,' she said crisply, 'He has no relatives and I'm the closest person to him. I didn't want to endlessly be told he was comfortable. I needed the full story. I am a doctor's—'

'Are you? Really?' He turned and strode down the corridor.

It was embarrassing to be caught out, but she had done it for good reasons. She was not going to be apologetic. She was a serious person and she had a lot to do as well.

When the nurse came out of Joseph's room, she smiled warmly. She thought she better be charming. She did not want everyone in the hospital to turn against her. 'May I go in now? And by the way, I just wanted to thank you for all you've done for my... for Mr Carter. I know how hard you work. And all for so little pay. And probably such a long way from your country.' The nurse looked confused. Maybe she didn't understand English very well.

Joseph looked better. The swelling in his face had gone down, although one eye was still completely closed. The bruises were beginning to turn from purple to that sickly yellow colour. The bandages round his skull were still there. They would have shaved his head: he would hate that. In the last few years his hair had begun to thin rather alarmingly and she guessed that it required a certain amount of work to get it as he wanted.

It was quiet inside his room, only the low hum of some machine. She was trying not to think about Sally's hospital room. Joseph was still hooked up to all those tubes. Sally had had no tubes at the end: she just lay there. She looked like a tiny, thin child, her bones jutting out, her skin covered in the soft down that comes when the body loses all its defences.

In the last hospital they had force-fed her, although they called it 'nutritional intervention'. 'Why don't we be grown up?' she said. 'It's feeding and you're forcing her.' Of the many bad times Shirley had had with Sally, she thought the day the force-feeding began was almost worse than the day she had died. How could they need such burly men to hold her down? You wouldn't have thought she could fight that hard. The tube down her throat, her look of terror, Alan in the corner of the room silently crying.

Like airports, hospital rooms were all the same: she sat down beside Joseph's bed as she had sat next to Sally's. She did not quite know what to do with Joseph. She put out her hand and rested it gently on his arm. He was awake more often now, but he could not really speak because of the damage to his face.

The doctor had said that all his functions would come back. Now he was awake, she needed to get through to him. She needed him back in the world. Shirley had glimpsed Sally twice since she had died, and both times Joseph had been part of it. First at the shiva when Joseph had understood that Sally wanted the food to go, and then in Manchester.

Sally had sent her to Joseph that night. How would Shirley have known that something had happened to him otherwise? If she had not found him in the room, he might be dead and they would be in Golders Green Crem reading passages from *The Prophet*. Maybe Sally would show herself through Joseph again.

After she left him, a sudden realisation flashed into her mind. Maybe Sally had put it there. Maybe she was pushing her in some unknown direction. Shirley had told everybody that she was Joseph's sister. She certainly felt that she was his only family, but now she suddenly realised that it was not true: he had a father. She knew she had to find Iz Herzl.

Maurice

It was more than ten days before Iz and Maurice met again. Maurice had considered going to his farm to look for him, but he knew Iz would not like that. He would want to keep him away from his friends.

Saturday was his day off. Maurice had got up late and he was sitting in the kitchen having a cup of tea. His uncle was sharpening his knives when there was a loud knock on the door. His uncle spun round as if it had been a gunshot. In the weeks Maurice had been there, no visitors had ever come to the farm. His uncle hobbled surprisingly quickly to the door and pulled it open aggressively.

Iz was standing there. 'I must see Maurice please. It is most important.'

Maurice saw that his uncle was holding up the knife he had been sharpening. Obviously you would need to protect yourself if there was a Jew-boy who might also be a Nazi spy standing menacingly on your doorstep.

'You stay there,' his uncle said. 'I don't want you coming in.' He turned to Maurice angrily, as if it was his fault. 'Do you know who he is? What does he want?'

Maurice stood up. 'Of course I know who he is,' he said contemptuously. 'He's my friend.'

He pushed past his uncle. Iz had moved off and was almost running up the track. Maurice shut the door in his uncle's face and ran after him.

'Isaac!' he shouted. 'What is it?'

Iz spun round so fast that his satchel swung round his body. 'I am going,' he said. 'They have informed me.'

Maurice had reached him. 'When? Not for a while, surely?'

'Tomorrow.'

'But… that's so soon.'

'They move quickly,' Iz said.

'Come into the barn.' Maurice said, and grabbed his arm. It was hot in there and smelled fetid. They sat down on a bale of hay.

Maurice felt a rising sense of panic. He wanted to shout: 'Do not go. You are my brother. If you go, I will wither away. I will become the boy I used to be before I met you. I will be forever rolling a stone up the hill alone like…' He could not remember whether it was Sisyphus or Hercules.

Iz was trembling. 'It's what I have wanted for so long, and now I am…' He didn't finish the sentence.

'What?' Maurice said desperately.

'I don't know.'

'Frightened? Doubtful?'

'Apprehensive, I think.'

Maurice thought, Yes, you have every reason to be apprehensive. It is messy and dangerous there. You might be killed. You do not need to go. Stay – there is so much we can do here. But Maurice knew that this was a test for him. What he said now would define his commitment and his purpose for ever. He could not just think about himself.

He put his hand on Iz's arm. He closed his eyes. 'It's what you have trained for, Isaac. Don't let it go to waste.' There was a painful knot in his stomach. 'Everyone has doubts. Everyone! Martin Luther had doubts. Trotsky had doubts.'

Iz looked confused. He was obviously not as familiar with them as Maurice was, not that Maurice was very familiar with them either. He fumbled for a name that Iz would relate to. 'Jesus!' he said. 'He didn't know whether he was really the Messiah or not.' Then he almost bit his tongue. He remembered that Jews didn't believe Jesus was the Messiah anyway. He hurried on: 'Just think how much you want it, how much you can do over there. Then the doubts will go.'

Iz put his head in his hands. 'You're right. Thank you. I must calm myself.'

'What will happen now?'

'I am doing something called Aliyah Bet. It is illegal immigration to Israel. The Jewish Agency arranges it.'

'How will you get there?'

'I am not absolutely sure.' Iz gave a little laugh. 'They don't issue you with an itinerary. Everything is secretive. Everything is done indirectly. People give messages to other people who pass them on, so the chain will not be discovered. They want us to be safe. I've never even met anyone at the Jewish Agency. It was Aviva, our dance teacher, who told me last night. I did not know she was even part of the organisation. Someone must have given her a message or telephoned her because she never goes to London. I must keep it secret. They don't even want me to tell the others on the farm. Sometimes people have just vanished overnight. I presume they were summoned, and they just left. Nobody asks any questions.'

'But you're telling me,' Maurice said.

'I had to tell somebody. No one will know. You are on the edge. You are an outsider. But I trust you. I think I would trust you with my life.'

Maurice felt his heart stop. 'But what happens now,' he said, trying to keep his voice from trembling. 'You go to the Jewish Agency in London and then what?'

'I will be given forged papers. Somehow they'll take me through France to the south, Marseilles I think, then on to a boat with others on Aliyah Bet. Then we head for Haifa. I left Germany on a boat and now I'm going to Israel on one. There's a certain symmetry in that, don't you think?'

'But what about the blockade?'

'It's dangerous, but some ships have got through. I will have to take that chance.'

'You'll be so alone.'

'I'll be alone but I will be looked after. I expect I will be given a secret address to go to in Haifa or Tel Aviv. Then I will meet others and we will be trained together. I'm sure I'll make friends. After all, we're all fighting for the same thing.'

Everybody would want to be Iz's friend, Maurice thought gloomily. He was going to be replaced. He would just become a dim memory.

They sat in silence for a moment. It was swelteringly hot in the barn. Maurice could feel sweat running down his back.

'I feel better,' Iz said. 'You have helped me very much. Thank you.'

I'm so pleased, Maurice thought rather sourly. He said, 'You know, I will…' But he was too embarrassed to go on.

'Yes, I will miss you, too,' Iz said.

'I hope I will hear from you sometimes.'

'Yes, of course. I shall write and tell you of my progress. I want you to know everything that happens out there.'

Maurice was not convinced that in a country at war there would be friendly postmen who said 'Good morning' to you and collected the mail four times a day.

Iz stood up. 'Oh, it's so hot! I'll tell you what I would like to do. I'd like to go swimming in the quarry one last time. Will you come? It is very refreshing.'

'That would be nice,' Maurice said, although he did not like swimming very much. 'I don't know where the quarry is.'

'I will show you. Through the woods and then up. It's been disused for years. It is a long walk, but we can talk.'

In fact, they walked quite a long way in silence. As they left the track and headed into the woods, Iz said, 'I am more cheerful now. It's going to be exciting, I think.'

'Yes,' Maurice said.

The path through the woods was overgrown, and they had to push their way through brambles and climb over fallen tree trunks.

'My friends at the farm – I have to drag them here. They think it is too difficult. They can be rather feeble,' Iz said.

Maurice was feeling rather feeble himself as he tried to keep up with Iz. There was shade where the sun could not get through the trees, but it was still hot. Iz began to hum softly.

'What's that tune?' Maurice asked. It was lovely.

'It's called "Hatikva". You might translate it as "The Yearning" or "The Hope". It's like our national anthem.' He laughed: 'A national anthem for a country that is not yet created.'

Then he began to sing the words.

When Iz had finished, Maurice asked, 'Is that Hebrew?' He had never heard it before.

'Yes, I sometimes sing in Hebrew. There are lovely folk songs. It helps me practise. My Hebrew is not as good as it should be.'

'What does the song say?'

'Oh, just what you'd think. Going back to our land, Jerusalem, Zion – that sort of thing.'

'You've got a wonderful voice,' Maurice said.

'I love music. I love singing. My parents were very musical. My brother Abram played the violin.'

Then Iz leaned in as if to tell Maurice a secret. 'Actually, I prefer the American songs. I love the blues. Such passion and anger! My favourite singer is Leadbelly – Huddie Ledbetter. All his songs: "Midnight Special". "Goodnight Irene". Just incredible. So many of those American martyrs were put in jail – him, the Scottsboro boys, Joe Hill. Like us Jews they fought against oppression.' He gave a little laugh and put his fist in the air. 'We should name our children after them! We should celebrate them in music for ever!'

'I love music, too. I sing,' Maurice said. 'I won a choral scholarship to my school.'

'That is very impressive. Well then: you must sing something for me now. But not your national anthem, please – I've had my fill of that in this country.'

For a moment Maurice could not think what he should sing, then he started. He was tentative at first, but after a few lines his voice became stronger.

> *Blow the wind southerly, southerly, southerly*
> *Blow the wind south o'er the bonny blue sea*
> *Blow the wind southerly, southerly, southerly*
> *Blow bonny breeze, my lover to me*

They told me last night there were ships in the offing
And I hurried down to the deep rolling sea
But my eye could not see it wherever it might be
The barque that is bearing my lover to me

He stopped and there was a silence. Maurice could see tears in Iz's eyes.

'There are some things that are beautiful in this country,' he said. 'I will miss it, I think.' Then Iz put his arm round Maurice's shoulder and they walked on.

There was a last barrier of thick bracken and when they had pushed through it, they came into a large clearing where the quarry was. There was a lake in front of them that extended about three hundred yards to the small cliff from which the stone had been excavated. The lake could not just be rainwater, there must have been some kind of spring. In the middle, there was a little island constructed from great slabs of stone piled on top of one another.

'The edge is rather muddy, but it is clear when you get further out,' Iz said. 'The water's cold, but that's good on a hot day.'

Iz began taking his clothes off. Maurice hoped he was not going to strip off completely, but he slipped his underpants off. Maybe being on a commune made you less self-conscious about your body, he thought. Iz stood with his hands on his hips, looking out over the water as Maurice undressed behind him.

Iz turned to him. 'It's beautiful, isn't it?'

Actually, Maurice thought it was rather eerie. 'Yes, lovely.'

Iz suddenly gave a little snort: 'You haven't got your helmet,' he said.

'What?' Maurice looked confused. Iz pointed down at his crotch.

'Oh,' Maurice said, going red.

'All Jews are snipped.' Iz made a scissor motion with his fingers, 'I thought English men stayed uncut. I expect they all work the same way, though.'

'Probably,' Maurice said. 'Actually, lots of people are… have that done to them. We had communal showers at school.' He was keen to move off this particular subject. 'Shall we go in now?' he said quickly.

Iz gave a great laugh and ran into the water, splashing and jumping up and down. 'Oh, so cold!'

Yes, it was. Maurice tried not to scrunch up his face in pain. He was the kind of swimmer who normally entered the water cautiously, but this time he felt he had to move more quickly to keep up with Iz.

'Let's go to the island,' Iz shouted. Of course he swam beautifully, great strokes of his arms pulling him sleekly through the water. Maurice followed behind him like a paddling dog. He didn't like putting his face under water, and he had never worked out how to coordinate his arms with his legs.

Iz reached the island and scrambled up on to it. He stood silhouetted against the sun and waved at Maurice, struggling towards him. When he reached the island he began to haul himself laboriously out of the water but Iz came to the edge and pulled him up with his hand.

The stones were warm, and they lay down beside each other on their backs.

'It will be hot in Israel,' Iz said thoughtfully.

'Yes.'

'But I think it can be quite cold in the winter. Of course, I imagine the Negev Desert would be hot most of the year round. That goes right down to the Red Sea.'

'Yes, I know.'

'The food is healthy, too. A lot of tomatoes and those little cucumbers. And eggs. There are many chickens on *kibbutzim*. They grow fruit there too, peaches and things. Much better food than here.'

'That wouldn't be difficult,' Maurice laughed, thinking about what he had eaten with his uncle.

'I wonder how long it will take me to get there.'

Maurice thought that he had never felt sadder in his life. Of course, Iz was excited about his new life starting tomorrow, but what about him? His new life was starting tomorrow, too, but it was going to be just his old life in disguise, returning to squash him like a slab of concrete.

'The Mediterranean can be rough, I hear. It wouldn't make a good impression if I was seasick on the boat.'

Maurice laughed. Revolutionaries were human, too. Iz should not have to impress people, he thought. They would have to impress him.

'What will I do, Isaac?' Maurice asked. It came out more desperately than he wanted.

'It's a pleasant life here, but you will not want to stay after you've learnt everything you can. Perhaps you will go to university and study something important.'

'Boys at my school were going to do Ancient Greek at university,' he laughed. 'Imagine that!'

'Well, most people are not suitable for revolutionary purpose, are they?'

Maybe Iz did not think he was suitable for revolutionary purpose either, but then he added, 'People aren't all like us,' and Maurice wanted to embrace him.

Maurice got up and moved to the other side of the little island. He stared at the cliff on the other side of the lake. Iz came over to him and put his arm round Maurice's shoulders.

'You are upset, I think.'

'You'll have comrades out there. You have a common cause. I have nobody. I can't do it on my own.'

'People will follow you because you have passion. Don't be downcast. Come and swim. It will refresh you. We can race.'

Maurice smiled. It was like being back at one of Arthur's birthday parties.

'I'll come in a bit,' he said.

Iz walked over to the other edge and stretched his arms up to a perfect point. Of course he would dive beautifully as well, Maurice thought. Iz slowly leaned forward, bent his knees and launched himself into the air. He gave a great shriek of laughter and went into the water like a knife. Because he had dived in so cleanly, there was almost no splash. The little indentation in the water closed and it was calm and glassy again.

Maurice moved over to the edge of the island and waited for Iz. He would help him out of the water and try to be more cheerful. He could ask some more questions about Israel: perhaps something about how their parliament, the Knesset, worked and what he thought of David Ben-Gurion.

He waited for a few moments. What was odd was that Iz did not seem to be coming to the surface. He was such a good swimmer that maybe he was swimming under the water and would come up somewhere else to surprise him.

'Isaac?' he called.

He leaned over and peered into the water. It was clear, but he could not see very far down. 'Isaac?' he said again. He went to the other side of the island, but there were no ripples there either. He suddenly realised that something awful was happening. He ran back to where Iz had gone in and began shouting his name over and over again. He went a little way into the water, leaned down and began ruffling the water with his hand as if that would make it clearer.

He launched himself in and began paddling frantically. He took a deep breath and put his head under the water. He opened his eyes but then some water got up his nose and he began coughing and he had to raise his head again. Panic seemed to prevent him moving his legs in any kind of rhythm to keep himself afloat and he kept slipping under. Now he tried to turn his body upside down, putting his backside and legs up in the air and swimming downwards by pulling himself with his arms. He had done it a few times before in the swimming pool at school and he had managed to touch the bottom, but that was only in the shallow end.

He kept his eyes open and he saw something in the murkiness that terrified him. A couple of the huge slabs of stone that made up the island must have slipped into the water. He could see them further down, standing upright against each other like an inverted V. He came back to the surface to get some air. He was shivering now, the cold of the water seeping into him, and he was breathing jerkily. He dived again and tried to pull himself deeper. It was very indistinct, but he thought he could see Iz's body lying beside the base of the slabs. There was no way Maurice could get down that deep, even if he had been a better swimmer.

How long could you hold your breath for? Iz would be able to hold it for longer than most people, but he would not be holding his breath if he had hit his head. The water would be pouring into his lungs. Maybe he had broken his neck. Five or six minutes had passed since he went into the water. Maybe it was longer: Maurice had lost all sense of time.

He sat on the edge of the island. He had no idea what to do now. He was trembling but he did not know whether that was because of the cold water or because he was frightened. It would have been better if he had his clothes on. He felt exposed and vulnerable. He decided he must go back in one last time.

With all his strength, he turned over and pulled himself down in the water and this time he managed to go deeper than before. Now he could see Iz's body lying on the bottom, white against the dark mud, but it was still at least fifteen feet below him and he knew he could never get down there. And even if he could, there was no way he would be able to pull his body up to the surface and drag it on to the island. And anyway – what would happen then? He would sit next to Iz and feel his body turning cold. It was easier for Iz to lie at the bottom of the lake. It would be awful to be beside Iz and know that he could not bring him back to life.

He sat on the stones for a while. The sun was getting lower in the sky. Before too long it would be dark. He did not want to leave because that would acknowledge that there was nothing more to be done, that Iz was gone. But sometimes, he thought, painful things had to be acknowledged whatever the cost. There were historic inevitabilities. Sometimes things were meant to happen.

He took a deep breath and launched himself into the cold water. He began to swim away from the island and found himself moving more confidently: he seemed to have found a way of coordinating his arms and legs so he could swim more easily through the water. It would not take him long to reach the shore.

He put his clothes on, and then he picked up Iz's satchel. He opened it and looked inside. He felt awkward doing it, but he knew Iz would not have minded: they were brothers after all. He put his hand in and began to empty it. Iz had wanted to hang on to the things he had, but there were not many of them.

There was a book in German: *Früchte des Zorns* by John Steinbeck. Maurice looked at the title page and saw that it was a translation of *The Grapes of Wrath*. There was his passport and identity card, an apple, a pair of gold-rimmed glasses. Maurice put them on and everything went a little blurred. They were not very strong: maybe that was why he had never seen Iz wearing them. There was a tattered map of Palestine with a circle drawn round Haifa. A little piece of paper with 'Great Russell Street' written on it was scrunched up at the bottom. Finally, he took out a photograph. It was of a boy in a sailor suit, maybe about seven, playing a violin that was too big for him with an intense expression on his face. Maurice suddenly began to cry, but whether he was weeping for Iz's brother Abram who was learning the violin, or Iz, or himself, he was not sure. He sniffed, wiped his nose on his sleeve and dried his eyes. You have to try to cut sentimentality out of your life, he thought. It is the future not the past you must concentrate on.

As he was putting everything back into the satchel, he opened the passport. The photograph must have been taken a few years before. Iz looked younger. He was wearing his glasses and his face was slightly fuller than it was now. His hair was short. Maurice ran his fingers through his own hair: it was longer than Iz's, but he would be able to cut it. He was suddenly frightened, but he felt curiously elated as well: he knew what he was going to do.

Iz's clothes, his Lenin cap and his shoes, his dungarees and shirt, were lying crumpled and untidy on the ground. He took his clothes off and put Iz's on. He gathered up his own clothes and took them into the woods and put them by a fallen tree. On top of the little pile he put his socks, the school ones that had name-tapes sewn on them saying 'Maurice Gifford'.

He wondered what would happen. It might be weeks before anyone came to the quarry, but he supposed that the body would eventually be discovered. He wondered how long it would take to rise to the surface. Nobody would look for Iz. For his friends at the farm, he would be another of the people who simply vanished overnight, gone in search of their destiny. He pulled the satchel over his shoulder and put on Iz's Lenin cap and began to walk back through the woods.

Back at the farm he packed a small bag with a few clothes. Iz had not brought much when he left Germany and it would be the same for Maurice. All the things he had found in Iz's satchel were still in it. He did not want to lose them. He sat down in front of the mirror with a pair of kitchen scissors and began to cut his hair. He made it shorter, but it looked a bit messy. That didn't matter: who on this kind of mission would have time to go to a proper barber? All over Europe there would be displaced people with bad haircuts.

He took Iz's passport out of the satchel and looked at the picture. He put the wire-rimmed glasses on and then the cap. It was obvious the photograph had been taken a while ago, so they would make allowances., It was rather faded and blurry: they would be able to believe it was the same person. Anyway, with thousands of people crossing borders and moving from one country to another, one more anonymous person should be able to slip through.

His uncle would not discover that he was gone until he returned to the farmhouse a few hours later. By then, Maurice would have vanished. In the kitchen, he bent down and pulled the saucepan out from the back of the cupboard under the sink. He took the money out and began to count it. He was amazed how much was there. How typical of the bourgeoisie to hoard money. He took

£450 and left about £100 in there for his uncle. He did not want to be ungenerous. His parents would be horrified that, on top of everything else, he was a thief, but they could not think worse of him than they already did.

It was nearly five. The main road was only about a mile away and he walked there as quickly as he could. Because of petrol rationing there were not many cars and it was half an hour before a lorry slowed down and stopped.

The driver rolled down his window. 'Where are you heading?'

'London. Great Russell Street.'

The man laughed. 'I'm not a taxi driver,' he said. 'I can take you as far as Elephant and Castle. You'll have to take the Underground from there.'

'Thank you,' Maurice said. He went round to the other side of the lorry and pulled himself up into the cab. 'This is very kind of you.'

'You from around here?'

'I'm German,' he said.

'German? If I'd known that I probably wouldn't have picked you up.'

Maurice laughed. 'Don't worry. I'm not a German spy. I'm a Jewish refugee. I've lived here a long time. I'm a citizen. I have a British passport.'

He closed his eyes. The hum of the lorry was making him sleepy. When he got to London he would find somewhere cheap to stay for the night. Of course, with all the money he had, he could stay in a swanky hotel but those kind of luxuries were not appropriate now. He did not know what time he was meant to arrive at the Jewish Agency tomorrow, but he would get there as early as he could in the morning. They might give him extra marks for punctuality.

Rose

I do not remember many people coming to the house in Muswell Hill in those days. Iz did not want to see anyone; he did not even have much desire to talk to the people who already lived there. But of course there were random people who rang the doorbell: people selling dishcloths or charity collectors or kids who wanted to be sponsored. Once in a while Jehovah's Witnesses came to the door, but Iz had advised – a long time ago when he was still in the business of dispensing advice to us – that we should tell them firmly that the family were Swedenborgians and close the door. If you said you were Catholic or Jewish, it would give them the chance to engage you in a theological debate. Saying you were a Swedenborgian would confuse them. I had looked it up: Emanuel Swedenborg was an eighteenth-century mystic and theologian who still had a small but faithful following.

The person who rang the doorbell that day did not seem to be a Jehovah's Witness so I did not have to say that we were Swedenborgians. Standing in the doorway was a grey-haired woman who was wearing a pin-striped trouser suit and a lot of big gold bracelets on her wrists. Carla or

Lally would never have worn that kind of outfit. Carla did not wear jewellery and Lally only wore her wedding ring.

The woman seemed surprised to see me. She cleared her throat. 'Is this the home of Mr Herzl?'

'Well…' I said, playing for time. It was possible that she was someone who had come to make outrageous and unreasonable demands of Iz. I had never actually met such people, but Lally believed that they were lurking behind every lamp post waiting to pounce.

'I'm sorry to disturb you,' the woman said. 'Is this a convenient time? I could come back – I only live fifteen minutes away.'

'A convenient time for what?' I asked as politely as I could.

'To see Mr Herzl.'

'And you want to…?'

'I want to see Mr Herzl,' the woman said again, as if I had not understood her the first time. Then she put her hand out. 'I'm sorry, how rude of me, my name is Shirley Isaacs.' I was not really used to shaking hands, but I did my best.

'How good to meet you,' the woman said. 'And you would be?'

'Rose Herzl.'

'That's nice. I love the name Rose. Is it a family name?'

What business was it of hers? 'No. I'm named after a character in *The Grapes of Wrath*,' I said, hoping that would silence her.

It didn't. 'That's a wonderful book! Actually, I have some connection with it.'

Despite myself, I was interested. 'Really?'

'Yes, some years ago my ex-husband and his writing partner nearly did a musical based on it, but they couldn't get the rights. They write musicals.'

That was rather a feeble connection, I thought.

'I'm sorry, this isn't really a very good time. Iz – Mr Herzl – is not very well.'

'Are you his granddaughter?'

'I'm his daughter.'

'Really? Well, I could talk to you, I suppose. You see, I have some news. It's important. Maybe you'd be able to pass it on to Mr Herzl, although I'd much prefer to talk to him personally, of course.'

I did not know what to do. I did not like being second best, but there was a part of me that wanted to hear what the woman might have to say.

'Please, can I come in? I won't stay long.'

It was only eleven. Lally would not be down till lunchtime. God knows where Carla and Joan were.

'Well…'

'Thank you. I'm very grateful.'

Reluctantly, I stood back to let the woman come in. I led her into the sitting room and closed the door.

'What a lovely room. So bright!' She walked over to the French windows. 'And what a super garden. It's so nice to be able to go straight out into the fresh air, isn't it?'

This kind of conversation did not play to my strengths. I did not see the point of small talk, particularly when it was as small as this.

'You said you had some news?'

'Yes, I do.' The woman paused: she seemed to be gathering strength. 'You have a brother called Joseph, don't you? I realise that you probably don't know him very well.'

'I don't know him at all,' I said. 'He's my half-brother, not my brother.'

A sad look passed over the woman's face. 'Family is so important. Just because he's only your half-brother doesn't mean you couldn't have a relationship with him.'

'Yes, I realise that,' I said sharply. 'I'm just pointing out that it isn't accurate to call him my brother, that's all.'

'Well... your half-brother Joseph...'

'I know,' I said. 'I know that something happened to him. I saw it in the papers.'

The woman called Shirley looked rather crestfallen. She obviously wanted to be the bearer of the bad news herself.

'I hope you don't believe all those newspaper articles,' she said. 'They're not accurate at all.'

'About what happened to him?'

'Well, no, the things about his private life. Getting attacked, that's all true.'

'Why are you involved in it?'

The woman looked offended. 'Actually, I was the one who discovered him. I was the one who called 999. I probably saved his life.'

'Oh, I see. Well, thank you. Is he going to be all right?'

The woman turned away. 'I don't know. The doctors don't know. He's been part of my life for a very long time. We were at school together. He was my best friend. He is my best friend.'

I had never heard grown-ups talking about having best friends. Girls at school did it all the time although the best friends kept changing.

'Could I trouble you for some Kleenex?' the woman said, wiping her eyes with the back of her hand.

'Yes, of course.' I went to Huddie's room and got some – there were always a lot of tissues there to wipe his face.

'I'm sorry, I must look awful.'

'No, you don't.'

'Thank you.'

'But why did you come? Did you think we wouldn't know about it?'

The woman hesitated. 'You must know that there has been some estrangement between your father and Joseph?'

I nodded cautiously.

'For many, many years. To the best of my knowledge – and Joseph told me everything – they only ever met once, when Joseph was very young.'

Lally had told me that. 'I know that they met. Didn't Joseph do something awful? That's what I heard.'

'What?' the woman said, outraged. 'That's a lie!'

I did not say anything.

'I'm sorry,' the woman said. 'But really, I don't think that's the case. I'll tell you why I came, Rose: Mr Herzl is old – you say he's not well.'

'No, he isn't.'

'I want it to be right, to make it all right.' She took a deep breath. 'What I'm asking for is your father to visit him in hospital.'

'Oh,' I said.

'You're obviously a highly intelligent girl. You'll under-stand why I'm asking.'

I nodded.

'If I can't see your father now, do you think it would help if I wrote a letter?'

'Maybe it's better to leave it alone,' I said cautiously. 'Wouldn't they have seen each other if they wanted to?'

'Well, it was a very difficult situation.'

'But has Joseph ever tried to see my father?'

The woman looked down. 'Well, no,' she said. 'But people don't always know what they want.'

'My father does.' I didn't want to actually say that nobody had even told Iz about Joseph.

There was a silence, then the woman said, 'Could I have a glass of water, please?'

When I came back from the kitchen, the woman was looking at the bookcases.

'What a lot of books!' she said pleasantly.

'They're my school books.'

'Anatomy books, medical encyclopaedias. How interesting. My father was a doctor, actually.'

'I'm going to study medicine at university. I want to be a neurosurgeon.'

'My goodness! That's quite a lofty ambition. When did you decide that?'

'When I was seven.'

The woman looked impressed. 'Someone who knows her mind, that's wonderful. Perhaps you got that from your father.'

I could not tell if that was meant to be sarcastic.

'My daughter wanted to be a doctor, too, actually,' she said.

I knew that it was polite to ask people about their lives so I asked, 'So is she a doctor now?'

'Well, no, not really.'

I was confused by that. You were either a doctor or you weren't.

I half wanted the woman to leave, but this was a rare experience: nobody ever asked me questions about myself, except for Huddie. Everybody in the house either talked about themselves or talked about Iz. The conversation with this woman seemed like the kind of conversation normal people had.

'Is your mother a singer like your father?'

'She's dead, but she did sing. And write songs.'

'Oh, I'm so sorry. And do you have brothers and sisters?'

'Just a brother.'

'How nice. And what's his name? Is he named after someone in *The Grapes of Wrath*, too?' She laughed. 'Tom, like Tom Joad?'

'Huddie.'

'What an unusual name.'

'He was named after a black blues singer.'

'Oh – that's interesting. Where are you at school?'

'Greenlanes. Do you know it?'

The woman looked round, surprised. 'Yes, of course I do. Actually my daughter went there. Isn't that a co-incidence?'

'Well, not really,' I said. 'You said you lived quite close. Tons of people in Muswell Hill go there.'

'And she wanted to be a doctor. That's another coincidence.'

'Well, that's not unusual. It isn't as if we both wanted to be taxidermists.'

'And you're the sister of my best friend.' The woman seemed curiously excited by all these connections.

'They're facts not coincidences. What's your daughter's name?'

'Sally. Sally Isaacs.'

'When did she leave Greenlanes?'

'Oh... when she was sixteen. She loved it there. She had a lot of friends. I hope she's not forgotten there.'

'Maybe some of the teachers remember her. I could ask when term starts, if you want.'

Maybe I was handling the conversation in the wrong way because the woman said rather firmly, 'Well... enough about Sally. Tell me more about you.'

'You know... I need to get back to work.'

A strange look of panic passed over the woman's face, as if her leaving was the worst thing that could possibly happen. She looked at me with an odd look on her face.

'May I ask you something?'

I shrugged. 'If you want.'

'What is your star sign?'

What an odd question, I thought. 'I don't believe in star signs. It's illogical to think that there are only twelve types of people in the world. Why would my destiny be the same as someone starving in Africa just because they were born during the same arbitrary time period as me?'

'Actually, there are many more variations than twelve. A lot of it depends on what specific time of day you were born and what day in the star sign your birthday is.' She gave a tinkly little laugh. 'I suppose you're going to tell me you don't believe in birthdays either?'

'Well, I don't think they matter much.'

'So when is yours?'

I had stopped enjoying talking about myself. I had begun to find the woman rather unsettling.

'Would you like me to guess?' she said.

'Why?'

'Let me just have a go. You've got nothing to lose.'

'Is this a magician thing, like a card trick?' I asked.

The woman put her hands out, palms up. 'No cards. Nothing about my person.'

'The odds are very high, you know.'

The woman gave a little laugh 'The odds! I wouldn't take you for a gambler.'

'I'm not. Gambling is about chance. I just know a lot about statistics. Do you want to know the odds on being on a plane taken over by terrorists?'

'I'd rather know the odds on the bus from the Broadway into town coming soon.'

'You can't do odds for "soon". All you could work out is the average waiting time, which wouldn't help you.

The probability of the bus taking the average time to come is no higher than it taking one minute or twenty minutes to come.'

'Right,' the woman said.

'The odds on you guessing my birthday are one in three hundred and sixty-five. Well, I suppose it would be one in three hundred and sixty-six if my birthday was February the twenty-ninth, which it isn't.'

The woman smiled. 'Maybe I should make it a bit easier on myself. Shall I try the month first?'

Rose shrugged. 'If you want: that's one in twelve.'

The woman closed her eyes. 'Okay... the month... the month... it's... let me think: it's...' She suddenly opened her eyes and looked straight at me. 'May.'

I nodded. 'That was lucky.'

'So – the date.' This time the woman did not spin it out. Without any hesitation she said, 'The twenty-third.'

I hated being surprised by things but I could not stop myself looking amazed. The woman was staring expectantly at me.

'Well?'

'Yes, it is.'

The woman gasped and put her hand to her mouth. 'And you were born in 1994, that's right isn't it? On the twenty-third of May.'

I stood up. 'I'd really like you to go.'

'There's something I need to tell you.'

'Please go.'

'No, I need to tell you something extraordinary...' Whatever she was going to say was interrupted by the door opening. Lally was standing there.

'What's happening? Rosie?'

I could not think what to say.

The woman stepped forward and put her hand out to Lally. 'I'm Shirley Isaacs and—'

I decided to confront things head on. 'She's a friend of Joseph Carter's and she wants Iz to visit him in hospital,' I said in a rush.

'*What*?' Lally said. 'If you don't mind me saying so, I really think that is the most astonishing request from a stranger.'

'I'm not really a stranger,' the woman said. 'Joseph is a dear friend of mine.'

'I meant a stranger to us.'

'Are you Mr Herzl's wife?'

'I'm not sure that's relevant,' Lally said.

'Joseph might die,' the woman cried. 'Don't you think his father should see him?'

'He behaved very badly to Iz, I'm afraid. It's hard to think of him as his son.'

'But Joseph is his son!'

'You have to earn the right to be the son of a man like Isaac Herzl.'

'No! That's not true,' the woman shouted in a shaky voice. 'It's the other way round: you have to earn the right to be the parent of a child. I had to. Isaac Herzl has to. He's no different from anyone else!'

Of all the things the woman might have said to Lally that was the worst. 'If you do not go now,' she said, 'I will have to call the police and say we have an intruder in the house. I'm sorry.'

The woman looked at me with a pleading look on her face. I was trembling. I had never heard adults raising their voices at each other before. Nobody ever raised their voice in our house. There was a moment of stillness and then the woman almost ran from the room.

Lally looked shaken, but resolute. They were all so sure of themselves in this house. They always thought they were doing the right thing.

'Lally – this is not your house. You don't own Iz,' I said angrily. 'That woman may be mad but it wasn't nice what you said to her.' That was not the kind of thing children said to adults, but it was true. Anyway, I was sick of being a child.

I turned from Lally and went out of the room, out of the front door and into the street. I could see the woman up the road and I ran after her.

'I'm sorry,' I said breathlessly when I caught up with her. 'I know you were only doing what you think is right.'

The woman turned round and put her hand on my arm. 'I need to see you again. I need to talk to you about something.'

I shook my head. 'No! I don't want to.'

'Rose…'

I turned from her and began walking away fast.

'Will you do one thing for me?' the woman shouted.

I did not stop.

'Will you and your brother at least talk to your father about Joseph?'

I stopped and turned round. 'My brother's dead,' I said.

I cared what Huddie thought and Huddie cared what I thought. We didn't much care what anyone else thought. We would have discussed the woman's visit and we would have decided that Iz should be told about Joseph. Lally and Carla would be cross with me, but Iz himself had always taught us that you should do what you believe is the right thing.

I felt nervous because I hardly talked to Iz these days, and we had certainly never talked about anything personal.

Of course, I knew from girls at school that at sixteen you were meant to avoid talking to your parents as often as you could – and more than that, you were never meant to tell them what you were up to because they would probably stop you doing it. Iz was not like that, and anyway, I wasn't really up to anything that he might disapprove of. It sometimes made me feel like a failure at being a teenager, but I couldn't change who I was. Anyway, I had seen some pornography that afternoon in Huddie's room: that was pleasantly transgressive enough to boast about at school if I had wanted to.

The next day, I waited till Lally had gone out to the shops to get her and Iz's lunch and I went up to his room. It was quiet and dark – the curtains had been closed against the midday sun. It smelt musty: an old-persony kind of smell.

'Iz?' I said.

In the corner of the room he stirred. Maybe he had been sleeping. 'Oh,' he said. 'It's Rose,' but not in a disappointed way, simply as if he was announcing my presence to someone else. Once his voice had been so clear and strong, but now it was throaty and muffled as if had been eroded like a pebble on the beach.

'How are you?' I asked him.

'Old.' He gave a mournful little laugh.

I couldn't think what to say next. There was a book on his lap, so I said, 'What are you reading?'

'Engels. *The Peasant War in Germany.*'

'I haven't read that. Shall I put it on my list?'

He smiled. 'It's heavy-going. I tried to read it when I was young. I thought it might be easier now.'

'Is it?'

'No.'

There was silence. Iz had always been hard to talk to.

Then he said suddenly. 'I forget things now. Did I tell you that I thought what you said about Huddie at the funeral was rather extraordinary?'

I liked him saying that. Although he used to be stridently opinionated about songs and causes and people's commitment to them, he never expressed approval and disapproval about us. He would probably have said that he wanted Huddie and me to decide things for ourselves, but I wondered whether it was simply that we were too far down the pecking order – there were more important things to express approval and disapproval about.

'Yes,' he said. 'It had gravitas. It was like a eulogy for a fallen warrior who died for his beliefs.'

The unexpected gift of approval he had given me had somehow got diverted on to the wrong path.

'I don't think dying of muscular dystrophy is dying for your beliefs exactly. He wasn't making a point by dying.'

I had forgotten how frustrating a conversation with Iz could be. People were always symbols to him. He was passionate about people, but I don't think he understood anything about them at all.

I had planned to tell Iz about Joseph as gently as I could, but in the end I just came out with it.

'Joseph Carter is very badly injured. He's in hospital.'

'Oh, Joseph.' He nodded his head slowly. 'Will he die?' he said in a voice that seemed only half-interested.

I should have known you could never predict Iz's reaction to anything. 'No. I don't think so.'

'Well, that's good. I can't imagine what kind of eulogy anybody would give him.'

'He got attacked.'

'Who by?'

'I think it was a friend, someone he knew, anyway.'

'You always have to be on your guard for that.'

'For what?'

'Friends betraying you.'

'It was a physical attack, Iz.'

'There are many different kinds of attack. A physical one is not always the most painful.'

'You could visit him in hospital if you wanted.'

'Oh no, I don't think so. He wouldn't want to see me.'

'Don't you feel any kind of bond with him?'

'Bonds aren't created by blood. I never had much of a bond with my parents. They disapproved of me so much that they sent me away.'

'But you were eight or nine! How could they disapprove of you? Sending you away saved your life, didn't it? They put you on that *Kindertransport* boat to England to get you away from the Nazis.'

He looked confused for a moment. 'Well, yes. And in fact, being sent away was the best thing that could have happened to me, so I suppose I am grateful to my parents. It helped me become the person I wanted to be. It wouldn't have happened if I'd stayed behind.'

I always found being a child rather a humiliating experience, but I suddenly reverted to the neediness of one. 'But you feel a bond with us, don't you?' I said pathetically. 'With Huddie and me.'

'The only kind of bond worth having is an ideological one. I hope we'll always have that. I think Huddie would have become a remarkable person, Rose. And you will, too.'

'Maybe that's because we're your children.'

He wouldn't even give me that much. 'I don't think so. You have to invent yourself. It's not about who your parents are. Sometimes a friend with a similar philosophy can help. It's good to have one person you can share everything with.'

'That was Huddie,' I said.

'You don't have many friends, do you?'

'No.'

'I didn't either. You question things like me. People don't like that. They just give you indifference when all you're looking for is truth.'

I was pleased: from Iz that was a kind of compliment.

'Did you have a friend?' I asked. 'Someone who helped you?'

'It was all so long ago,' Iz said dismissively. When he didn't want to talk about something he always said it was too long ago.

'But you can't have forgotten.'

There was a silence. I think he was deciding whether to go on with the conversation or not. Finally he spoke.

'No, I haven't forgotten. He was someone I met just before I went to Israel.'

'What happened to him?'

'We lost touch.'

'It must be sad not to have ever seen him again if he was such a friend.'

'Yes,' he said, 'but you have to cut sentiment out of your life.'

'But you must think about him sometimes.'

He nodded. 'Yes, I do.'

I smiled. 'So you do look into the past.'

He thought for a moment and shrugged. 'I try not to. It might make you want to go back there. You have to keep moving forward. I always did. I didn't know what would happen if I stopped. There was so much to do. I had concerts to give. There were countries to go to.'

He lifted his arm and pointed at the big table where Lally's scrapbooks and piles of old newspapers were. 'Look at that. Those are all the concerts and countries stuck in a book. I feel like a moth with a pin through it.'

'Isn't it nice to have a record of your achievements?'

'Do any of them matter? I only do it to give Lally something to do. She's led a sad life.'

'Because of you?'

'I don't know why you want to talk about these things. I'm tired.'

'Lally told me that you had a baby with her that died.' This was like going into a room that had always been locked. This was dangerous territory.

'She shouldn't have told you,' he said sharply.

'I just want to know the truth about things.'

'Don't confuse facts with the truth.' he said. 'They're not the same thing. You have to go now, Rose. I'm tired.'

I couldn't stop now. 'The day Huddie died, when you were in his room – what were you thinking?'

Iz did not answer for a moment, then he said, 'I was thinking about his name.'

'I don't understand.'

'I should never have called him Huddie.'

'Why not?'

'I loved Huddie Ledbetter. He was the greatest blues singer there's ever been. I remembered that I had thought of calling Lally's baby Huddie if it was a boy.'

'So that's what you called our Huddie. I think that's nice.'

'Huddie Ledbetter died of motor neurone disease, then Lally lost the baby, then Huddie died. There are historic inevitabilities.'

I was suddenly angry. 'There's no logic to that. It's ridiculous. A name can't be jinxed! Huddie isn't jinxed!

Is everyone called Huddie going to die of some strange disease?'

'Who else would call a child Huddie?' he said quietly.

'You brought us up to believe in certainties not superstition! You wouldn't tell me not to walk under ladders. If something awful happened to me afterwards, it wouldn't be an historic inevitability. With Huddie, it was just a genetic malfunction.'

'But that is an historic inevitability.'

'No! It's just chance.'

'I don't think there is chance. Everything is meant to be. It wouldn't mean anything if it was all random. There are links that cause things to happen. A chain of events make revolution happen. A chain of events make people become the people they're meant to be.'

'What about free will? What if you didn't want to be the person you became?'

He turned away. 'It's too late by then. You can never go back.'

Then Lally was in the doorway. 'What's going on?'

'We're looking into the past, Lally,' I said. 'I know that's forbidden.' I got up and pushed past her.

What Iz and I had had was not a conversation that would be picked up where we left off. I knew I would never talk to him like that again.

Shirley

Shirley was in bed. She had been in bed since yesterday when she got back from Iz Herzl's house. She had not even taken her make-up off. This was the first day that she had not visited Joseph and it made her feel guilty and ungrateful because Joseph had helped put her on the trail that she had followed. She thought it was a combination of his and Sally's energies that caused it to happen, like a ball being tossed back and forth between them.

In Manchester, Sally had led her to Joseph. Shirley had told Rose that she had saved his life, but that was not true. It was Sally who had ensured she got to Joseph's room before it was too late. All she had done was dial 999.

If Joseph had died, she would not have gone to Isaac Herzl's house to suggest he went to the funeral. What would have been the point? But because Sally had made sure that Joseph did not die, it had given her the reason to go to the house. The idea had not even occurred to her until yesterday at the hospital. It was like a leaf that had landed on her shoulder, gently blown in her direction by Joseph and Sally. Without them, it might have been blown by some other gust of wind and landed in the gutter. And then she would not have found Rose.

Sally and Rose looked quite different from each other. That did not faze Shirley at all: it was not a lookalike competition. Sally had been small and dark-haired. Rose was tall and had mousy-blond hair. Until she got ill, Sally spent a lot of time on clothes and make-up. Rose certainly didn't, with her sloppy jeans and baggy sweatshirt and chopped hair. In fact, she could do with a makeover, Shirley thought: maybe sometime she could treat her to a day at the Sanctuary. But the best difference between Rose and Sally was that she was not particularly thin – you could even say that she was almost on the verge of chubby.

Shirley was both excited at having found Rose and terrified about losing her, like some cruel fairy tale in which you found the gold, but then an evil wizard made it vanish. Shirley thought that she normally made a good impression on people, but she knew that was not the case yesterday with Rose: she must have seemed like a madwoman to her. It was fair enough to knock on the door and suggest politely that a father should take some responsibility for his son. Anyone might do that. But all that talk about horoscopes and birthdays, and then guessing the day right – what could Rose have thought about that, with her obsession with statistics? If she had been gambling in a casino with those odds, Shirley could have bought a mansion.

What she could not tell Rose was that, unlike gambling, her guess had not just been lucky. It was not exactly that she had been certain, but after finding out about Greenlanes and then her ambition to be a doctor, a path through the woods had suddenly opened up and Shirley followed it. Anyway, she had had nothing to lose. If Rose's birthday had been some other day, Shirley would have just smiled and politely taken her leave and Rose would have just thought that she was a strange woman who liked playing silly games. And she would have left the house before that awful woman arrived.

Shirley had known immediately that it was a strange household. Her antennae were finely tuned to that kind of thing. When Sally was alive, theirs had been such a happy house. She could not imagine what went on in the Herzl household. No wonder Rose seemed so odd. That woman looked like a little old lady, but she had crazy eyes. And Iz Herzl? Was he locked in the attic like Mrs Rochester in *Jane Eyre*, not allowed to see people and singing his Hebrew songs to himself? Rose seemed like a lonely child, her head always in one of those medical textbooks. Her brother was probably her only friend and now he was dead. If only she got the chance, Shirley knew she could fill that void.

She and Rose were obviously so similar: Shirley talking about Sally without mentioning that she was dead, Rose doing the same thing about her brother until the very end when she had told Shirley in the street. How old was he when he died? What did teenagers die of apart from anorexia? Shirley knew that there were fewer of them, but boys could be anorexic, too. It was unlikely, though, and Shirley did not need another link between Rose and Sally: she had enough already. Maybe the boy had been on drugs or had got meningitis. Maybe he was hit by a car as he was running away from that awful house.

But at least she had found Rose, a girl born on the day Sally had died. She was very lucky except that it had all gone wrong. She thought about what she should do now. The first thing was to make the bed and have a bath, do her hair and put her make-up on. She might see if her hairdresser could fit her in later. Whatever was going to happen next, she wanted to look her best.

Later, she was sitting in the kitchen. She had opened another bottle of the wine she had bought for David's visit and had made herself a meal. After she had finished, she got her headed notepaper out: she was going to write Rose a letter. That was really all she could do – she could hardly go round to the house again. That woman would probably get a restraining order against her.

Rose was obviously an unusual and clever girl: she would not respond to something conventional – 'I was so sorry to hear about your brother's death. My thoughts are with you' or a flowery condolence card with a message inside saying 'With Deepest Sympathy'. She had to somehow get through Rose's shell. She thought the best way was to be as revealing as she could about herself, to hold nothing back, and then maybe Rose would do the same. She began to write:

Dear Rose,

Firstly, I want to apologise for my behaviour when I came round to your house yesterday. I must have seemed very strange to you and I would like to reassure you that I am actually a very normal person who lives in a nice detached house not far from you in Highgate with Virginia creeper all over the front and a little driveway with a garage at the end of it, not in an attic with cats.

You will have realised how upset I was about your half-brother being in hospital. I visit him every day. It was with the best intentions that I came to your house. I simply thought – and still do – that your father and Joseph should be reunited and bring the years of pain to an end for both of them.

But there was more to my strange behaviour, and
while none of it is an excuse, I feel I should explain it
to you. Firstly, my husband recently left me after thirty-
eight years of what I thought to be a happy marriage.
I will get over that in time, of course, but I will not
pretend it has not been painful. The other thing I should
have told you yesterday is that my daughter Sally is dead.
I sometimes find that difficult to talk about. She died
sixteen years ago. She had anorexia – a terrible, terrible
curse. With the funny coincidence of you both being at
Greenlanes and wanting to be doctors, you reminded me
of her a little bit. I don't really know any girls of your age
so I enjoyed talking to you.

And you must forgive my silliness over your birthday. I know you think star signs are very trivial but I'm
rather intrigued by them, I'm afraid. Sometimes I read
my horoscope and am amused to be told that I will meet
a tall dark stranger or that my finances will improve
because Mars is in the ascendant! Because of my interest
in that kind of thing, trying to guess people's birthdays is
a bit of a party trick of mine. Of course, I'm almost never
right, so you can imagine my surprise when, by some
amazing fluke, my guess was correct! I have always been
a lucky person, although not recently. As you pointed out,
the odds are completely against it but then people win the
lottery, don't they? You are a very clever young woman
and I expect you know the odds for that, too!

I am leaving the most difficult part of this letter to the
end. I was shocked when you told me that your brother
had died and while I do not want to indulge in any
superficial condolences, I just wanted to say that I know
from my own experience that the death of a young person
brings with it grief that is without bounds. But despite

*everything, your brother will never leave you, as my
daughter has never left me.*

    *Nobody in your family owes me anything, but I think
that they owe something to Joseph. If your father changes
his mind about visiting, please tell him that his son is at
the Princess Grace Hospital in St John's Wood.*

    Or perhaps you would like to come?

    I send you every good wish.

Yours very sincerely
Shirley Isaacs

Shirley had to have several goes at it before she got the
letter as she wanted it. She had told the truth as best she
could but obviously there were some things she could
not say. Shirley knew that the one thing that would scare
Rose off would be to tell her what she knew about her
and Sally. She could not tell Rose that she had been born
the day Sally died, and she needed to add some detail to
pretend that she was interested in everybody's birthdays
and not just Rose's. Actually, she had no interest in star
signs and certainly never read her horoscope. And guessing birthdays was her party trick? Well, that was the best
she could come up with, ridiculous though it was.

    Even though the last post had gone, she walked down
the road to the postbox and put the letter in. She did not
want to change her mind about sending it. She was not
going to falter now.

Rose

There were two reasons I finally went to the hospital myself to see Joseph: one was plain curiosity; the other was Huddie. He would not have let me get away with not going.

I had a strange feeling walking down the corridor. I was nervous about seeing Joseph because I did not know what I was meant to feel about meeting a new brother. I turned a corner, and I almost jumped. Shirley was there, sitting on a chair. She stood up, with a great smile on her face.

She grasped my hand. 'Oh, Rose, I'm so glad you've come. How have you been?' she said.

'I've been fine, thank you.'

'Would you like a cup of tea? We could talk for a while before you go in to see Joseph.'

'Well, he's the reason I've come, so maybe I should just go in now.'

Shirley put her hand on my arm as if to stop me. 'I'm so sorry about your brother,' she blurted out. 'Can I ask when he died?'

'A couple of weeks ago.'

Shirley gasped. 'It must be so raw. You must have wept and wept.'

'No, not really.'

'Oh Rose – don't hold it all in.'

'I don't think crying means you care more. Anyway, I don't cry. Huddie cried a lot when he was small, but I never did.'

'Had he been ill for a long time?'

'Well… for ever, really,' I said. 'He had Duchenne.'

Shirley obviously didn't want to ask what that was, so I told her. 'It's a form of muscular dystrophy. It always kills you.'

'How awful!'

'Only in comparison with other people's lives. And there's no point comparing anyone else to Huddie.'

'I hope he had a wonderful send-off. I think that's really important.'

'Where would we be sending him off to?'

'I just meant—'

'If you meant was the funeral good, yes, I think it was. It didn't take long.'

'I hope there was some music. With your family… did your father sing?'

'He doesn't sing any more. I'll go in now.'

'Take as long as you like. Then we can have a chat.'

I knew Joseph might be unconscious, but I knocked on the door anyway. I didn't know the etiquette for that kind of thing. The room was quite dark. I stood by the bed for a while and then I pulled up a chair and sat by the bed. There was an IV drip stand on the other side, like a coat stand.

I had no idea what to do. Finally, I said, 'Hello, I'm Rose. Rose Herzl. We have the same father: Isaac Herzl.' I paused because I was leaving a moment for him to say something, but all he did was move a little and his eyes opened. Then I went on: 'I know you haven't seen him for a long time and I've come to see you instead because… well, he's old and he isn't great on his feet.' I thought it was okay to tell an ill person a small white lie. 'I'm sixteen and I had a brother – well, he was your brother, too – called Huddie. He was fifteen and he died a few weeks ago, but he might have to come to see you as well except he was in a wheelchair. He died at home, not in hospital,' and then I added hurriedly, 'not that being in a hospital means you're going to die, of course. I'm planning to be a doctor. I'm going to study medicine at university.'

I did not know what else to tell him, or whether there was any point in telling him anything at all, but I would have felt bad if I had just sat there in silence. I did not want him to think that I was just there because you were expected to visit family in hospital. I waited for another five minutes by his bed, and then I got up.

Well,' I said, 'Goodbye.' Then, feeling foolish, I added, 'It was very nice to meet you and maybe we can do it again sometime.'

As I reached the door handle, I heard him say something. It was muffled, but I could tell what it was: he had said, 'Rose.'

I turned in surprise. 'Yes, I'm Rose.' I went back to his bed, but his eyes were closed. I touched his hand and said, 'Joseph?' but he did not speak. Maybe he had been sleep-talking.

Shirley was hovering outside. I wouldn't have been surprised if she had been listening at the keyhole.

'How was it?' she asked. 'What did you think? About him, I mean.'

'I'd like to have seen if he looked like me or my brother, but it was hard to tell because of the swelling and bruising.

Huddie and I didn't really look alike but siblings often don't. Everybody has two versions of their genes and they can be different. Which version a child gets from their parents is totally random. I'm going to study medicine, but I'm interested in genetics as well.'

'Right,' Shirley said, nodding her head.

'He said my name.'

Shirley gasped. 'That's amazing! He hasn't really been able to say anything up to now. He must have responded to you. He doesn't really know any children. He knew Sally. He loved her. There must be some special connection—'

I picked up my rucksack and put it over my shoulder. 'I have to go now.'

'Please stay.'

'I can't.'

'Why?'

I had hoped to escape without having this conversation, but maybe it was inevitable. 'Because I know what you think and I don't want you to go on thinking it,' I said.

'What I think?'

'About me and your daughter.'

'I don't think anything, Rose. It's just nice talking to a girl Sally's age.'

'I looked up the old pupils at Greenlanes. She died on the day I was born. You think that means we're linked in some way, but it doesn't.'

'But isn't it an amazing coincidence!' she said desperately.

'No! A coincidence is identical twins from Kazakhstan who are separated at birth and meet in Oxford Street. Do you know how many people are born every day? The number of people in the world who'd be born on the same day as your daughter died?'

'No,' Shirley said reluctantly.

I reached into my rucksack and rummaged around. I was pretty sure my calculator was in there.

'I think there are about 7 billion people in the world.' I began tapping numbers in. 'Fifty per cent of them will be women so that makes 3.5 billion. Say fifty per cent of the women are of child-bearing age: that makes 1.75 billion. Let's say women have their babies between the ages of fifteen and forty-five and they have an average of two children over that thirty-year period. That's one in fifteen. Divide 1.75 billion by fifteen and that's 116,666,666 babies a year. Divide that by 365 and you have 319,634. That's the amount of babies born in the world every day.'

There was a silence. Finally, Shirley said, 'That was impressive, Rose.'

'I like solving that kind of problem.'

Shirley nodded. 'And what about Muswell Hill?'

'What about it?'

'How many people do you think live in Muswell Hill?'

I shrugged my shoulders. 'I don't know… 25,000? 30,000?'

Shirley gently took the calculator out of my hand.

'I'm quite at good at these things,' she laughed. 'I did all the accounts for the… club I used to belong to.' She began tapping. 'Okay – let's call it 25,000 people. Half of them are women so that's 12,500. I think you said half would be of child-bearing age so that's 6,250. You divided by fifteen, so that's… 416 born every year. Divide that by 365 and it's… 1.14. Shall we round that down to one? Isn't that what people do?' She looked at me. 'So there was one person in Muswell Hill born on the day that Sally died. Of course, it could be just another coincidence.'

I couldn't bear this. I couldn't bear the lack of logic. 'What difference does it make if it's Muswell Hill?' I almost shouted. 'It's got nothing to do with distance. If you really believe that your daughter has a soul or something that gets released when she dies, it wouldn't go into somebody just because they're up the road. It doesn't go by bus. It doesn't get tired if it has to travel too far! It can probably go at the speed of light. It could get to China as quickly as it could from one end of Muswell Hill to the other.' I put my head in my hands. 'This is so ridiculous. It isn't me you want, it's somebody else.'

'Don't you think it's possible?'

'No, of course I don't! There aren't spirits! You're dead or alive. It's like a light switch – you're on or you're off.'

'There are things in the world that can't be explained, Rose.'

'No there aren't! Unexplained things are just things that haven't been explained *yet*. They'll get explained when more research has been done, when we've got the technology or whatever.'

'Oh, Rose, you must have faith in something.'

'I'm a Swedenborgian!' I shouted. I grabbed the calculator back from Shirley and threw it into my rucksack. 'I've got to go. You're dragging me into some world that doesn't exist. People need something concrete to rely on, like a compass or the position of the stars or prime numbers. Without them you're lost. You're just floundering around in the dark, trying to force things into being the way you'd like them to be. If there were spirits, Huddie would be with me now.'

'I think he is,' Shirley said quietly. 'Only you won't let yourself see him.'

I looked at her, then turned and ran up the corridor and pushed through the door at the end, making it bang hard against the wall.

Joseph

When he began to feel pain, Joseph knew he was coming back from wherever he had been. Dreams didn't hurt but real life was all about pain. His face ached, if he moved his stitches hurt, his arm in plaster itched. The doctor said that was all good: his body was healing, the nerves were reconnecting. That might be a good thing – he suspected that his nerves had probably been disconnected for most of his life.

Later, Shirley told him what had happened in a tone of awe. She asked him if he remembered the girl being in his room – his sister Rose.

'Yes, I remember someone being there.'

'You said her name. You said "Rose"! It was the first time you really spoke. Maybe she willed you to do it. She's a very extraordinary person.'

'Oh, Shirley – what are you talking about? It wasn't some kind of spiritual experience. It was just me getting better. Why did she come to the hospital?'

Shirley seemed to have to think about that for a moment. 'Well, I just thought I'd send a letter to your… well, the Herzl house in general, telling them that you were in hospital.'

'I wish you hadn't done that, Shirley,' Joseph said. 'What? You thought that the great man would come and visit me?'

'Well, I didn't know. Anyway, Rose came, so that's good.'

'Why do you think she's so extraordinary?'

'Actually, I think she's rather like Sally. Well, maybe it *was* just a coincidence that it was the day she saw you that you spoke for the first time. Anyway, whatever happened, she came and you're getting better.'

And it was true: he was getting better. A nurse fed him soup, but when could move his jaw and bring his hand up to his face, he began to be able to feed himself. He knew he must look awful, but it did not matter much. Luckily there weren't any mirrors in the room, not that he could have got out of bed to check his appearance even if he had wanted to. Maybe his face would be scarred, but that might look distinguished at his age. It was only young people who were meant to look beautiful, like Gaz.

What happened that night had mostly come back, not every detail but enough. He got the gist of it, as if he had been reading an abridged book or listening to the highlights of an opera. He tried not to think about it, but he did think about Gaz. In a relationship not character-ised by much tenderness, it was the few tender moments they had had before that last night which were in the sharpest focus for Joseph, like the few days of a holiday when the sun came out. Gaz's skin, Gaz's brown eyes, Gaz's shyness: his voice sometimes so soft that Joseph had to lean towards him to hear. He tried not to remember the times when his voice was so loud and aggressive that Joseph had to lean away from him, the times when Gaz was anything but shy.

Why couldn't you just have the good part of a person? It seemed to be all or nothing. What was wrong with eating the best things on the plate and throwing the rest of it away? Joseph was sick of thinking in metaphors, but that was what he was good at. That was what songs in musicals were like: you're younger than springtime, all the hurts you wanted healed grown to flowers in the field, you're going to wash some man right out of your hair. He just wanted things to be unadorned by metaphor, just simple and direct. What a childish wish that was: a wish that ignored all the complicated realities of life – the unrealistic hopes, the unrealised ambitions, the untold secrets.

His had been untold because he had always suspected that the more secrets you revealed the more dignity you would lose. With Gaz, he had discovered that it was true. Both your secrets and your dignity are gone if you get involved with someone like Gaz. When I met him I entered a different world, Joseph thought, I went through some strange portal.

There was a time when there had been a kind of playfulness between them, certainly a kind of make-believe that could be left behind afterwards when you returned to real life. But before long it stopped being make-believe: it became the only reality he and Gaz had. And then the drugs – at first to make them feel good, and then to stop them feeling bad. Gaz took drugs all the time, but then his life was harder than Joseph's. He had to lie to his family but he was good at lying. Joseph didn't really care whether the things Gaz said were true or not. He knew one thing: what he felt for Gaz was not a lie, it was the only thing that was true. That was the problem.

He wondered what had happened later that night in Manchester. He and Gaz had talked to Michelle on the way up to the room and she knew his name; the hotel staff would have seen them go upstairs. Gaz would have panicked. He would not have stayed in Joseph's room for long. He would have been a dishevelled boy acting suspiciously, running out of the hotel with his hoodie up. His fingerprints would be all over the room. There was nobody else the police could be looking for and they would find him – Gaz was not good at flying under the radar.

The curious thing was that Joseph did not feel anger towards Gaz. In fact, he felt sorry for him, sorry that he would probably go to jail. People might say Joseph had it coming, that it was a consequence of that kind of lifestyle, but he did not really have the kind of lifestyle everybody presumed him to have. No, what had happened was not about consequence: it was about something else. It was about what Joseph had been looking for. He wondered whether what had happened on that night was what he had wanted all along, some kind of final, painful comfort, some kind of release from the songs and the hotel rooms and the loneliness and the things he wondered about his father. He did not blame Gaz – how could you blame someone for knowing what you really wanted?

Shirley spent a lot of time complaining about the hospital and Joseph's doctor. Joseph rather liked him, but after all these years he was used to Shirley's likes and dislikes, her irrational opinions and her barely contained anger. She was determined to get him out of there as quickly as possible. She wanted him to recuperate at her house in Muswell Hill.

He was walking now, up and down the corridor with crutches in one of those hospital gowns that looked like a dress without a back. Soon he would be able to walk with just a stick. The bruises on his face and body were fading. He was not sure he really wanted to go to Shirley's but he would not be able to cope in his flat on his own for a while. She was excited about him moving in – she would have something to do now instead of being on her own thinking about Alan or Sally.

'Oh, Joseph – it'll be such fun, won't it? I can start cooking again. We'll watch lots of DVDs. I'll pamper you. Maybe when you're better we can go on a holiday. Somewhere sunny, somewhere that'll put some colour in your face.' Shirley paused, and then she said, 'You could stay in Sally's room. Nobody's slept there since she died. She loved you, she'd want you to be there.' She gave a tinkly little laugh. 'Maybe you'll feel her spirit.'

'Well, I won't stay for too long.'

'You'll stay as long as you have to, and that's that.'

They had talked cautiously about what had happened that night in Manchester.

'How did you find me?' he asked.

'I was so upset. I had just discovered what Alan had done…' Shirley paused, as if she was trying to remember what had happened then. '…and, well, I took a walk along the corridor to pull myself together and I passed your room and the door was open. And I found you.'

They were both aware that there was an unmentioned part of the story. It was only when Joseph seemed to be getting better that the subject was raised.

'Joseph: I wanted to ask you…'

'Yes?' he said.

'Well, you don't have to tell me, you know how I respect people's privacy. The boy: did you know him? I mean from before.'

'Yes, I did. I knew him from London.'

She nodded her head. 'Was it an argument? An argument that got out of hand?'

'Something like that.'

'But it was so violent!'

'Yes,' Joseph said. 'Do you know what's happened to him?'

'Only what I've read in the papers. He's been arrested. Apparently there was CCTV everywhere – in the corridor and the stairs and the lobby.' She laughed. 'The only thing in that bloody hotel that worked. I think he's on bail. There'll be a trial.'

He nodded.

'You know the police want to interview you? I asked the doctor to say you weren't well enough yet.'

'Well, I think I am well enough. They might as well do it sooner rather than later.'

When two detectives came a few days later, Shirley was with Joseph and she greeted them as if she was the hostess. She placed chairs round the bed and offered to get them a cup of tea. There was an awkward moment when it became clear that she was planning to stay. Politely, one of the detectives said that she would have to leave the room.

'I just thought I could help,' she said crisply.

'Help?'

'I was the one who found Joseph. I was the one that dialled 999.'

He looked down at his notes. 'Yes, we have a record of the interview you gave to our Manchester colleagues after you found Mr Carter.'

'Well then – you'll understand how involved I am.'

'We need to interview Mr Carter about the incident itself, not what happened after the incident. I presume that, if you had any more information about the incident, you would already have told us.'

'I am Mr Carter's carer. I don't want this to be too tiring for him.'

'If Mr Carter needs care, I'm sure he will be able to tell us himself. And then we will just come back another day to complete his interview.'

There was a short silence. Shirley stood up. 'I'll be just outside,' she said. 'If you need me.'

There was no preamble. One detective did all the talking.

'Do you know that a man has been arrested in connection with the alleged attack on you?'

'I had heard that, yes.'

'How long have you been in hospital for, Mr Carter?'

'About a month.'

'Your injuries must have been very serious.'

'I seem to be recovering pretty well.'

'Good,' the detective said. 'That's good.'

'Yes.'

'We need to ask you about the night of March the twenty-seventh.'

'Yes.'

'Did you know Gavriel O'Donnell before that date?'

'Yes, I did. Do the police always ask questions that they already know the answer to?' Joseph said. 'I'm a writer. I've written these kind of interrogation scenes myself.'

'This is not an interrogation scene, Mr Carter. It's an interview scene. You're not being accused of anything.'

'Shall I just answer the questions you're circling around? I know what you want to ask.'

'If you'd like.'

'He came up to Manchester to see me. He didn't force his way into my hotel room. I invited him there. We had an argument. We had a fight. It got out of hand. That's it. There's nothing else that's relevant really.'

'When Mr O'Donnell was arrested, he appeared to be unharmed. It sounds like rather a one-sided kind of fight.'

'I'm not going to press charges,' Joseph said suddenly.

The detective laughed grimly. 'If you don't mind me saying so, you must be a very forgiving person, Mr Carter. This is not a black-eye kind of situation where you can tell people you walked into a door. It doesn't matter whether you want to press charges or not. It's for the Crown Prosecution Service to decide what action is appropriate in the public interest. You will need to write down as much as you can remember for a statement. I'm afraid there will be a trial and you will be summoned to appear.'

Joseph closed his eyes. He did not want to think about a trial. He knew that it would be the last time he would ever see Gaz. He had read in reports of trials that sometimes the accused kept their eyes averted and could not look at the accuser. Since Joseph was not accusing Gaz of anything – it was the legal process that was doing that – he hoped that Gaz would look at him. He would like that to happen.

Back in Muswell Hill, as she said she would, Shirley pampered him. Joseph thought he would go mad. He felt like James Caan in *Misery*, which Alan and he had once considered turning into a musical. She hovered around him all day, bringing him breakfast in bed before he wanted to wake up, making him mid-morning coffee which he did not want to drink, preparing elaborate meals that he did not want to eat. In the afternoons he said that he had to take a nap, but even that was not much of an escape: within an hour she was bringing him a cup of tea and home-made biscuits, sitting on his bed chatting. It felt as if Shirley was the one coming back to life rather than him. He was grateful to her for her support and loyalty, but he did not really want to be there. The trouble was he did not want to go either. It's the Stockholm syndrome, he thought gloomily.

The only good thing was she tended to go to bed early. Sometimes, just to have someone else to talk to apart from her, he called Alan late at night. Alan was not allowed to come to the house; Shirley would not see him. He was in a terrible state. Joseph had been shocked when Shirley had told him, but underneath the shock he was a little hurt that Alan had not confided in him. However well you knew someone you never really saw what went on behind the flickering net curtains of their lives. While on the surface it seemed a terrible betrayal, he was not going to judge Alan. Joseph loved Shirley in his way but he could see that nearly forty years of being married to her might drive you over the brink into madness. He imagined that Alan's woman might be someone rather voluptuous with a bit of life in her, someone who might drink a little too much and get giggly, someone you could fall into like a soft cushion in a way that would be impossible with Shirley. But, of course, the problem was that Alan's bond with her was almost unbreakable. He wanted Shirley to allow him back, but that was not a service she would provide.

One night, after he had drunk too much whisky, Joseph made a different kind of call: he found himself dialling Gaz's number. He was sober enough to block his caller ID. He knew that Gaz would probably not answer the call if he saw Joseph's name come up. He had no idea what he would say.

Gaz's phone rang for a long time, then, just as Joseph was about to hang up, he answered. Joseph felt his stomach tighten. Gaz did not say anything. The only sound on the line was a faint rushing noise, as if Joseph was holding a conch shell to his ear.

Finally he said, 'Gaz?'

There was nothing. 'Gaz? It's me. It's Joseph.' His voice was trembling.

He waited and then at last Gaz spoke.

'I can't talk to you.'

'Please.'

'I'm not allowed to talk to anyone.'

'Who says?'

'The police. Anyone to do with the case. I can't talk to them.'

'Just for a moment.'

There was a silence.

'How are you, Gaz?'

'Like I'm going to be feeling great? I'll be sent to jail. That's what the solicitor guy says.'

'I didn't want to press charges. I've told them as little as possible, but I couldn't say you didn't… do it.'

'Thanks a lot.'

'There's no way I could get out of it.'

'They'll stitch me up. You'll stitch me up.'

'I won't. I'll try not to. We just have to keep it simple. Just say we had an argument and you lost your temper. The more detail you go into, the worse it will sound for you. You'll probably have to go to jail, but if we get our story straight it might not be for too long. I don't want that for you. I'm not going to say anything bad about you.'

'They'll ask me things.'

'They have to ask you things – it's a trial. Make sure they know it wasn't premeditated.'

'What?'

'You didn't plan it. It was a spur-of-the-moment thing. I think that makes it better. Well, less bad, anyway. You'll get a shorter sentence. You just have to stay calm, don't let them rattle you.'

Gaz grunted.

'Where are you?' Joseph said.

'I can't see you.'

'I'm not asking to see you. Are you with your parents?'

Gaz gave a grim laugh. 'Of course I'm not with my parents. They won't speak to me. They won't have me in the fucking house.'

'So where are you?'

'My brother's. He's been cool.'

'What are you doing with yourself?'

'What do you mean?'

'What are you doing all day?'

'I pray. I read the Bible.'

'Really?'

'Why shouldn't I?' Gaz said aggressively. 'I just took the wrong path, that's what my brother says. He told me that if you're punished in this world, God doesn't punish you again in the next world.'

'That's a good way of looking at it,' Joseph said as encouragingly as he could.

'You don't believe in religion, that's your problem,' Gaz said sulkily.

'I just want everything to be all right for you.'

'It can't be all right!' Gaz shouted.

'There are courses you can do in prison. You can get some qualifications.'

'Yeah. Right.'

'Are you okay for money? Do you want me to send you some?'

'You can't have my address.'

'Gaz – I don't want your address. I'm just trying to help you.'

'Nothing to spend it on. I don't go out.'

There was a pause. Joseph could not think of anything more to say.

'I didn't mean it all to happen,' Gaz said suddenly. 'It was just that…'

'I know,' Joseph said, 'I know.'

Then he could hear Gaz crying, and the line went dead.

Rose

Shirley had written a letter to me that came a few days after I had seen her at the hospital.

> *Dear Rose,*
>
> *I just wanted to let you know that your brother, Joseph, is much better. It actually began to happen the day you visited him. I am going to ask him to come and live at my house until he is fully recovered.*
>
> *Perhaps your father, even if he wishes to know nothing else about his son, might like to know that he is, at least, out of danger.*
>
> *I regret how we parted that day, but I want you to know that I will think about you and your brother Huddie as often as I think about my daughter, Sally. When you become a doctor, Rose, as you will, I know that you will have an extraordinary life and achieve extraordinary things.*
>
> *Shirley*

For some reason I had not thrown it away. In fact, I had taken it out several days later and read it again, not that there was much to be discovered in it from a second reading. I did not often get letters. Maybe it was partly because of the letter that I decided to go and see Joseph giving evidence in court. I was still doing things because I would have something to tell Huddie afterwards. It would be a long time before I stopped doing that.

I needed to leave early, before Lally arrived. I did not want her to ask where I was going. Carla and Joan would be too preoccupied to even know that I had left the house. I got there an hour before it was meant to start just to be on the safe side. There seemed to be quite a lot of people there already. I had never been to a trial so I was not sure what to do. I went inside and asked someone who looked official: he told me that there was a public gallery I could sit in.

When I got there and looked out over the courtroom, I was surprised that it looked so different from what I imagined it to be from reading books. I suppose I thought it might be like the courtroom in *Bleak House* – cobwebby and dim, with dark wood panelling and cadaverous old barristers. Instead, it was very modern – a light teak floor and bright fluorescent strips along the ceiling and new chairs. It was like a conference room waiting for the delegates to arrive.

Just before it started, there was a movement at the other end of the public gallery and I turned. Shirley Isaacs slipped in and sat down. I moved my body to the side and lowered my head. I did not want Shirley to see me. I did not want to talk to her and then get another regretful letter.

There was some dull stuff first, short bursts of witnesses just setting the scene: what time someone had seen Mr Carter and the defendant walking through the hotel lobby and getting into the lift, what time the police and the ambulance had been called, what state the hotel room had been in. The barristers kept saying, 'No further questions.' Everybody seemed rather bored. This obviously was not the main event.

I watched the boy called Gavriel O'Donnell. Although I had read in the papers he was twenty-two, he did not look it – he could have been someone I was at school with. He did not react to anything that was being said. In fact, he never raised his head up from the book he had on his lap, his finger running across the page and his lips moving as if he was a child learning to read. It could hardly be a novel that he was reading; maybe it was the Bible. He was probably trying to make a good impression.

There was a lull and then Joseph Carter was called. In the hospital, I had not been able to tell what Joseph looked like. Now I saw him clearly, and my heart jumped a beat. He was taller and thinner, but he looked exactly like Iz, but an Iz who had had a makeover – a dark suit and tie and neatly cut, thinning hair.

I presumed it was the defence barrister who began asking questions. 'Mr Carter,' he began.

'Yes,' Joseph said.

'Would you say that Mr O'Donnell was a friend of yours?'

'Yes. In a way.'

'And how long had he been a friend for?'

'About nine months.'

'So a new friend then?'

'Well…'

As Joseph did not seem to be completing the sentence the barrister went on. 'Do you have many friends who are twenty-two, young friends?'

'In my world, in the theatre, I meet a lot of people through work – young actors or singers or dancers.'

'I see. And was Mr O'Donnell a young actor or singer or dancer you met through work?'

There was a pause. 'No,' Joseph said. 'Not exactly.'

'You've had a very impressive career, Mr Carter.'

Joseph did not say anything.

'Broadway shows, a hit in the West End at the moment.'

'They haven't all been hits,' Joseph said.

'But it's a glamorous world, isn't it – First Nights, photographers, stars, autographs?'

'I'm afraid nobody asks the writer for an autograph. It's not so glamorous if you're inside that world.'

'I understand that, of course, but I wonder what it must appear like if you're not inside that world. It could seem very glamorous, couldn't it?'

The barrister waited.

'Perhaps,' Joseph finally said.

'Particularly for an impressionable and vulnerable young man from a very different world to yours, a devout world, a world of prayer.'

Joseph shrugged his shoulders. 'I don't know.'

'But you did know that Mr O'Donnell was a vulnerable young man.'

'It depends what you call vulnerable, I suppose.'

'Wouldn't you call a young man who made two suicide attempts and was sectioned in a psychiatric hospital vulnerable?'

Joseph looked amazed. 'I didn't know that.' He looked at the boy as if for corroboration, but he did not look up from his book.

'But you knew he had problems.'

'I knew that there were some problems with his family.'

'Could that have been because the lifestyle and the world you introduced him to were so different from his own strongly Christian background?'

'Actually, he wasn't really interested in my world at all. He had no interest in the theatre or seeing plays.'

'Mr O'Donnell has said that he was your guest on numerous occasions at some of the best restaurants in London. Expensive food, fine wines, that kind of thing.'

'Yes, sometimes he was.'

'Had he been to many of those kinds of restaurants before you met him?'

'No. I don't suppose so.'

'And on those occasions did you always pay the bill?'

'He had no money.'

'That's very generous of you.'

Joseph remained silent.

'He must have felt in your debt, that he owed you something.'

'I don't think he looked at it like that. I didn't look at it like that.'

'At these restaurants, Mr O'Donnell has said, you encouraged him to drink alcohol.'

'I didn't encourage him.'

'But you drank alcohol together?'

'We were eating; yes, we sometimes had wine.'

'You know that his faith does not allow alcohol?'

'It's not my faith. I'm not an expert on what you can do and can't do.'

'Would you say that Mr O'Donnell is a devout man?'

'No, I don't think he is particularly devout.'

'Did he observe the important events in the Christian calendar as his faith requires?'

'I don't think so.'

'Like fasting and abstinence during the period of Lent.'

'I don't know. I don't think so.'

'But he has said that you celebrated the end of Lent together in the traditional way.'

Joseph sighed. 'I'm not sure I would call it the traditional way exactly.'

'Would you say he was less devout after he met you?'

'I don't know.'

'How did you meet Mr O'Donnell?'

There was a silence. 'In a club,' Joseph finally said.

'Was this a club you frequented often?'

'No. I only went once.'

'And what was the purpose of going to the club?'

'To meet people, I suppose.'

'Men? Women? Was it a mixed establishment?'

'It was mostly men.'

'Was it a crowded marketplace?'

'It was not a marketplace. It was a club.'

'And did you meet many people there?'

'No.'

'But you did meet at least one person there. Mr O'Donnell.'

Joseph looked down. 'Yes.'

The atmosphere in the courtroom suddenly seemed charged. I could not believe what Joseph was being asked. Were you even allowed to ask those kind of questions? The barrister was like a magician: he proffered a deck of cards to Joseph over and over again, asking him to choose any one he wanted, but each time, in answering the question, Joseph picked the same card – the one that the barrister had predicted, the one that made everything he said sound terrible.

'Mr O'Donnell has said that he began to be confused about his sexuality after he met you. You say you are not an expert on his faith, but you presumably know that homosexuality is forbidden by the kind of strongly Christian sect he belongs to.'

'Yes, I suppose so. I don't know if he was confused or not.'

'Was it a meeting of equals, would you say?'

'I don't know what you mean.'

'You are a mature man, an experienced man. You're fifty-six years old, Mr Carter. Mr O'Donnell is twenty-two. He is impressionable. His world is the Christian world. He did not have experience of *your* world until he met you. Would you say that drugs played an important part in your relationship?'

'We took drugs sometimes, yes.'

'Provided and paid for by you. Like the alcohol.'

'Yes,' Joseph said quietly.

'Would you say that Mr O'Donnell's judgement was impaired by the drugs and alcohol you provided for him, that he became more malleable?'

'I don't know.'

'The night of the twenty-seventh of March: Mr O'Donnell has said that he hitch-hiked to Manchester to see a friend and that he ran into you outside the theatre where your play was on.'

'That's not true. He had specially come up to see the play.'

'Really? Even though, as you said earlier, he had no interest in the theatre or seeing plays? Mr O'Donnell has told the police that you coerced him into coming back to your hotel by telling him that you could provide drugs and alcohol for him.'

'That's not true.'

'But back at your hotel you did provide drugs and alcohol for him, didn't you?'

Joseph did not say anything.

'Is that correct?'

'Yes.'

'Mr O'Donnell has said that he tried to resist your advances at the hotel.'

'It wasn't like that,' Joseph said.

'What was it like, Mr Carter?'

Joseph seemed to be shrinking before my eyes. He put his head in his hands.

'You knew that Mr O'Donnell had been arrested and charged?'

Joseph nodded.

'And yet two weeks ago you telephoned Mr O'Donnell. Did you know that he was not allowed to discuss the case?'

'No, I didn't.'

'But didn't he tell you that on the telephone and yet you asked to continue the conversation?'

Joseph nodded.

'During that conversation did you use the phrase, "If we get our story straight…"?'

'It wasn't what it sounds like.'

'But you did use it?'

'Yes, I think so.'

'And he has testified that you offered him money during that conversation.'

'I was concerned for him.'

'I see.'

Joseph suddenly roused himself, and for the first time he raised his voice a little. 'I cared about him.'

'You cared about him? Really? I would say that you were simply exploiting him for your own sordid purposes,' the barrister said contemptuously.

Even if Joseph had wanted to answer the question, he was denied the opportunity. The barrister turned his back on Joseph and said, 'I have no further questions.'

Iz had brought us up to distrust lawyers. He had told me about them getting the innocent convicted and the guilty set free. He had told me about trials in which people were arrested because of their political beliefs and were manipulated by lawyers into sneaking on their friends to save themselves, about show trials in Russia where innocent people were put on trial purely to get rid of them.

The stories Iz told about his past were few and far between but I remembered one that had particularly struck me when I was a child, in the days when he still told us stories. It was about a trial that Iz had been involved in. I was only five or six. It might have been Iz's strange idea of a bedtime story: it sounded a bit like a fairy tale in which there was good and evil, and bad people doing horrible things to good people. The details and the background were very vague. It was not even clear exactly who was on trial nor did he really say what the charge was: at one point it seemed to be about someone not being allowed to have different beliefs from someone else but at another point it seemed to be about setting fire to a building. There was someone who manipulated the truth and there was someone else who lied to save their own skin and there was a guilty verdict. It was only at the end of the story that I realised that Iz was the one on trial: when I asked what had happened after the trial, he said, 'I was sent a long, long way away.'

I realised that what had happened in Iz's story was happening to Joseph now – there was a lawyer who was manipulating the truth and there was someone who was obviously lying. The difference was that Joseph was not the one on trial but he was going to be found guilty anyway.

What surprised me was that I found myself on Joseph's side from the start. He could have just been an accomplished liar, but I knew he was not. I believed in him, and I initially dismissed the thought that it could be just because he was my brother – there was no logic to that. Then I realised that I would have been on Huddie's side whatever terrible thing he had done. I would always have believed in him.

At the end, when the barrister had said he had no further questions, Joseph lowered his head. He had been reduced to nothing and I could not bear it. When the recess was called, I got out of the public gallery as fast as I could. As I went through the door, I heard my name being called: it was Shirley, of course. I kept going as fast as I could. I didn't want to see her, but mostly I never wanted to see a courtroom again. I did not think Iz was right about everything, but now I knew he had been right about this, right to be frightened of lawyers and trials.

Joseph

The day after the trial ended, the newspapers stopped being delivered to the house. When it was time for the news on television, there was a programme Shirley wanted to watch on the other channel.

Finally, Joseph said to her, 'Shirley, I am a grown-up. You don't have to protect me from what people are saying.'

'Oh, it'll blow over,' she said dismissively. 'People have short memories.'

'I don't have a short memory. Why should other people?'

'It'll only upset you, Joseph. Why put yourself through it? Don't think about it.'

'You can't just refuse to think about the things that are painful,' he said crossly.

'Oh Joseph – you've had a horrible time. You're not yourself.'

He gave a grim laugh. 'I am myself. That's the problem.'

What he said to Shirley about painful thoughts was not really true: of course you could refuse to think about them. He had spent most of his life doing that: not thinking about the theatres emptying after one of his and Alan's flops; not thinking about the frightening things he had wanted, the things he had found with Gaz; and his father: that was what he mostly tried not to think about.

How often did people think about their parents? For what percentage of the fifty minutes on their therapist's couch did they talk about them? But most people had something to say or think when they talked or thought about their parents: the day their father forgot to pick them up from school, say, or the painful divorce after their mother's affair or any of the other small or large betrayals parents inevitably inflicted on their children.

There was a place where most people stored these things, a big, untidy cupboard that needed cleaning from time to time. Joseph's cupboard was as spacious as anyone else's but there was nothing much to put in it. You needed a lot of painful memories about your parents to fill it up and he only really had one: the meeting of twenty minutes or so when he met his father for the first and last time more than forty years ago.

He supposed that people might change their interpretation of painful events as they got older, become more generous: the father did not pick the child up from school that day because he was suicidally depressed; the mother's affair happened because she was trapped in an abusive marriage. Your parents were sad, flawed people, but it was just possible that they had done the best they could. Joseph found it hard to come up with some late-flowering reinterpretation of the meeting with his father in the coffee bar in Soho. His father was be a sad, flawed person, but he had not done the best he could.

It was time to face things: he went up to the study on the top floor where he and Alan used to work, switched on the computer and googled 'Joseph Carter + Gavriel

O'Donnell'. There were more references than he would have thought, but then, of course, everybody likes a prurient story: 'I Gave My Attacker Drugs', 'Devout Christian Seduced by the High Life', 'Champagne Lifestyle of Left-wing Activist's Son'.

The unnamed colleagues and friends who had expressed shock at the 'brutal attack' on Joseph before the trial, who had lauded his 'extraordinary talent', who had said that he was 'one of the best-loved people in the London theatre world', were now saying something different: it was 'well known in theatrical circles' that Joseph 'allegedly dabbled in recreational drugs'. He had been warned about the dangers of his 'promiscuous lifestyle'. It was alleged that he had sometimes been seen with 'young boys'. If only he had had a promiscuous lifestyle, he thought, life might have been more fun. And there hadn't been any boys, young or not. Just Gaz.

They had picked the worst possible photographs of him coming out of the courtroom. Gaz, on the other hand, looked wide-eyed and innocent. Sometimes he was shown in photographs as a schoolboy: neat hair, tie, blazer, a happy, gap-toothed grin. Somewhere, Joseph thought, there must be an instantly accessible database containing photographs of murderers, terrorists, rapists and high-school shooters looking angelic in their school uniforms.

What seemed to get less coverage was what had happened at the trial after Joseph's appearance in court. Although the prosecuting barrister had pulled some of Gaz's evidence to pieces, cast doubt on his depiction as the devout innocent who had unwittingly been exploited, some of the papers seemed more interested in discussing the 'mitigating circumstances' that had made Gaz's sentence shorter than it might otherwise have been. That's me, Joseph thought, I am the mitigating circumstance.

When he had slowly began to come back to life in the hospital, he had found flowers everywhere and cards from practically every member of the *Taste of Honey* company. Now there was nothing – no cards, no flowers, no letters – only two abusive scrawls which had been sent on from the theatre: 'You fucking pervert scum', and 'He who causes the faithful to stray from the true path shall be destroyed by God.' Shirley whisked them away and put them in the new shredder she had bought to get rid of all Alan's letters to her over the years.

After a week, a note came.

Joseph,

You've been having some pretty awful reviews. So sorry, amigo. I'm still distraught about the Shirley situation. Thank you for listening to me. How can someone be so unforgiving and uncompromising?

I feel awful, Joseph: that silly musical of Pollyanna has run into trouble – surprise, surprise – and they've asked me to do some new songs. I really wanted to say no, but I need to do something to keep myself sane. Please don't be upset. I want to get back to work with you as soon as you feel able.

Keep well, and talk soon.

Alan

Joseph did not know what else was going to be thrown at him. It was as if he was playing that card game, Hearts, and had picked up too many of the bad cards. But if you played skilfully enough you could do the most difficult thing of all and Shoot the Moon – it meant turning the game on its head and winning by making sure you got all the bad cards. Maybe he could do that.

A few days later another bad card arrived, a phone call. Shirley brought the phone into his room and practically threw it at him. 'It's Kevin,' she snarled. 'Well, his assistant, anyway. He's too frightened to talk to me.'

'Yes?' Joseph said.

'I've got Mr Lever for you.'

Kevin took over. 'Joseph, mate – how are you?'

'Not great, Kevin.'

'Well. No. We're all thinking of you. Everyone. All the boys and girls.'

'So how is the show going?' Joseph asked wearily.

'Houses haven't been so great since… well, I didn't think I'd ever say you could have too much publicity. Don't think I'm blaming you.'

'No.'

'But listen – good news: I'm putting the finance together for New York.'

'The show's a bit English, isn't it?'

'Well, that's the thing. We've got to make it more American. It'll work over there. *Honey*'s a universal story. Race relations, gay rights. It's got it all.'

'That's not really what it's about, Kevin. It's about the girl. It's not a political statement.'

'We've got to get under the surface, scratch a bit deeper.'

'So what do you want me to do?'

'That's the good thing. Absolutely nothing.'

'What do you mean?'

'We've got to get an American writer in.'

Joseph closed his eyes. 'Oh.'

'Someone who understands that world.'

'What world? Bolton in the sixties?'

'No, *Baltimore* in the sixties. Or maybe Chicago. When they did *The Full Monty* on Broadway, they set it in Buffalo or somewhere. And we might move it up to the seventies, give it a bit of sparkle.'

Joseph did not say anything.

'It'll be expensive to get someone. What do you think about David Mamet?'

'I'm not sure it's his kind of thing, Kevin. Perhaps you should try Arthur Miller,' Joseph said sarcastically. 'If he's still alive.'

'What did he write again? Apart from the play about the witches. And we'll have to think about credit. You won't want your name on it if someone else comes in. Shared credit doesn't look good. And royalties. We'll have to think about a little reduction. Not much, maybe one per cent. Let's not talk about it now. I'll touch base with your agent.'

Before Kevin could go on, Joseph hung up.

Days went by. Everything was a blur. Sometimes drink helped, but not always. In fact, he would have liked to have some coke as well, but he knew that had happened in a different world, one that was lost to him – like Gaz. Could you miss the things that destroyed you? Joseph had an uneasy feeling that you could.

Shirley had been uncharacteristically tactful. In the taxi home after the trial, after people had fired questions at him on the steps of the court, after photographers put cameras up against the glass of the car, all she had said was, 'That boy…' And then shook her head. She had not asked him any questions, not that there were many questions left to ask after what had been revealed in court. She did not even say it was so unfair. He was grateful for that.

But finally, as he knew she would eventually, she reverted to the Shirley he knew. In a way he was relieved: it was time.

In the kitchen, she suddenly slammed the dinner plates into the sink.

'Joseph – you've got to stop doing this. You've got to stop hiding. Stop feeling sorry for yourself. Where's your fight?'

'I'm not sure I ever had much fight.'

'Never apologise, never explain.'

'But Shirley – I was made to explain. In court. That didn't go so well.'

'Everybody has a secret life. You think other people's secret lives are any better than yours?'

'No, but their advantage is that their secret lives are still secret.'

She waved her hands in the air. 'Let's… I don't know… we could go to the show! Why not? It'll be good for both of us. Hold our heads up high. We've got nothing to be ashamed about. My husband left me for someone he met on the Internet. Please! *That's* humiliating.'

'I don't think I'm up to that yet.'

'Joseph – I know people say you're not meant to compartmentalise your life, but I think it makes things easier. You must feel so much anger about that boy and what he did. I don't blame you. You've just got to find somewhere to put it. I mean, I did with Sally – I don't lead my life full of bitterness and rage.'

They were silent for a moment, and then Shirley said, 'You know I'm not one to look on the bright side, Joseph…'

'No,' he said.

'There's something I didn't tell you. Your sister, Rose – that day in court. She was there. I only caught a glimpse, but it was definitely her.'

Joseph sighed. 'Is that the bright side, Shirley?'

'She cared enough to come. That's something, isn't it?'

'A girl who happens to be my sister – half-sister – who doesn't know anything about me suddenly has a crash course and knows everything about me in the space of an hour? Is that good?'

'That stuff's not everything. It's nothing really. You're not defined by it, Joseph.'

'She doesn't know me. What else does she have to go on?'

'But she wants to know you. Why else would she have been there?'

'Then why didn't she talk to me afterwards?'

Shirley looked away. 'Because I was there and I don't think she likes me very much. I'm too… intense for her. Anyway, it's not me she wants, it's you. She's been to see you twice now. She came to the hospital, too, didn't she?'

'Have you heard from her since?'

'Well, no.'

When Shirley had left him, he thought about his sister. He knew so little about families. Maybe there were strange bonds between siblings, maybe they could get inside each other's heads. But surely that was because they had lived together, they knew their likes and dislikes, they knew what they were going to say before they said it because they had heard them say it before. It was just familiarity. There could be none of that between him and the girl called Rose. There was nothing she could want from him. There was nothing he could give her. They shared Isaac Herzl's blood, but that would be too thin to forge a bond between them.

Rose

Sometimes, in books or newspapers, you read stories about a particular day that changes somebody's life. These days always seem to be very ordinary: the school run or the coffee morning or the Monday trip to the supermarket. Then, on this very ordinary day, the teenager takes out a gun at Burger King, the wife finds images of underage girls on her husband's computer, the father who's lent his child the car sees the outline of the policemen's helmets through the frosted glass in the door.

A few weeks after Joseph's appearance in court there was a day like that for me and what happened conformed to some of the constants of those kind of days: someone at the door for one thing; the bringing of bad news for another. But that was later, far into the evening of that day.

Although it was the holidays, I always did some school-work in the mornings. I had moved into Huddie's room, and had brought all my books and work and pens there. His wheelchair still was in the corner.

As usual, at about nine o'clock, I heard the lock in the front door turn. As usual, it was Lally. 'How's Rosie this morning?' she said cheerfully.

'Rosie's okay this morning. How's Lally this morning?'

'Oh, very good. Super walk up the hill. It's going to be hot,' she said. 'This is just the kind of day we would have taken Huddie out into the garden, isn't it? He did enjoy that.' Tears came into her eyes and she put her hand on my arm. 'Our lovely, lovely boy.' Lally wiped her eyes and then said briskly, 'Well, I must get on. The clippings are already up to 1973.'

I could hear her going up the stairs and knocking on Iz's door. Then Lally called out, 'Carla! Is Iz up with you?'

Why would he be up with Carla and Joan? He did not cope well with stairs. He never even came downstairs much.

I went out into the hall. Carla and Joan were standing with Lally outside Iz's study. 'What do you mean he isn't there?' Carla said.

'I mean he isn't there!'

'Perhaps he's gone out for a walk,' Joan said.

'You know he hasn't been out for a long time,' Lally said sharply. 'Where would he go?'

They came downstairs. 'Have you seen him, Rose?' Carla asked.

'No, I've been in here with the door shut.'

'This is terrible,' Lally said. 'He never goes out. I'd worry about him crossing the road!'

'He may not be great on his legs, Lally, but he's not blind,' I said.

'This isn't helping anything,' Carla said. As usual, she was going to be the calm one. 'Let's sit down and think about what could have happened. What was he like yesterday, Lally?'

'Well, he seemed distracted. Actually he seemed a bit upset yesterday, but you know what he's like: not one to share the secrets of his soul.'

'No,' Carla said.

'I think I need a cup of tea,' Joan said. 'Is there any of that Red Zinger? Or the chrysanthemum? You have some too, Carla. It's very calming.' Actually, it was Lally who needed calming: she was shaking.

'Rose…' Joan said imperiously. I knew that Joan was going to ask me to make the tea so I quickly said, 'I'll go upstairs and see if he's taken his stick.'

In the corner of his room there was an umbrella stand where he kept his stick. It wasn't there. I called out, 'No, it's gone,' and Lally let out a great wail from downstairs. Actually, I thought it was quite good news: it would have been much worse if he had gone out without his stick.

I stayed in Iz's room for a while. I did not want to have to be with the others. The room was south-facing and sun was streaming in. It showed up the dust that floated in the air and lay on the surfaces. Lally did everything for Iz, but it would be unreasonable to expect her to clean his room as well. Despite Joan's belief that Carla had been reluctantly forced into being a housewife, she certainly didn't do it either. Still, it didn't matter – Iz did not care about that kind of thing.

There was a lot of stuff in the study, books in piles on the floor as well as in bookcases, and mountains of yellowing newspapers and magazines all over the place. Iz had been in this house for fifty years and had not thrown much away. Lally had lived in it with him, then our mother, then Carla. Lally would have taken her things with her when she left, but what had happened to our mother's? You would have thought Iz might have saved something for me, like a ring or a necklace, but there was nothing.

By the wall, there was a big trestle table with pairs of scissors and pots of glue. The current scrapbook was lying open, waiting for Lally to go on filling it up with the events of 1973 and beyond. There was only one chair at the table. It would only be Lally doing the clipping. Iz would be sitting in the chair looking out on to the garden, and while he stayed silent she would be keeping up a chatty commentary on this article or that old concert review.

What I wished was that one of the scrapbooks could be a photo album like other people had, not just pictures of Iz holding rifles in Israel or speaking in Trafalgar Square but ones of him with me and Huddie. The trouble was, Iz thought that kind of thing was frivolous.

I ran my fingers along the books in the bookcases until I came to Iz's ones. I had not actually read them but I was going to at some point. Maybe I would start with *From Bondage to Freedom: The Legacy of Huddie Ledbetter*. I was less interested in *The Diaspora in Song* because I did not like folk music. And there were his records on the bottom shelf – *Anthems of the Jewish Partisans* and *Send for the Fiddle: The Songs of West Virginia*. I was certainly not planning to listen to those.

Iz's bed was at the other end of the room. The blankets were on the floor. Lally tidied it all up for him when she arrived in the morning. I sat down on the bed and looked at the little table next to it. His reading glasses were on it and a water glass. On top of a pile of books there was a tattered old hardback with no dust jacket. I opened it to see what it was: *Früchte des Zorns* by John Steinbeck. I did German at school so I knew what it was: *The Grapes of Wrath,* the book in which Iz had found my name: Rose of Sharon.

At the back of the book, there were two things: an old faded photograph of a little boy in a sailor suit playing the violin with 'Abram Herzl' written on the back and an envelope on which Iz's name and address were written in neat handwriting, postmarked a couple of days ago. I pulled the letter out.

Dear Friend,

I address you thus because it is my hope that we are still friends, despite not having met for more than sixty years. More than that I do not know what I should call you — what Christian name, that is. I would feel awkward calling you Isaac Herzl, but you obviously do not wish to be called Maurice Gifford, your name when I knew you, before you vanished so suddenly from all our lives when we were seventeen.

I quickly folded up the letter. I did not want to read on. I had a sudden instinct that something awful was about to happen.

When I got downstairs, they were all arguing. I was shaking.

'I don't think Iz would like us to call the police,' Lally said.

'What do you suggest?' Carla said.

'You know what he feels about them.'

'Oh, Lally – we're not in Chile. He's not going to become one of the Disappeared.'

'He's disappeared already! But he couldn't have got too far. He walks slowly.'

'He might have gone somewhere in a taxi,' Joan said.

'Iz only uses public transport,' Lally said sternly.

I could not bear to be with them. I got up. 'Has anyone thought of just walking around and seeing if we can find him?'

Charles Elton

They all looked at one another as if that was a surprising notion. 'I'll go,' I said. I could not get out of the room fast enough.

It was hot outside. The letter made me feel sick. I tried not to think about what it meant. I had it with me now, pushed deep into the back pocket of my jeans. I just wanted to keep moving. I decided that Iz would not have just gone out for an aimless walk. He had not done that for years, and even then Lally always went with him. No, he would have had a purpose: he would be going somewhere specific. There was nothing he could possibly want in Muswell Hill so he would need the tube or bus. I began walking towards Highgate tube, which was the closest. At Highgate, there were only a few people around. I put my head into the ticket office and tried to describe Iz. I mentioned things that would make him stand out: his age, the beard, the stick, maybe his cap. The man first said 'No', then 'I don't know', then 'Maybe'.

When I got back, the women were still sitting round the kitchen table bickering. I had had enough. 'Just call the police,' I said angrily. 'I know Iz is always saying they're a totalitarian organisation, but once in a while they get cats out of trees or look for missing persons. Do you have any other ideas? You've just been sitting here faffing about.'

'Well,' Joan said huffily. 'Miss Bossy.'

'No,' I said. 'Miss Logical,' and went into my room – Huddie's room – and slammed the door. I took the letter from my back pocket and sat down in Huddie's wheelchair.

The reason I write to you now is really a selfish one. I have been ill – oesophageal cancer – and I do not have much time left. There are a small number of people in my life that I wish to make amends to. Along with my son, who I have not seen for many years, you are one of them.

I know that you will soon be eighty because your birthday is the week after mine, which you may remember because you came to so many of those carefree parties. Treasure hunts and rowing races! What a different era it was.

We have both lived a long time, and I hope it has been the life you wanted. Mine – more or less – has been, although it was a much more conventional one than yours. I studied medicine at Oxford and joined my father's – and your father's – medical practice until I retired. Now I live a solitary life in the north of Scotland.

I had the privilege of working alongside your father for a few years. He was an inspirational medical practitioner and I learnt so much from him. And he had so many passions – I remember his delight when a coat of arms was bestowed on your family. There was a lot of sherry drunk that day, I can tell you! But he was never the same after your mother died of cancer in 1955.

Your father's suicide soon after was a very painful event for all of us. I had always suspected that he suffered from depression, but people did not talk about those things then and he was a very private person. He never talked about what happened to you after you left in 1947. It was reported in the papers that you had simply vanished. There was a lot of gossip: people said you had died or were on the run from the police because you had stolen a great deal of money. I knew that was not true. The one thing I know about you is that your integrity has never been in question. You have shown that by your life and work for which I am full of admiration, even though my political persuasions go in other directions.

The strange thing is that I have known for many years who you were. There was a report on the television about a demonstration you were involved in and I saw you singing. When I heard your voice I knew it was you. A voice is like a fingerprint – you cannot change it. Of course it was nearly fifteen years since I had last seen you and you had changed, but as soon as I heard you sing, I could see past the beard and the long hair and I knew that you were Maurice. Of course I never told anybody. You had your reasons for doing what you did and I knew that they would be good ones.

That brings me to the reason for this letter: what happened the last day I saw you at school, the last day I ever saw you – I betrayed you. My parents put great pressure on me and, while it is no excuse, I was frightened. The thing I loved and respected about you is that you were never frightened of anything, and on that awful day you behaved with such dignity. I hope after all these years you will forgive me.

And now I must close. In many ways, I would rather you did not answer this but I cannot tell you how many good wishes I send you, my dear friend Maurice. Please remember me with affection if you can.

As always

Arthur Mayall

After I had finished it, I went into Huddie's bathroom, locked the door and did something I could hardly remember ever doing before: I cried, but it was more out of panic than anything else. It was as if Iz had adopted us after our real father, the person called Maurice, had died. Now, without him and without Huddie, I had nothing.

Later, Carla knocked at the door. I was back sitting in
Huddie's wheelchair. Carla came and stood behind me,
putting her hands on my shoulders.

'Are you okay, Rose?'

'Yes.'

'What a day! Well, we did call the police. We should
have done it much earlier, of course. You were right. I
hope he's okay. Lally thinks they're going to waterboard
him when they find him.' She looked round the room.
'All Huddie's things – what are we going to do with them?'

I shrugged. 'I don't think we need to keep his wheelchair or his respirator to remember him by. Or ten pairs
of tracksuit bottoms.' We were silent for a moment and
then I said cautiously, 'Carla – you still sound American
after all these years. How come Iz sounds so English when
he comes from Germany?'

'Why?'

'Well, there was a copy of *The Grapes of Wrath* in German
by his bed. I keep forgetting that he even is German. Has
he ever spoken German to you?'

'No, I don't think he has. He doesn't talk about Germany.
I wouldn't if my parents were killed in the camps like that.
Of course, he came over on the *Kindertransport* when he
was about eight so he started English early. I think he's
just got a good ear for languages: he picked up pretty
good Hebrew in Israel after the war. But you're right – if
you didn't know, you'd think he was English, wouldn't
you? No accent at all. Well, we all know how clever he is.'

I was playing Racing Demon in the kitchen with Lally
when the doorbell rang. It was nearly midnight. Carla
came down the stairs, trailed by Joan. We could see a
silhouette through the glass of the door.

Before the policeman had even come in, Lally was saying, 'Is he all right? Is he all right?'

'Mrs Herzl?'

Carla normally took Lally's presence in the house with good grace, but she said 'Actually, I'm Mrs Herzl,' rather sharply. 'Let him come in, Lally.'

We all sat down at the kitchen table. The policeman cleared his throat and said, 'We've found Mr Herzl. He's in hospital.'

'But he's all right?' Lally said.

'By the time we got there he had collapsed. He fell and hit his head.'

Lally gasped and put her hand up to her mouth.

'What do the doctors say?' Carla asked.

'They're doing some tests,' the policeman said rather evasively. 'They say he's stable. I think you should call them.'

'But what was he doing?' Lally said.

'He was at a school in Godalming, a private school for boys.'

'Godalming?' Carla said, as if it was the Galapagos Islands. 'What on earth was he doing there?'

Lally was confused. 'A private school? Iz has never believed in private education.'

'But what was he doing at a school?' Carla asked.

The policeman looked rather awkward. 'Schools are very careful about security these days. They called us to say there was a man behaving strangely.'

'Strangely?' Carla said.

'Well, they considered an unknown man loitering around a school for several hours to be strange.' The policeman paused. 'Could we have a word with you in private, Mrs Herzl?'

Carla looked surprised. 'No, it's fine, you can say anything you want to all of us.'

'Very well. It's rather delicate.'

We all waited.

'Have you known him to do this kind of thing before?'

'What kind of thing?' Carla asked.

'Loitering around schools. We have to take that kind of thing seriously when young people are involved. Does he have a computer? We might need to take it away.'

'I don't understand what…?' Carla said, a look of confusion on her face.

'They're asking if he's a paedophile, Carla,' I said.

Lally got to her feet. 'Oh, this is terrible,' she moaned. 'Do you know who Isaac Herzl even is? It's so unfair to make unfounded allegations about such an extraordinary man! And he's done such remarkable things for you people,' she said, pointing at the policeman, who was black. 'He was at Sharpeville, he marched at Selma with Dr Martin Luther—'

'Lally,' I said. 'Sit down. They're only doing their job.'

I turned to the policeman. 'My father is not a paedophile, I promise you. In fact, he has no interest in children at all. Anyway, if he wanted to hang around schools, he wouldn't need to go to Godalming. He could come to my school, which is practically round the corner and I can tell you he's never done that in his life. Anyway, aren't schools like Eton and Harrow tourist attractions? They must be full of people loitering around. Do you bring all those Japanese tourists in for questioning? He doesn't have a computer but you can search the house if you want to. You won't even find a photograph of me and my brother. The only photo of a child you'll find is of a little boy in a sailor suit playing the violin.'

'Was there a reason why he might have gone to the school?' the policeman said.

'He doesn't do anything without a reason.'

I sat in Huddie's dark room. It was at times like this – times when I was confused and a little frightened – that I missed him the most. Who else would I have been able to talk this over with? Not Carla or Lally. What I had read in the letter was unbelievable, but I knew that did not necessarily make it untrue. Huddie and I would have worked out the truth of it. We would have treated it like one of our problems: if x equals Iz Herzl and y equals Maurice Gifford, what would the square root of the sum of x and y be?

I imagined Huddie in the room with me. He would tell me to turn the computer on and say, 'Google Maurice Gifford.'

I might protest: 'There'll be thousands and thousands! It'll take hours.'

'I'll just have to cancel my marathon. Put the name in quotes. That'll weed out people called just "Maurice" or "Gifford".'

I was imagining him speaking fluently, but I knew I would have had to ask him to repeat things and take time to let him dribble his saliva out and wipe his mouth.

I tapped it in. 'There are 2,100 entries.'

'What's coming up?'

'There seem a lot for a Lord Gifford who was a Tory in the House of Lords.'

'A Tory? He's not going to have anything to with Iz. Filter him out.'

'Then we're down to 1,220 hits. Now there's a lot of stuff about some colonel called Maurice Gifford.'

'The army? No way.'

I would laugh. 'Listen to this: he was wounded in the second Matabele war in South Africa. He had the bullet that shot him in the arm set in gold and then he gave it to his wife as a wedding present!'

Huddie would gurgle with laughter, which would make him cough. I filtered the colonel out. '434 hits. That's more manageable.'

'Okay – go through them one by one.'

It took some time. A lot of them could be easily discarded – a dentist called Maurice Gifford in Pasadena, or references to the Facebook pages of various different Maurice Giffords. I went on scrolling through the entries. 'There's a record of a school choir, each year's members. A Maurice Gifford was a member from 1943 to 1947. Somewhere called St George's College.'

'Where?'

'In Godalming…' We would look at each other, or rather I would look at Huddie because he found it hard to move his neck. 'Maybe that's what Iz was doing: he was going back to his old school…' I felt my heart quicken. It was odd to feel excited to be on the trail of something I did not want to be true.

'He sang! He was in the choir,' Huddie would say. 'It says he joined it in 1943. Say that was the year he went to the school so he'd probably have been thirteen. The letter said he vanished when he was seventeen. That would have been 1947, the year he stopped being in the choir. Put it into the search.'

I added '1947'. I found an entry heading which was a piece from a Kent newspaper, the *Ashford Gazette*, dated 15 August 1947. It was a blurred facsimile and I had to increase the magnification to read it properly. It was only five lines long and headed 'Missing Boy Sought by Police'. In a village in Kent called Runton, a Maurice Gifford, seventeen, had vanished with £450 stolen from his uncle, a local farmer called Jack Gifford. So far, the police had been unable to trace the boy.

Further on, there was another entry dated six months later: 'Body Found in Quarry'. The decomposed body of a man had been discovered in a lake in a disused quarry two miles outside Runton. He was thought to be Maurice Gifford, aged seventeen, a farm worker already wanted for questioning by the police in connection with a theft. He was thought to have drowned. There were no suspicious circumstances.

'Do you think it's the same person? He can't be both a choirboy in Godalming and a farm worker in Kent, can he?' I would say.

'Go on through the entries.'

I got to the last page. 'No, there's nothing else.'

There did not seem anywhere else to go. We might have stopped then, except on a whim I looked up Iz's entry in Wikipedia again. I read it through carefully. It covered all the things I already knew but near the beginning of the entry there was a sentence that I would never have taken any notice of before: Isaac Herzl had trained to fight in Palestine on a Jewish-funded farm in Runton, Kent.

I would turn to him and read the entry and we would look at each other in amazement, but of course there was no Huddie. I was alone in the dark with nobody to talk about what we had discovered or what we would do with it.

The next day Carla, Lally and I had taken the train down to Godalming to see Iz. When we got to the hospital, a doctor took us into a small room and asked us to sit down. I had a sinking feeling.

'Mr Herzl is comfortable,' he began.

'When can he come home?' Lally said.

'He's had a stroke.'

Lally gasped.

'What does that mean?' Carla said in her calm voice.

'There are many different kinds of stroke,' the doctor said.

'And what is this one?' I asked. I was the only one in the family who knew anything about medicine.

'We think it's occurred in the brain stem. It affects both sides of the body. He is paralysed from the neck downwards and shows signs of aphasia. He has difficulty expressing himself, though he may understand what you're saying to him. He may improve over time but that's by no means certain. He will need significant care.'

'We're used to that in our house,' I said.

We went into the ward to see him. He had a big gash on his forehead where he had fallen, but otherwise he looked fine. Although his eyes were open, he certainly was not talking and did not react to us at all, not even when Lally practically threw herself on top of him. Carla and Lally were still perplexed about why Iz had gone to Godalming. I was not: I presumed that he was simply going home.

A few days later it was just like old times in the house in Muswell Hill: a new carer had arrived to look after Iz who was using Huddie's wheelchair and wearing his tracksuit bottoms. It was lucky we had not given them all away. I had moved out of Huddie's room and was in Iz's old room on the first floor. The ground floor was the invalid's floor.

Lally was staking her claim to be the one who would look after Iz: there was already tension between her and the carer. The first thing Lally got him to do was to move all the furniture down from Iz's study and then pack all the archives up in boxes. She thought he had not been careful enough.

'These are irreplaceable things!'

'Oh, Lally, he's not the removal man.'

She did not like him being in the room while she was doing the scrapbooks so she kept sending him out of the house for pointless errands.

'It's just that he's so intrusive, Rosie.'

'He's a carer, Lally! You can't just let him sit outside the room like a dog and then call him in when Iz needs his trousers changed. Anyway, if he went, there'd just be another carer. Maybe a woman this time. Would you prefer that?' Lally would certainly not prefer that.

After Lally had gone in the early evening, Carla went into Iz's room to spend some time with him. Joan never set foot there. She was busy preparing another of their 'Evening of Sister Songs' which was happening in a few days. I had heard them practising and once I had sneaked in to listen. There were six women, and, in front of them, Joan was standing conducting. I had thought that it was meant to be Carla's time, but now she seemed to have become just another member of a group led by Joan.

I was in the kitchen when Carla came out of Iz's room. She sat down at the table and poured herself a glass of wine.

She let out a sigh. 'Oh, I don't know, Rose, I hope he's happy. Well, as happy as he can be. Do you think he even understands what we're saying to him? It's funny, he looks so distinguished, doesn't he? In his wheelchair he's like the Lincoln Memorial in Washington – you know, the huge marble statue of him sitting in a chair.'

'Well, he is distinguished.'

'I worry that people have forgotten him, all he did. Maybe he's become irrelevant.'

'Lally's not going to let that happen,' I said, and we laughed.

'You have no idea what he was like when I met him. I was terrified when my father said he was coming to dinner in Boston. He had such a reputation. Of course, he was married to your mother then. I only got to know him when I came over here a few years later. And you two – you and Huddie were gorgeous, so tiny and frightened. Iz didn't want more children, but I had you. Iz gave me so much then.'

'And now?' I said carefully.

Carla looked away. 'Things change, Rose.'

'Yes, I know that.'

'Iz was the love of my life, really he was, but he didn't make loving him easy.'

I nodded.

'I need to sing again, Rose. I need Joan. I hope you can understand that.'

I nodded again.

'You know, it's the future not the—'

'Carla – if one more person says that to me again, I'm going to throw up,' I said.

I tried to think what Huddie would have wanted, and it took me a few days to work out what that would have been. I was not a timid person, but I felt nervous about it. Still, I had decided and I was going to do it.

Before leaving, I went into Huddie's room – I did not think of it as Iz's room yet – and went over to the open French windows where Iz was sitting in his wheelchair facing the garden. I drew up a chair and sat beside him and put my hand on his. It felt completely neutral, neither hot nor cold. It had been a long time since I had touched him. I began to talk to him, even though I knew he could not respond and probably would not even be able to understand.

'You never told us what kind of people you wanted us to be, Iz. You never helped us. If we'd have known,

Huddie and I would have tried. Maybe you wanted us to write songs or to be singers like you, but we wouldn't have been good at it. Anyway, I don't believe in rhyme. Everyone thinks there's some logic to it but there isn't. You're shoehorning words together to make them sound smooth. You wouldn't write a political speech in rhyme, would you? You'd want to pick the exact words and you couldn't necessarily make them rhyme. It's often the wrong words that are the ones that rhyme.

'I don't know where you come from, Iz. I know it's not Germany. I don't even know who you are. I read that letter your schoolfriend sent you. I'm not going to tell anybody, I promise you. It would be nice to think that you'd have told me about it one day, but I don't suppose you would have done. I would have loved to have a secret that only you and Huddie and I shared. I'd like you to have made us understand how you became the person you are even though once you'd been someone completely different. I can't work that out. Maybe Huddie could have understood it, but it's too late now. I used to think that when Huddie died he would just be gone, that he would have packed his bags and left, but now I'm not so sure. You should have got to know him better. You were careless with him. You were careless with all your children, Iz.'

I got up and kissed him on the top of his head, where his hair was thick and white. As I went out of the house, I could hear the sound of Carla and Joan practising. It was a hot day and the sun felt warm on my face. I was not going far, only about fifteen minutes away. When I turned the corner and saw the nice detached house with Virginia creeper all over the front and a little driveway with a garage at the end of it, I suddenly felt frightened. There was no real logic to what I was doing.

I waited in the porch for a moment before I rang the doorbell. I could hear footsteps and then the door opened. I don't think I have ever seen someone look as surprised as Shirley.

'Rose...' she said.

'I've come to see Joseph.'

She nodded. 'Come in.'

As she took me through the house, I saw a small photograph in a frame on a table. I stopped and picked it up.

'Is this your daughter? Is this Sally?'

'Yes,' she said.

'She looks just like you.'

'I'm sorry,' she said. 'I'm sorry about all those things I said about you and Sally. You must think I'm a very foolish woman.'

I shrugged. 'In my house, everybody is always certain that the things they believe in are true. I don't know what's true and what isn't any more. You did those calculations about Muswell Hill the other day; maybe there was a special child born the day Huddie died as well. I don't believe it but that doesn't mean I wouldn't like it to be true.'

'You don't have to believe it. Just don't let go of Huddie.'

'I'd never let go of Huddie.'

'Then we're not so different, Rose.' She turned away from me. 'Go in,' she said. 'Go in and see Joseph.'

I knocked on the door and went in. He was sitting at a desk with his back towards me writing something.

'Hello,' I said. 'I'm Rose Herzl.'

He turned round. 'I know.'

'I came and saw you when you were in hospital.'

'I remember. Thank you for that. And you came to my trial.'

'Don't say that. It wasn't your trial. It was unfair. It was like Stalin's Show Trials where innocent people got destroyed. You'd know all about them if you'd been brought up by Iz. He told me that something like that happened to him once but I'm not sure anything he's said is really true.'

I couldn't think what to say next, so I pointed at the desk and said, 'What are you writing?'

'A song.'

'For one of your musicals?'

'No, it's not my song. When I'm bored I rewrite other people's songs. This one's an old one called "Manhattan".'

'Don't you write songs of your own?'

'I did, yes.'

'What's the song about?'

'Well, the original song is about how lovely New York was. I've added things about 9/11 to make it more topical.'

'Oh, like a political song. Like Iz's kind of song.'

'No, I wouldn't be very good at that. The verse I'm doing now is more about what people did there in the old days, something about sailors meeting girls at the harbour. I'm stuck: I can't think of anything which rhymes with "Girls at Manhattan's dockside".'

I thought for a moment. 'That's not so difficult. What about: "With curls under hat and peroxide"?'

He threw his head back and laughed. 'Oh,' he said, 'you're a songwriter, too.'

And then I told him about the choirboy at the school in Godalming in 1947 and the friend called Arthur who was old and dying in Scotland. I told him about the boy who worked on his uncle's farm in Kent and the boy who drowned there and the boy who went to Israel. I asked him if maybe he would come with me to those places and see what we could find. I told him that without Huddie I did everything on my own, and I did not want to do this on my own.

Then, afterwards, I walked with him back to our house. He walked slowly and sometimes I had to take his arm. When we got there I took him into Huddie's room where Iz was, still by the French windows looking out over the garden. I turned the wheelchair round so he was facing us. I did not know whether he would understand me or not.

'This is Joseph,' I said, 'Joe Hill Herzl.'

Thank You

Maria Alvarez   Richard Barrowclough   John Brown
Yvonne Cardenas   Marjorie DeWitt   Abraham Elton
Lotte Elton   Charles Fox   Sue Freathy
Judith Gurewich   Emily Heller   Lucy Heller   Zoë Heller
William Humble   Brent Isaacs   Sally Lever
Imogen Parker   Jeremy Pfeffer   Stewart Plant
Jonathan Powell   John Preston   Alexandra Pringle
Felicity Rubinstein   Ian Simpson   Adrian Smith
Sarah Spankie   Gillian Stern   Jeremy Treglown
Nicholas Underhill   Nina Underhill   Naomi Pope

A Note on the Type

The text of this book is set Adobe Garamond. It is one of several versions of Garamond based on the designs of Claude Garamond. It is thought that Garamond based his font on Bembo, cut in 1495 by Francesco Griffo in collaboration with the Italian printer Aldus Manutius. Garamond types were first used in books printed in Paris around 1532. Many of the present-day versions of this type are based on the *Typi Academiae* of Jean Jannon cut in Sedan in 1615.

Claude Garamond was born in Paris in 1480. He learned how to cut type from his father and by the age of fifteen he was able to fashion steel punches the size of a pica with great precision. At the age of sixty he was commissioned by King Francis I to design a Greek alphabet, and for this he was given the honourable title of royal type founder. He died in 1561.